THE GHOST STORIES OF CHARLES DICKENS VOLUME 1

'My own mind is perfectly unprejudiced and impressionable on the subject of ghosts. I do not in the least pretend that such things cannot be. . .'

Charles Dickens

The horrors of the 'penny dreadful' magazine, *The Terrific Register*, which made the young Dickens 'unspeakably miserable and frightened the very wits out of my head' and the stories recounted to the impressionable child at the knees of his nursemaid were to have a lasting and fearful influence.

Dickens's story of Scrooge, *A Christmas Carol*, is arguably the most famous ghost story in all literature – with it he began the tradition of 'the ghost story at Christmas'. What is less well known is quite how deeply the supernatural pervaded the rest of his writing: half a dozen such stories can be found in the *Pickwick Papers* alone.

Peter Haining's remarkable collection brings together famous and long-lost tales for the first time.

About the editor

PETER HAINING is a well-known writer and anthologist whose books have been published all over the world. He has written extensively on the supernatural and published a number of ghost-story collections. He has been a lover of Dickens's work since his childhood, and now delights in reading stories such as those in this book to his own three children. He lives in a sixteenth-century house (reputed to be haunted) not far from the Suffolk town immortalised in *Pickwick Papers* as Eatanswill.

THE GHOST STORIES OF CHARLES DICKENS VOLUME 1

Edited and introduced by Peter Haining

CORONET BOOKS
Hodder and Stoughton

First published in Great Britain 1982
by Michael Joseph Ltd, with volume 2, as
THE COMPLETE GHOST STORIES OF CHARLES DICKENS
Coronet edition 1984

British Library C.I.P.

Dickens, Charles, *1812–1870*
[The complete ghost series of Charles Dickens.
Selections] The ghost stories of Charles
Dickens.
Vol. 1
I. Title II. Haining, Peter III. The
ghost stories of Charles Dickens
823'.8 PR4572

ISBN 0-340-36426-2

Printed and bound in Great Britain for
Hodder and Stoughton Paperbacks, a
division of Hodder and Stoughton Ltd.,
Mill Road, Dunton Green, Sevenoaks,
Kent (Editorial Office: 47 Bedford
Square, London, WC1 3DP) by
Cox & Wyman Ltd, Reading
Photoset by Rowland Phototypesetting Ltd,
Bury St Edmunds, Suffolk

CONTENTS

For
JOHN & MARGARET KENT

'I wants to make your flesh creep!'
The Fat Boy in *Pickwick Papers*

INTRODUCTION

Among Dickens's good things should not be omitted his telling of a ghost story. He had something of a hankering after them, as the readers of his briefer pieces will know; and such was his interest generally in things supernatural that, but for the strong restraining power of his common sense, he might have fallen into the follies of spiritualism. As it was, the fanciful side of his nature stopped short at such pardonable superstitions as these of dreams, and lucky days, or other marvels of natural coincidence; and no man was readier to apply sharp tests to a ghost story or a haunted house, though there was just so much tendency to believe in any such, 'well-authenticated', as made perfect his manner of telling one.

JOHN FORSTER
The Life of Charles Dickens
(1874)

Charles Dickens's fascination with ghosts and the macabre which he reveals in the pages of his books and stories can be seen today as one of the most inevitable elements to have emerged in his writing. For in his very earliest years he was introduced to the grim and the ghoulish through the stories told to him by his nursemaid, a remarkable young woman called Mary Weller, whom he referred to in later life as Mercy, 'though she had none on me'.

If we remember ourselves when young, or think of our own children now, open-mouthed and wide-eyed while being indulged with tales of giants and demons, ghosts and monsters—the staple ingredients of fairy stories which, generation after generation, are fed to young and impressionable minds—it is not hard to visualise the young Dickens partaking of the same fare in much the same manner. In his case, however, both the storyteller and the tales she told were to have a far more profound effect than that on most children. For it is not overstating the case to say that the macabre stories which Mary Weller recounted to the youngster at her knee were so powerful and terrifying as to colour his imagination permanently and shape much of the brilliant and enduring fiction which he later created. (Indeed, Andrew Lang, the contemporary novelist and critic, has no hesitation in declaring that Mary, 'was obviously a true genius as a narrator'.) The world of the supernatural to which he was introduced became vividly real to him, and through the medium of his stories he has made it likewise chillingly authentic for us. It is equally true to say that the ghost stories of Charles Dickens not only represent some of the high points of the genre, but have proved enormously influential upon many subsequent practitioners of the art of supernatural fiction.

The impact of Mary Weller's stories on young Charles's imagination is not a matter of speculation, as one so often finds when tracing the formative influences in any great writer's life. Dickens himself in a number of letters, as well as in certain of his stories (*vide* the first item in this book), speaks of her exceptional gifts which became evident to him very soon after she had entered the employ of the Dickens family when he was just five years old. Mary's skill as a storyteller is all the more remarkable when we learn that she was just thirteen years old at this time!* Although to all outward appearances she was a hard-working and conscientious servant, in the privacy of the nursery she had no compunction whatsoever in filling her young charge's head with the most macabre and weird stories.

Writing much later as an adult, Dickens tell us that Mary was employed as his nurse for six years, until he was eleven. During this time she found many opportunities to speak of her interest in death and murder, in ghosts and demons – and even in cannibalism! The images which she conjured up in her stories imprinted themselves indelibly on his receptive mind: throughout his writing life he gave every indication of trying to exorcise these dark thoughts by pouring them into his stories. As Professor Harry Stone, the Dickens authority, has written in his study, *Dickens and the Invisible World* (1979), 'When Mary came to the Dickenses she brought with her a fantastic budget of weird stories and country superstitions, and she also brought with her a baleful imagination that embroidered and personalised everything that she related. Dickens proved an ideal audience, and Mary Weller practised on him endlessly.'

From among the many grim tales she spun, one – 'Captain

* It is an interesting fact to ponder that another young girl, Mary Shelley, played a vastly influential role not only on one writer, but on the entire development of the modern horror story, when she wrote her classic novel, *Frankenstein* (1816) while still in her teens.

Murderer and The Devil's Bargain' – particularly fascinated and frightened him, and it has been seen by several authorities as particularly influential on much of his later fiction. The tale is actually two stories in one as well as being something of a summary by Dickens of the other horrific yarns Miss Weller had in her repertoire. Dickens wrote the tale as an episode for his book, *The Uncommercial Traveller* (1860), and the critic Mary L. Pendered has written that, 'All Grimm's gruesome tales rolled into one could not beat this story for sheer blood-curdling.' She also confirms the story's importance on his future development, telling us, 'Dickens describes his horrors and nightmares after listening to these two stories: how they haunted his dreams, and he became morbidly afraid to put his hand in his pockets for fear of finding a rat there. But I have no doubt whatever he enjoyed them. A normal child's thirst for the horrible is insatiable, as his nurse evidently knew. I can't help thinking he enjoyed writing them, too, when he was grown up!'

Although not strictly a ghost story in the tradition of the others included in this collection, I feel it is essential to include 'Captain Murderer and The Devil's Bargain' in this book, as nothing else that Dickens wrote could better illustrate his early, crucially important influences; in turn, its influence on the stories that he wrote later will become evident to the reader as he progresses from one story to the next.

I must also say here that it would be wrong to think that Mary Weller was the sole influence on the macabre side of his nature. Charles's paternal grandmother, Elizabeth Bell Dickens, was also an accomplished fairy-story teller, and the household contained a library wherein rested numerous books of fantasy and the supernatural. In his teens, Dickens also discovered a weekly 'penny dreadful' magazine called *The Terrific Register*, which was enormously popular with the reading public of the day and served up sixteen pages of horrors complete with a ghoulish engraving of some act of murder or sadism. He tells us that the publication made him, 'unspeakably miserable, and frightened my very wits out of my head'. He thought that the price of one penny, 'considering there was an illustration to every number, in which there was always a pool of blood, and at least one body, was cheap'.

Finally, of course, one must not overlook the grim surroundings in which Dickens lived and for a time worked during his formative years in London: the sprawling slums, sweat-shop factories and grimy streets teeming with the brawling, coarse and impoverished inhabitants of the metropolis. Their dark world of despair made an ideal backcloth for the weaving of tales of ghosts and hauntings: not a street was without its grim house of mystery, not an alleyway free from some legend of ghastly happenings.

All these factors notwithstanding, Dickens evidently believed Mary Weller to have been his single greatest influence, for as he wrote in 1837, 'If we all knew our own minds (in a more enlarged sense than the popular acceptation of that phrase), I suspect we should find our nurses responsible for most of the dark corners we are forced to go back to, against our wills.'

These, then, were the major elements which brought about Charles Dickens's interest in the macabre. We can now look at the various stories which were the products of his vivid and lively imagination. . . .

Pickwick Papers, which was issued in monthly instalments beginning in March 1836, was the first of Dickens's novels to contain ghost stories. This marvellous account of the exploits of Mr Pickwick, Alfred Jingle, Serjeant Buzfuz, Slammer, The Fat Boy, Mr Winkle, Sam Weller and the rest is one of the most entertaining works from this author, highlighted in my opinion by the five ghost stories interjected into the main narrative. Each is told by a man thrown by circumstances into the company of Mr Pickwick and his friends, and each tale has a completeness that makes it possible to extract it without difficulty. This feature has led to the suggestion that Dickens might well have originally written them as individual short stories, but then pressed them into service in the *Pickwick Papers* when the need to meet punishing deadlines for each month's instalment grew critical. It was, after all, his first writing commission and he was still a newcomer at the game. However, this is an argument that we shall have to accept will probably never be satisfactorily resolved.

G. K. Chesterton, who was a great admirer of Dickens, has called the *Pickwick Papers* a 'wild promise' of the books that are to follow. 'He is still in the youthful whirl of the kind of world he would like to create,' Chesterton writes in *Criticisms and Appreciations of Charles Dickens* (1911). 'He has not yet really settled what story he will write, but only what *sort* of story he will write. He tries to tell ten stories at once; he pours into the pot all the chaotic fancies and crude experiences of his boyhood; he sticks in irrelevant short stories shamelessly as into a scrapbook; he adopts designs and abandons them, begins episodes and leaves them unfinished; but from the first page to the last there is nameless and elemental ecstasy—that of the man who is doing the kind of thing that he can do.'

Let us look briefly at the ghost stories to be found in *Pickwick*. The first we come across is 'The Lawyer and the Ghost', which is related to Mr Pickwick by a little old man named Jack Bamber who has devoted his life to the legal profession, which provides its setting. The tale is, actually, a preface to a much longer story called 'The Old Man's Tale About the Queer Client', which recounts a man's obsessive search for revenge. Next comes two stories from a remarkable character known as The One-Eyed Bagman, a short, jovial middle-aged fellow who twice bumps into Mr Pickwick during the course of the narrative. 'The Queer Chair' is about a wayfarer haunted by a most unusual piece of furniture at an inn; 'The Ghosts of the Mail' is the story of a mail coach and its unearthly passengers. The fourth tale, 'A Madman's Manuscript', is another departure for Dickens, taking us into the realms of insanity and the mind of a man haunted by spectres. 'The Story of the Goblins Who Stole a Sexton', told by Pickwick's friend Mr Wardle of Dingley Dell, is the last of the ghost stories in *Pickwick* and was appropriately published in the Christmas instalment dated December 1836. It is undoubtedly the best of the group and, as more than one commentator has already pointed out, is in several respects a prototype for Dickens's forthcoming full-length story, *A Christmas Carol*. The main character, Gabriel Grubb, is a miserable, solitary, mean-spirited soul whose adventure occurs on Christmas Eve—a festival he despises. Instead of enjoying himself, Grubb chooses to work in the graveyard, and for good measure roundly abuses a carol-singer he meets on the way there. He receives his come-uppance at the hands of a 'strange, unearthly figure' who pops up from behind a gravestone and reveals what the future has in store for him unless he mends his ways. Even stated as simply as this, the reader will no doubt appreciate the parallels with the later tale of Scrooge. These similarities will be underlined when actually reading the two tales, although both have their own special and unique qualities. (As a matter of interest, Professor Stone has also found certain similarities between 'A Madman's Manuscript' and *Oliver Twist*, the novel which Dickens wrote immediately after *Pickwick*, in 1837–38. The professor writes, 'After the murder of Nancy, her staring eyes haunt Bill Sykes at every step. Like the murderous madman in "A Madman's Manuscript", Sykes cowers and tries to hide, but he has no relief.')

In his third novel, *Nicholas Nickleby* (1838–39), Dickens once again interrupts the narrative with two short stories, one a melancholy fable, 'The Five Sisters', and the other a light-hearted ghost story entitled, 'Baron Koëldwethout's Apparition'. In this second tale the author demonstrates another facet of his developing talent: the ability to write a humorous adventure of the supernatural. The story is related by a 'merry-faced gentleman' whom Nicholas and Wackford Squeers (the brutal schoolmaster) meet when they are detained at a roadside inn as a result of an accident to the stage coach in which they are travelling. The critic W. H. Auden, who numbered *Nicholas Nickleby* among his favourite works by Dickens, believed the author had a purpose in introducing this story into the main body of the narrative—a purpose already put to good effect in *Pickwick Papers* and to be employed again from time to time in later books. Writing in *The Dyer's Hand & Other Essays* (1963), he says, 'Dickens's primary reason for introducing these stories was, no doubt, that of any writer of a serial—to introduce a novel entertainment for his readers at a point when he feels they would welcome an interruption in the main narrative.'

It was with the publication of *A Christmas Carol* in December 1843 that a great landmark occurred in the literary career of Charles Dickens. The passage of time since that date has proved it not only his finest ghost story, but arguably the most famous of all his works. On top of this it began a tradition amongst publishers—still widely observed today—of issuing a special volume for the Christmas season, in particular one with a ghostly or supernatural theme.

In announcing the tale of the miser Scrooge and his transformation at the hands of supernatural agencies, Dickens called the work 'A Ghost Story of Christmas'—and as a result of its extraordinary success he went on to produce four more titles for the season, all of which he referred to as 'Christmas Books'. They were *The Chimes* (1844), *The Cricket on the Hearth* (1845), *The Battle of Life* (1846) and *The Haunted Man* (1848). Of the five stories, however, only two, *A Christmas Carol* and *The Haunted Man*, can be counted as ghost stories: *The Battle of Life* is an analogy, while the other two rely on dream sequences for their fantasy elements. All, though, enjoyed considerable popularity with the public. As a direct result of this acclaim, Dickens continued the tradition throughout the rest of his life, though his later contributions were all short stories and a number were ultimately gathered together into a posthumous collection suitably titled *Christmas Stories* (1871). The stories are a lively mixture of comedy, pathos and the supernatural, with just three specifically about ghosts: 'The Haunted House', 'The Trial For Murder' and 'The Signal-Man', all of which are included in this volume, and to which we shall come in due course.

What had inspired Dickens to write these Christmas tales was a growing conviction that while the festive season was a time for mankind to be happy and joyful, it was a moment for re-assessment and, if necessary, change. He also thought he had found a way of combining both these elements in story form. How successfully he achieved this, in a way both unique and enduring, has been explained by G. K. Chesterton in his study of Dickens. '"A Christmas Carol" is a happy story first,' he says, 'because it describes an abrupt and dramatic change; it is not only the story of conversion, but of a sudden conversion; as sudden as the conversion of a man at a Salvation Army meeting. Popular religion is quite right in insisting on the fact of a crisis in most things. . . . Again the story owes much of its hilarity to the fact of it being a tale of winter and of a very wintry winter. There is much about comfort in the story; yet the comfort is never enervating: it is saved from that by a tingle of something bitter and bracing in the weather. Lastly, the story exemplifies the kinship between gaiety and the grotesque. Everybody is happy because nobody is dignified. We have a feeling somehow that Scrooge looked even uglier when he was kind than he had looked when he was cruel.'

The actual plot for *A Christmas Carol* apparently occurred to Dickens in the October of 1843, and he committed it to paper in a frenzy of excitement, later confessing to his friend Professor Felton that as he wrote it he 'wept, laughed and wept again, exciting myself in a most extraordinary manner in the composition'. Just before delivering the manuscript to his publishers he also added a brief preface which read:

> I have endeavoured in this Ghostly little book, to raise the Ghost of an Idea, which shall not put my readers out of humour with themselves, with each other, with the season, or with me. May it haunt their houses pleasantly, and no one wish to lay it.

The book proved an instant success, the first edition of 6,000 copies selling out within days. Second and third editions followed, and within a year sales had passed the 15,000 mark. Dickens was naturally overjoyed. 'A most prodigious success,' he wrote to another friend, the actor William Macready; 'the greatest, I think, I have ever achieved.' The critics also shared the public's delight, William Thackeray for example declaring, 'It seems to me a national benefit, and to every man and woman who reads it, a personal kindness.' Thackeray also recounted in his review the story of what happened to one reader, a Scottish philosopher who, 'naturally does not keep Christmas'. After he had finished the story, said Thackeray, the man, 'sent out for a Turkey and asked two friends to dinner – this is a fact! What a feeling is this for a writer to be able to inspire, and what a reward to reap!' Dickens himself was probably most delighted with a personal letter he received from Lord Francis Jeffrey, the eminent Scottish judge and critic; for the sentiments this man expressed about the book were closest to those which he had set out to elicit. 'You should be happy yourself,' wrote Lord Jeffrey, 'for you may be sure you have done more good by this little publication, fostered more kindly feelings, and prompted more positive acts of beneficence than can be traced to all the pulpits and confessionals in Christendom since Christmas 1842.' Not surprisingly, the success of *A Christmas Carol* led to it being swiftly adapted for the stage as well as being unmercifully pirated. (In these days, before proper copyright protection existed, Dickens had to fight tenaciously in court to preserve his work from unlawful reprinting, and the battle cost him hundreds of pounds which he was unable to recover from the culprits.) The theme was also widely imitated by other writers in volumes bearing such titles as *Christmas Eve with the Spirits* and so on. It is interesting to speculate that with all this furore over his creation, Dickens might just have had some inkling that he had started something which was to prove an enduring fashion.

No description of this remarkable work is required here: it stands as one of the masterpieces of English literature, a joy to each new generation as they discover it, and rightfully lauded as the book which founded the tradition of telling ghost stories at Christmas. Writing in an introduction to a library of Dickens's works published in 1910, J. A. Hammerton also noted that, 'The "Carol" and its successors have made the name of Charles Dickens synonymous with that of Father Christmas, and each succeeding Yuletide it is safe to say that the Spirit of Christmas, which seems to take possession of us all, is the spirit of Dickens. Indeed, one might be apt to think of him as the originator of the old English Christmas, which had its countless votaries many generations before he was born; but what he did was to give enduring expression to all that it stood for, of good fellowship and kindness of heart. He attached to it new ideas and gave it a place in literature.'

Interestingly, also, in some quarters *A Christmas Carol* is credited with having 'invented' the idea of white Christmases! For, according to Professor Hubert Lamb of the climactic research unit at East Anglia University, snowy Christmases are actually very infrequent, and the belief in them, 'owes a good deal to Charles Dickens and *A Christmas Carol*'. Professor Lamb found the explanation for the belief during research into past weather records, which showed that for the first eight years of Dickens's life there was a white Christmas every year with either snow or white hoar frost. Though this may well have left a vivid memory of Christmas weather with Dickens, says the professor, it was very much a freak period. 'The idea of a white Christmas is fairly mythical, you see. Christmas Day and the days either side have a rather good sunshine record. The most characteristic picture is of a rather quiet, sunny period between more disturbed winter weather.'

Although Dickens continued to produce 'Christmas Books' for the next three festive seasons, it was not until the winter of 1848 that he gave his public another ghost story, *The Haunted Man*. The reason for this break in theme has been most acceptably explained by Professor Harry Stone. 'Dickens seems to have been discontented with the overt fairy-tale machinery of his "Christmas Books",' he writes. 'The intrusive ghosts and spirits of the "Carol" had given way to the carefully generated bell goblins of "The Chimes", which in turn yielded to the more domesticated (and limited) crickets and kettles of "The Cricket on the Hearth". In the next Christmas book, "The Battle of Life", he dispensed with supernatural machinery altogether. "The Battle" is not only the least typical of the Christmas books but the least successful.'

Small wonder, then, that Dickens allowed the next year to pass without a Christmas book, and then when he did search for a new topic he returned to the formula which had made the story of Scrooge such a success. Indeed when he announced his new plan to his biographer, John Forster, he told him, 'I have been dimly conceiving a very ghostly and wild idea, which I must now reserve for the next Christmas book.' In *The Haunted Man* he once again portrayed a melancholy figure who is visited on Christmas Eve by a ghostly agency which forces him to re-examine his past in order to improve his future. But unlike the various spirits in *A Christmas Carol*, 'the ghost here is a thorough-paced Gothic creation with an evil smile upon its face,' to quote Michael Slater in his article on 'The Christmas Books' in *The Dickensian*, January 1969. Mr Slater believes that *The Haunted Man* is more than just a ghost story, but also something of a revelation about the state of Dickens's mind at this period of his life. And of course it is true that there are other immediately apparent similarities between the author and his central character, Redlaw, a learned teacher.

> Redlaw is a man haunted by memories of past sorrow and wrong. He comes eventually to rejoice in these painful memories instead of bitterly resenting them for they are, he learns, the necessary basis of love and compassion in the human breast. Dickens, we know, was at this time brooding on his past. He had written, probably in 1847, some chapters of an autobiography, in which he revealed to Forster the scars which the debtors' prison and the blacking factory of his boyhood had left upon his memory. The domestic disillusionment that was to lead to separation from his wife in 1858 was growing and Mrs Winter had not yet appeared to convince him that the seemingly cruel denial of his first serious aspirations as a lover was, in fact, a fortunate escape. He seems in 'The Haunted Man' to be seeking to argue himself out of a barren feeling of bitterness and regret. But to exorcise his 'Phantom' by means of art he needed greater freedom than the framework of a 'Christmas Book' allowed him. The following April he began *David Copperfield.*

(Mr Slater might also have mentioned that Dickens's sister Fanny died lingeringly of consumption during the summer of 1848 and some critics have seen *The Haunted Man* as 'a dirge to her memory'.)

This argument shows us clearly enough why *The Haunted Man* was destined to be the last of the 'Christmas Books'; with an author less steeped in the supernatural and the macabre, it might also have been the last work of this kind he ever wrote.* But

* Like *A Christmas Carol* before it, *The Haunted Man* was also imitated and parodied by other writers—the most famous example being Brett Harte's burlesque, *The Haunted Man by Ch—r—s D—ck—ns*, published in 1870—and it similarly found its way on to the stage. Charles Dickens's son has written that it was a 'great success' when first presented at The Adelphi in London, and he added, 'I well remember the strangely weird effect of the very cleverly-managed first appearance of O. Smith as the ghost.'

Dickens had learned an important skill from writing them – how to blend fantasy and realism into powerful themes about the mysteries of life – and this can be seen at work in many of his subsequent novels. He had seen, too, how the supernatural could be employed to point up all the other elements of a story. So, although his stature and success grew with each book that followed – *David Copperfield* (1849–50), *Bleak House* (1852–53), *Hard Times* (1854), *Little Dorrit* (1855–57) and *A Tale of Two Cities* (1859) – he could not resist returning to the ghost theme in the occasional short story, and it is these tales which make up the remainder of the collection.

It is perhaps not to be wondered at that, after having exposed the traumas of his present circumstances in *The Haunted Man*, Dickens should sometimes dwell on his early and happier childhood days. (Mary Weller notwithstanding!) From such reflections came perhaps the most delightful of all his supernatural stories, *A Child's Dream of a Star*, published two years later in 1850. In it the spirit of a little girl becomes an angel and awaits that of her brother. Writing in *The Dickensian* in January 1922, Walter Dexter pointed out how Dickens was 'haunted' by his childhood, and says that this particular story reflects his happy days when he was living at St Mary's Place in Chatham. Dexter adds, 'In "A Child's Dream of a Star", he refers very touchingly to these days . . . From an upper window on one side of the house, the Church and Churchyard of St Mary's were visible, just as described in this charming story.'

I have to admit that the story has long been one of my favourites, and I think it provides the ideal kind of 'interlude' after the dark and sombre adventures of Redlaw that the author himself would have approved of.

For the Christmas number of *Household Words* (see below) that same year, Dickens returned to the subject of the festive season in a piece called 'A Christmas Tree'. In this lengthy discourse he introduces a fanciful section about the different kinds of ghosts that might be experienced at this time of year. I have extracted the section—giving it the title 'Christmas Ghosts'—and included it here because, apart from its own intrinsic worth as a piece of storytelling, splendidly evoking memories of Christmas, it throws still further light on Dickens's own attitudes to such things.

Charles Dickens's dedication to hard work has been marvelled at by successive generations of writers, for apart from producing the monthly instalments of his various novels year in and year out, he also travelled a great deal, gave public readings of his work, was involved in private theatricals and wrote plays, undertook speeches, kept up a voluminous correspondence, produced a great many pamphlets, contributed to various periodicals and even edited one of the most popular magazines of his time! This weekly publication was called *Household Words*. Dickens edited it from 1850 to 1859 (when it was retitled *All The Year Round*), and remained in the job until 1870 when the post was assumed by his son. With one exception, all Dickens's further ghost stories were first published in this magazine.

The exception is 'To Be Read At Dusk', which he contributed to *The Keepsake* in 1852. It is another off-beat ghost story which, perhaps because it did not appear in the pages of *Household Words*, has frequently been overlooked by critics and anthologists; indeed the fact that it was included in the anthology of Dickens's short stories called *Collected Papers*, published in 1903, is often missed when the contents are listed (*vide* Gilbert Pierce's definitive volume, *The Dickens Dictionary*, 1908).

Because of his own predilection for ghost stories, Dickens encouraged his contributors to *Household Words* to write such stories for his special Christmas issues; a number of famous writers of supernatural fiction were first published in his pages, including Lord Bulwer Lytton, Mrs Elizabeth Gaskell, Amelia Edwards and Wilkie Collins, author of the classic mystery story, *The Woman in White* (1859–60), who also became a close personal friend. Little need be written here of the friendship of these two great writers, beyond the fact that they collaborated on a number of items and did much to encourage each other's work. One such collaboration occurred in August 1857 when the two men decided to seek a break from their exhausting work schedules and take a rambling holiday in the Midlands of England. For two weeks Dickens and Collins wandered about as the fancy took them, and out of their experiences came the idea for a series of five fanciful pieces for *Household Words* which they decided to call *The Lazy Tour of Two Idle Apprentices*. There has subsequently been much debate as to who wrote what in this collaboration, but, from the point of view of this writer, there can be no doubt that it was Dickens's hand that created the ghost story which interrupts the journey of the two men while they are staying at the King's Arms Inn in Lancaster. Despite the obvious stylistic qualities which point to it being his work, Dickens admitted as much when he mentioned it in a letter to his long-time correspondent, Baroness

Angela Burdett-Coutts on October 24, 1857. 'It is a very odd story,' he told her, 'with a wild, picturesque fancy in it.' In my opinion there can be no fairer, or more accurate, description of 'The Bride's Chamber' than that, and I am sure the reader will feel the same when he reaches it!

The whole series of five pieces which make up the *Idle Tour* appeared in *Household Words* in October 1857, but strangely have never enjoyed separate book publication, although they have occasionally been included in collected editions of Dickens's works. Once again Professor Stone has seen autobiographical traces relating to Dickens in 'The Bride's Chamber'—in particular the destruction of an unwanted wife, and the hopeless love of the young man for the beautiful, imprisoned young girl in the chamber of the title. In 1857 Dickens himself was hopelessly in love with a teenage actress, Ellen Ternan, who had toured with the production of his play, *The Frozen Deep*, and he saw his wife as standing in the way of this happiness. (Part of the reason for the tour with Wilkie Collins had been to put this business temporarily to one side.) Professor Stone also believes that there are elements to be found throughout the whole story of *The Lazy Tour* which Dickens was to utilise and enlarge when he came to write *Great Expectations* in 1861.

In 1859, the year in which the title of *Household Words* was changed to *All The Year Round*, Dickens also decided to try an experiment by giving an overall title to the special Christmas Extra number (he called it 'The Haunted House') and solicited chapters on this theme from various of his contributors. It has to be said that the resulting publication was a disappointment—a fact that was perhaps predictable with diverse hands at work—and only three of the eight chapters can be said to fulfil Dickens's concept. Of these, two had been written by Dickens himself and the other was a story by Mrs Elizabeth Gaskell entitled 'The Ghost in the Garden Room', which was very derivative of Dickens's style and had, in fact, been substantially edited by him before publication. In its theme of a young man who suddenly inherits wealth, squanders it, and descends into a life of crime, there were echoes of the master's own earlier work. 'The Mortals in the House' and 'The Ghost in Master B.'s Room' give us a clearer picture of his (unfulfilled) objective, and as one might expect with such a writer—skilled as he was already at the independent episode in longer works—both read quite satisfactorily on their own.

The December of the following year, 1860, saw the publication in one volume of seventeen of the pieces which Dickens had contributed over the years to *Household Words* and its successor, *All The Year Round*. The book was called *The Uncommercial Traveller*. Among the items was Mary Weller's story, 'Captain Murderer and The Devil's Bargain', and an out-of-the-ordinary ghost story called 'Mr Testator's Visitation'. Mr Testator is another of Dickens's unhappy lawyers, an impoverished fellow who lives in dreary chambers in Lyons Inn, London. The story centres on the eerie character who visits him, and Dickens teases us by leaving us to make up our own minds as to just who or what the 'Visitor' might be.

Five years were to pass before Dickens wrote another ghost story—the composition of the superb *Great Expectations* and *Our Mutual Friend* fully absorbing him during this time—but when he did take up his pen he produced in quick succession two tales which have become his best-known short ghost stories, and by far the most anthologised of all his examples of short fiction. They are 'The Trial For Murder' and 'The Signal-Man'.

'The Trial For Murder' appeared as a section in *Doctor Marigold's Prescriptions*, the Christmas Extra number of *All The Year Round* for 1865. It was listed as the sixth of the good doctor's 'Prescriptions' and was subtitled, 'To Be Taked With A Grain Of Salt' (a title it still sometimes enjoys when anthologised). It is supposedly written by a literary character whom Dr Marigold comes across during his travels, and purports to be an account of the circumstances preceding a trial for murder. The narrator, who serves on the jury at the trial, is haunted by the apparition of the murdered man—although no one but he can see it—and the spirit has apparently returned to ensure that justice is done. It is a beautifully constructed, atmospheric piece, written by a man thoroughly comfortable with the supernatural as well as being at the top of his literary powers.

The same verdict can also be applied to 'The Signal-Man' which Dickens inserted as an episode in *Mugby Junction*, the title of *All The Year Round*'s Christmas Extra for 1866. It is the account of an incident on one of the branch lines leading from the place called Mugby Junction. (For this reason, the story is very often anthologised as 'No. 1 Branch Line: The Signalman'.) The tale is supposedly related by a curious character called Barbox Brothers who is always wandering about in the vicinity of the railway junction hoping to pick up tit-bits of information to tell his bedridden friend named Phoebe. It is while exploring Branch

Line No. 1 that he meets the signalman of the title who tells him about a strange apparition which appears to him near the mouth of a tunnel just before any fatal accident is about to occur. Brothers' predicament in the face of this extraordinary confession, together with its consequences, form the gripping climax of this brilliant ghost story.

The story of the signalman has been exciting the attention of Dickens scholars for years because of a persistent rumour that it was based on a real event. Early suggestions that it might have been discounted because the description does not tally, and there is no deep cutting as mentioned in the story. But it is possible that the source may have been a train crash which occurred in 1861—five years *before* the story was written—on the South Downs. This was the first railway accident in the United Kingdom in which more than twenty passengers were killed and as such it made headline news. It occurred in a locality that Dickens knew well, and he could hardly have escaped reading about it. T. S. Lascelles, who spent many years investigating the background to the story, finally wrote his conclusions in *The Dickensian* of May 1960: 'I think this accident—if a real accident was in Dickens's mind at all—was clearly a train accident in a tunnel in which passengers were hurt. I can find no such accident until 1861 when the serious collision involving excursion trains occurred in the Clayton tunnel under the South Downs near Hassocks, on the London–Brighton line. There is a deep cutting there and a long pathway down to where the signalbox was in 1861. The collision was due to a misunderstanding on the telegraph, combined with other things, between the signalmen at each end of the tunnel; twenty-three passengers were killed. Two excursion trains were involved, the date was August 25th. These unfortunate people were brought out from the tunnel past the signalbox at the south end, the location, etc., of which was in fact very like the description in the Ghost tale.'

There the mystery remains for the moment—a mystery every bit as fascinating and intriguing as the story itself!

Of the three remaining items in the collection, two I believe to be remarkable and unacknowledged additions to the canon of Charles Dickens's works—and his 'ghost' writings in particular.

The first, simply titled 'Four Ghost Stories', appeared in *All The Year Round* on 14 September 1861. As was the usual practice, the contribution appeared anonymously, and it has subsequently been allowed to disappear into oblivion. This, I maintain, is a terrible fate for an item I believe to be the work of Dickens *himself*. My conviction that this is a lost work by the master is based not only on its theme (in which we know Dickens was fascinated) and its stylistic similarities with the rest of his writing (which will be immediately apparent to the reader), but on Dickens's own confession that it *is* his work in a letter to his biographer, John Forster. Remarkable as these facts are, the matter does not end there. For, as Forster tells us in his biography of Dickens, the author discovered that his piece of fiction was actually *fact*—that, unknowingly, he had written a ghost story that had, in truth, 'happened' to somebody! This revelation was made to Dickens by the person in question, who, on reading the story in *All The Year Round*, wrote to him accusing him of stealing the idea! But let Forster explain the extraordinary affair in his own words:

> The story was published in September, and in a day or two led to what Dickens will relate. Writing to Lord Lytton on September 15, 1861, he says, 'The artist himself who is the hero of that story has sent me in black and white his own account of the whole experience, so very original, so very extraordinary, so very far beyond the version I have published, that all other like stories turn pale before it.' The ghost thus reinforced [i.e. the portrait-painter's own story] came out in the number published on the 5th of October, and the reader who cares to turn to it, and compare what Dickens wrote to me in the interval (17th of September) will have some measure of his readiness to believe in such things. 'Upon the publication of the ghost story, up has started the portrait-painter who saw the phantoms! His own written story is out of all distance the most extraordinary that was ever produced; and it is as far beyond my version as Scott is beyond James. Everything connected with it is amazing; but conceive this—the portrait-painter had been engaged to write it elsewhere as a story for next Christmas, and not unnaturally supposed, when he saw himself anticipated in *All The Year Round*, that there had been treachery at his printers. 'In particular,' says he, 'how else was it possible that the date, the 13th of September, could have been got at? For I never told the date until I wrote it.' Now *my* story had NO DATE; but seeing, when I looked over the proofs, the great importance of having *a* date, I (CD) wrote in, unconsciously, the exact date on the margin of the proof!'

In the light of this, the reader will not be surprised that I have included both Dickens's 'Four Ghost Stories' and the remarkable 'fact-is-stranger-than-fiction' sequel entitled 'The Portrait-Painter's Story'.*

The last item brings us into contact with another area of ghostly phenomena that interested Dickens—spiritualism, which was rampant in the country during the latter part of his life. While, as we have seen, he was fair-minded on so much to do with the supernatural, he found himself deeply sceptical on the subject of contact with the dead, and over the years carried numerous articles on the topics of mediums, apparitions and 'spirit rappings' in both *Household Words* and *All The Year Round*. Indeed, his involvement in this issue was to continue until his death.

His own generally scathing tone, and the exposés which several of his contributors provided for his columns, naturally made Dickens a target of attack for the spiritualists (or 'Rappers', as he called them). Several papers have been written on this aspect of his life, so I will not labour the point here. He allegedly wrote half a dozen anonymous articles himself for his journal, and the one I have selected for inclusion is perhaps the most suitable on two counts.† Firstly, it is couched in the form of a satire and the events it recounts take place yet again at Christmas; secondly, it forms

* In his biography of Dickens, Forster also quotes a letter from the author which describes another strange experience verging on the supernatural. Dickens's letter is dated 30 May 1863, and says, 'Here is a curious case at first hand. On Thursday night in last week, being at the office here, I dreamed that I saw a lady in a red shawl with her back towards me (whom I supposed to be E). On her turning round I found that I didn't know her, and she said, "I am Miss Napier". All the time I was dressing next morning, I thought—What a preposterous thing to have so very distinct a dream about nothing! and why Miss Napier? for I never heard of any Miss Napier. That same Friday night, I read. After the reading came into my retiring-room Mary Boyle and her brother, *and* the lady in the red shawl whom they present as "Miss Napier"! These are all the circumstances, exactly told.'

† The other articles which have been attributed by various authorities to Dickens are: 'The Ghost of the Cock Lane Ghost Wrong Again', which is an attack on the wrongful use of Dickens's name in connection with some London seances (15 January 1853); 'A Haunted House', which is a comedy about the Houses of Parliament (23 July 1853); 'Rather A Strong Dose', containing some general remarks about spiritualism and table-rapping (21 March 1863); and 'The Marty Medium', a critique of the medium Daniel Dunglas Home's book, *Incidents In My Life* (4 April 1863).

part of an argument that Dickens *may* have planned to employ spiritualism of a kind in the last of his novels, the unfinished *Mystery of Edwin Drood*. 'Well-Authenticated Rappings' appeared in the 20 February 1858 issue of *Household Words* and, according to N. C. Peyrouton in *The Dickensian*, 'purported to be an account of his own sittings and revealed that he had not softened his attitude'.

Mr Peyrouton has made a detailed study of Dickens's involvement with spiritualism and it is these essays that have convinced him that the subject was going to emerge in *The Mystery of Edwin Drood*—if not to actually provide the solution to the crime. Writing in *The Dickensian* of May 1959, he says

> During much of 1869 and until his death on June 9, 1870, Dickens was engaged in the planning and writing of *Edwin Drood*. For the first time in a major work he had introduced the supernormal. There are suggestions of oriental mysticism woven about the Eurasian Landless twins, the hypnotic powers of John Jasper and his dream apparitions . . . Let us look briefly at what might have been. Perchance Dickens planned for Edwin to return as a ghost to haunt his Uncle Jack (the cover may depict Jasper discovering Edwin in the crypt—not the disguised Helena as has been hitherto often been suggested). Or it may be that Jasper was a Spiritualist, that Helena discovered this and masqueraded as Edwin in order to exploit his fear and force a confession. Possibly, but admittedly far-fetched, the disembodied spirit of Edwin might be working through Tarter or Datchery or even Jasper himself to bring down his murderer. But surely any such thing was only to have seemed to be—an appearance not a reality. If Dickens did elect to write a novel of the supernatural he would have taken unusual care that it could not be construed as an endorsement of Spiritualism and Spiritualists; he would expose the fraud or leave the solution of the mystery inexplicable as, in quite a different sense, it is.

It is a wry fact to have to note that, although believers in spiritualism had been joined in such a bitterly fought battle with the sceptic Dickens during his lifetime, after his death several of them claimed to have evoked his spirit. Now, they said, he was a believer! Among this number was none other than Sir Arthur Conan Doyle, creator of that famous fictional solver of mysteries, Sherlock Holmes, and, of course, a dedicated proponent of spiritualism. In September 1927, according to *Light* magazine, Sir Arthur revealed that he had spoken with the spirit of Charles Dickens at a seance held in his country house in the New Forest. The contact had been made through a planchette board which first indicated Dickens's presence when it spelt out the word, 'BOZ', his pen-name. After several exchanges about Dickens's existence on 'the other side', Sir Arthur said he enquired about the unwritten ending of *Edwin Drood*, which had long fascinated him. At this, he said, the 'ghost' of Dickens replied, 'The poor chap had a hard time. I always hoped you would put Sherlock on his track! I don't know which is better—to solve the mystery in your notebook or let it remain a mystery!'

The mystery of *Edwin Drood* still remains a mystery today, of course—as, in my opinion, should any tale that the creator's hand cannot resolve. Ghosts, too, remain a mystery to tantalise and fascinate us: indeed, if a solution to them *should* be found, think what havoc that would wreak on a large body of our literature!

The nineteen stories I have discussed (leaving aside 'The Portrait-Painter's Story', which of course does not qualify) represent the complete ghost stories of Charles Dickens. He does, it must be said, make mention of ghosts and hauntings in many of his other works, but after the most intensive research I am sure that all the *short stories* as such are included here: which makes this the first volume of its kind.

So now let me leave you to enjoy these marvellous stories, and with some of Dickens's own words on the subject of ghosts. They are words I would address to anyone whose mind is closed on such matters. For if a man such as he can feel as he does after a lifetime of involvement, then I for one will not dispute his sentiments:

'My own mind is perfectly unprejudiced and impressible on the subject of ghosts. I do not in the least pretend that such things cannot be.'

PETER HAINING
Christmas 1981

CAPTAIN MURDERER AND THE DEVIL'S BARGAIN

There are not many places that I find it more agreeable to revisit, when I am in an idle mood, than some places to which I have never been. For, my acquaintance with those spots is of such long standing, and has ripened into an intimacy of so affectionate a nature, that I take a particular interest in assuring myself that they are unchanged.

I never was in Robinson Crusoe's Island, yet I frequently return there. The colony he established on it soon faded away, and it is uninhabited by any descendants of the grave and courteous Spaniards, or of Will Atkins and the other mutineers, and has relapsed into its original condition. Not a twig of its wicker houses remains, its goats have long run wild again, its screaming parrots would darken the sun with a cloud of many flaming colours if a gun were fired there, no face is ever reflected in the waters of the little creek which Friday swam across when pursued by his two brother cannibals with sharpened stomachs. After comparing notes with other travellers who have similarly revisited the Island, and conscientiously inspected it, I have satisfied myself that it contains no vestige of Mr Atkins's domesticity or theology, though his track on the memorable evening of his landing to set his captain ashore, when he was decoyed about and round about until it was dark, and his boat was stove, and his strength and spirits failed him, is yet plainly to be traced. So is the hill-top on which Robinson was struck dumb with joy when the reinstated captain pointed to the ship, riding within half a mile of the shore, that was to bear him away, in the nine-and-twentieth year of his seclusion in that lonely place. So is the sandy beach on which the memorable footstep was impressed, and where the savages hauled up their canoes when they came ashore for those dreadful public dinners, which led to a dancing worse than speech-making. So is the cave where the flaring eyes of the old goat made such a goblin appearance in the dark. So is the site of the hut where Robinson lived with the dog and the parrot and the cat, and where he endured those first agonies of solitude, which—strange to say—never involved any ghostly fancies; a circumstance so remarkable, that perhaps he left out something in writing his record? Round hundreds of such objects, hidden in the dense tropical foliage, the tropical sea breaks evermore; and over them the tropical sky, saving in the short rainy season, shines bright and cloudless.

Neither was I ever belated among wolves, on the borders of France and Spain; nor did I ever, when night was closing in and the ground was covered with snow, draw up my little company among some felled trees which served as a breast-work, and there fire a train of gunpowder so dexterously that suddenly we had three or four score blazing wolves illuminating the darkness around us. Nevertheless, I occasionally go back to that dismal region, and perform the feat again; when, indeed, to smell the singeing and the frying of the wolves afire, and to see them setting one another alight as they rush and tumble, and to behold them rolling in the snow vainly attempting to put themselves out, and to hear their howlings taken up by all the echoes as well as by all the unseen wolves within the woods, makes me tremble.

I was never in the robbers' cave where Gil Blas lived, but I often go back there, and find the trap-door just as heavy to raise as it used to be, while that wicked old disabled Black lies everlastingly cursing in bed. I was never in Don Quixote's study, where he read his books of chivalry until he rose and hacked at imaginary giants, and then refreshed himself with great draughts of water, yet you couldn't move a book in it without my knowledge, or with my consent. I was never (thank Heaven!) in company with the little old woman who hobbled out of the chest, and told the merchant Abudah to go in search of the Talisman of Oromanes, yet I make it my business to know that she is well preserved, and as intolerable as ever. I was never at the school where the boy Horatio Nelson got out of bed to steal the pears; not because he wanted any, but because every other boy was afraid: yet I have several times been back to this Academy, to see him let down out of window with a sheet. So with Damascus, and Bagdad, and Brobdingnag (which has the curious fate of being usually misspelt when written), and Lilliput, and Laputa, and the Nile, and Abyssinia, and the Ganges, and the North Pole, and many hundreds of places—I was never at them, yet it is an affair of my life to keep them intact, and I am always going back to them.

But, when I was in Dullborough one day, revisiting the associations of my childhood, my experience in this wise was made quite inconsiderable and of no account, by the quantity of places and people—utterly impossible places and people, but none the less alarmingly real—that I found I had been introduced to by my nurse before I was six years old, and used to be forced to go back to at night without at all wanting to go. If we all knew our own minds (in a more enlarged sense than the popular acceptation of that phrase), I suspect we should find our nurses responsible for most of the dark corners we are forced to go back to against our wills.

The first diabolical character who intruded himself on my peaceful youth (as I called to mind that day at Dullborough) was a certain Captain Murderer. This wretch must have been an offshoot of the Blue Beard family, but I had no suspicion of the consanguinity in those times. His warning name would seem to have awakened no general prejudice against him, for he was admitted into the best society, and possessed immense wealth. Captain Murderer's mission was matrimony, and the gratification of a cannibal appetite with tender brides. On his marriage morning, he always caused both sides of the way to church to be planted with curious flowers; and when his bride said, 'Dear Captain Murderer, I never saw flowers like these before: what are they called?' he answered, 'They are called Garnish for house-lamb,' and laughed at his ferocious practical joke in a horrid manner disquieting the minds of the noble bridal company, with a very sharp show of teeth, then displayed for the first time. He made love in a coach and six, and married in a coach and twelve, and all his horses were milk-white horses with one red spot on the back, which he caused to be hidden by the harness. For, the spot *would* come there, though every horse was milk-white when Captain Murderer bought him. And the spot was young bride's blood. (To this terrific point I am indebted for my first personal experience of a shudder and cold beads on the forehead.) When Captain Murderer had made an end of feasting and revelry, and had dismissed the noble guests, and was alone with his wife on the day month after their marriage, it was his whimsical custom to produce a golden rolling-pin and a silver pie-board. Now, there was this special feature in the Captain's courtships, that he always asked if the young lady could make pie-crust; and, if she couldn't by nature or education, she was taught. Well! When the bride saw Captain Murderer produce the golden rolling-pin and silver pie-board, she remembered this, and turned up her laced-silk sleeves to make a pie. The Captain brought out a silver pie-dish of immense capacity, and the Captain brought out flour and butter and eggs and all things needful, except the inside of the pie; of materials for the staple of the pie itself, the Captain brought out none. Then said the lovely bride, 'Dear Captain Murderer, what pie is this to be?' He replied, 'A meat-pie.' Then said the lovely bride, 'Dear Captain Murderer, I see no meat.' The Captain humorously retorted, 'Look in the glass.' She looked in the glass, but still she saw no meat, and then the Captain roared with laughter, and, suddenly frowning and drawing his sword, bade her roll out the crust. So she rolled out the crust, dropping large tears upon it all the time because he was so cross, and when she had lined the dish with crust, and had cut the crust all ready to fit the top, the Captain called out, '*I* see the meat in the glass!' And the bride looked up at the glass, just in time to see the Captain cutting her head off; and he chopped her in pieces, and peppered her, and salted her, and put her in the pie, and sent it to the baker's, and ate it all, and picked the bones.

Captain Murderer went on in this way, prospering exceedingly, until he came to choose a bride from two twin sisters, and at first didn't know which to choose. For, though one was fair, and the other dark, they were both equally beautiful. But the fair twin loved him, and the dark twin hated him, so he chose the fair one. The dark twin would have prevented the marriage if she could, but she couldn't; however, on the night before it, much suspecting Captain Murderer, she stole out and climbed his garden wall, and looked in at his window through a chink in the shutter, and saw him having his teeth filed sharp. Next day she listened all day, and heard him make his joke about the house-lamb. And that day month he had the paste rolled out, and cut the fair twin's head off, and chopped her in pieces, and peppered her, and salted her, and put her in the pie, and sent it to the baker's, and ate it all, and picked the bones.

Now, the dark twin had had her suspicions much increased by the filing of the Captain's teeth, and again by the house-lamb joke. Putting all things together when he gave out that her sister was dead, she divined the truth, and determined to be revenged. So, she went up to Captain Murderer's house, and knocked at the knocker, and pulled at the bell, and, when the Captain came to the door, said: 'Dear Captain Murderer, marry me next, for I always loved you, and was jealous of my sister.' The Captain took it as a compliment, and made a polite answer, and the marriage was quickly arranged. On the night before it, the bride again climbed to his window, and again saw him having his teeth filed sharp. At this sight she laughed, such a terrible laugh at the chink in the shutter, that the Captain's blood curdled, and he said: 'I hope nothing has disagreed with me!' At that, she laughed again, a still more terrible laugh, and the shutter was opened and search made, but she was nimbly gone, and there was no one. Next day they went to church in a coach and twelve, and were married. And that day month she rolled the pie-crust out, and Captain Murderer cut her head off, and chopped her in pieces, and peppered her, and salted her, and put her in the pie, and sent it to the baker's, and ate it all, and picked the bones.

But, before she began to roll out the paste, she had taken a deadly poison of most awful character, distilled from toads' eyes and spiders' knees; and Captain Murderer had hardly picked her last bone, when he began to swell, and to turn blue, and to be all over spots, and to scream. And he went on swelling and turning bluer, and being more all over spots and screaming, until he reached from floor to ceiling, and from wall to wall; and then, at one o'clock in the morning, he blew up with a loud explosion. At the sound of it, all the milk-white horses in the stables broke their halters and went mad, and then they galloped over everybody in Captain Murderer's house (beginning with the family blacksmith who had filed his teeth) until the whole were dead, and then they galloped away.

Hundreds of times did I hear this legend of Captain Murderer in my early youth, and added hundreds of times was there a mental compulsion upon me, in bed, to peep in at his window as the dark twin peeped, and to revisit his horrible house, and look at him in his blue and spotty and screaming stage, as he reached from floor to ceiling, and from wall to wall. The young woman who brought me acquainted with Captain Murderer had a fiendish enjoyment of my terrors, and used to begin, I remember—as a sort of introductory overture—by clawing the air with both hands, and uttering a long low hollow groan. So acutely did I suffer from this ceremony in combination with this infernal Captain, that I sometimes used to plead, I thought I was hardly strong enough and old enough to hear the story again just yet. But, she never spared me one word of it, and, indeed, commended the awful chalice to my lips as the only preservative known to science against 'The Black Cat'—a weird and glaring-eyed supernatural Tom, who was reputed to prowl about the world by night, sucking the breath of infancy, and who was endowed with a special thirst (as I was given to understand) for mine.

This female bard—may she have been repaid my debt of obligation to her in the matter of nightmares and perspirations!—reappears in my memory as the daughter of a shipwright. Her name was Mercy, though she had none on me. There was something of a ship-building flavour in the following story. As it always recurs to me in a vague association with calomel pills, I believe it to have been reserved for dull nights when I was low with medicine.

There was once a shipwright, and he wrought in a Government Yard, and his name was Chips. And his father's name before him was Chips, and *his* father's name before *him* was Chips, and they were all Chipses. And Chips the father had sold himself to the Devil for an iron pot and a bushel of tenpenny nails and half a ton of copper and a rat that could speak; and Chips the grandfather had sold himself to the Devil for an iron pot and a bushel of tenpenny nails and half a ton of copper and a rat that could speak; and Chips the great-grandfather had disposed of himself in the same direction on the same terms; and the bargain had run in the family for a long long time. So, one day, when young Chips was at work in the Dock Slip all alone, down in the dark hold of an old Seventy-four that was haled up for repairs, the Devil presented himself, and remarked:

'A Lemon has pips,
And a Yard has ships,
And *I*'ll have Chips!'

(I don't know why, but this fact of the Devil's expressing himself in rhyme was peculiarly trying to me.) Chips looked up when he heard the words, and there he saw the Devil with saucer eyes that squinted on a terrible great scale, and that struck out sparks of blue fire continually. And, whenever he winked his eyes, showers of blue sparks came out, and his eyelashes made a clattering like flints and steels striking lights. And hanging over one of his arms by the handle was an iron pot, and under that arm was a bushel of tenpenny nails, and under his other arm was half a ton of copper, and sitting on one of his shoulders was a rat that could speak. So, the Devil said again:

'A Lemon has pips,
And a Yard has ships,
And *I*'ll have Chips!'

(The invariable effect of this alarming tautology on the part of the Evil Spirit was to deprive me of my senses for some moments.) So, Chips answered never a word, but went on with his work.

'What are you doing, Chips?' said the rat that could speak.

'I am putting in new planks where you and your gang have eaten old away,' said Chips.

'But we'll eat them too,' said the rat that could speak; 'and we'll let in the water and drown the crew, and we'll eat them too.'

Chips, being only a shipwright, and not a Man-of-war's man, said, 'You are welcome to it.'

But he couldn't keep his eyes off the half a ton of copper, or the bushel of tenpenny nails; for nails and copper are a shipwright's sweethearts, and shipwrights will run away with them whenever they can. So, the Devil said, 'I see what you are looking at, Chips. You had better strike the bargain. You know the terms. Your father before you was well acquainted with them, and so were your grandfather and great-grandfather before him.'

Says Chips, 'I like the copper, and I like the nails, and I don't mind the pot, but I don't like the rat.'

Says the Devil fiercely, 'You can't have the metal without him—and *he*'s a curiosity. I'm going.'

Chips, afraid of losing the half a ton of copper and the bushel of nails, then said, 'Give us hold!' So, he got the copper and the nails and the pot and the rat that could speak, and the Devil vanished. Chips sold the copper, and he sold the nails, and he would have sold the pot; but, whenever he offered it for sale, the rat was in it, and the dealers dropped it, and would have nothing to say to the bargain. So, Chips resolved to kill the rat, and being at work in the Yard one day with a great kettle of hot pitch on one side of him, and the iron pot with the rat in it on the other, he turned the scalding pitch into the pot, and filled it full. Then, he kept his eye upon it till it cooled and hardened, and then he let it stand for twenty days, and then he heated the pitch again, and turned it back into the kettle, and then he sank the pot in water for twenty days more, and then he got the smelters to put it in the furnace for twenty days more, and then they gave it him out, red-hot, and looking like red-hot glass instead of iron—yet there was the rat in it, just the same as ever! And the moment it caught his eye, it said with a jeer:

'A Lemon has pips,
And a Yard has ships,
And *I*'ll have Chips!'

(For this Refrain I had waited, since its last appearance with inexpressible horror, which now culminated.) Chips now felt certain in his own mind that the rat would stick to him; the rat, answering his thought, said, 'I will—like pitch!'

Now, as the rat leaped out of the pot when it had spoken, and made off, Chips began to hope that it wouldn't keep its word. But, a terrible thing happened next day. For, when dinner-time came, and the Dock bell rang to strike work, he put his rule into the long pocket at the side of his trousers, and there he found a rat—not that rat, but another rat. And in his hat he found another; and in his pocket-handkerchief another; and in the sleeves of his coat, when he pulled it on to go to dinner, two more. And from that time he found himself so frightfully intimate with all the rats in the Yard, that they climbed up his legs when he was at work, and sat on his tools while he used them. And they could all speak to one another, and he understood what they said. And they got into his lodging, and into his bed, and into his teapot, and into his beer, and into his boots. And he was going to be married to a corn-chandler's daughter; and when he gave her a workbox he had himself made for her, a rat jumped out of it; and when he put his arm round her waist, a rat clung about her; so the marriage was broken off, though the banns were already twice put up—which the parish clerk well remembers, for, as he handed the book to the clergyman for the second time of asking, a large fat rat ran over the leaf. (By this time a special cascade of rats was rolling down my back, and the whole of my small listening person was overrun with them. At intervals ever since, I have been morbidly afraid of my own pocket, lest my exploring hand should find a specimen or two of those vermin in it.)

You may believe that all this was very terrible to Chips; but even all this was not the worst. He knew, besides, what the rats were doing, wherever they were. So, sometimes he would cry aloud, when he was at his club at night, 'Oh! Keep the rats out of the convicts' burying-ground! Don't let them do that!' Or 'There's one of them at the cheese downstairs!' Or, 'There's two of them smelling at the baby in the garret!' Or, other things of that sort. At last he was voted mad, and lost his work in the Yard, and could get no other work. But, King George wanted men, so before very long he got pressed for a sailor. And so he was taken off in a boat one evening to his ship, lying at Spithead, ready to sail. And so the first thing he made out in her, as he got near her, was the figure-head of the old Seventy-four, where he had seen the Devil. She was called the Argonaut, and they rowed right under the bowsprit, where the figure-head of the Argonaut, with a sheep-skin in his hand and a blue gown on, was looking out to sea; and sitting staring on his forehead was the rat who could speak, and his exact words were these: 'Chips ahoy! Old boy! We've pretty well eat them too, and we'll drown the crew, and will eat them too!' (Here I always became exceedingly faint, and would have asked for water, but that I was speechless.)

The ship was bound for the Indies; and, if you don't know where that is, you ought to it, and angels will never love you. (Here I felt myself an outcast from a future state.) The ship set sail that very night, and she sailed, and sailed, and sailed. Chips's feelings were dreadful. Nothing ever equalled his terrors. No wonder. At last, one day, he asked leave to speak to the Admiral. The Admiral giv' leave.

Chips went down on his knees in the Great State Cabin. 'Your Honour, unless your Honour, without a moment's loss of time, makes sail for the nearest shore, this is a doomed ship, and her name is the Coffin!'

'Young man, your words are a madman's words.'

'Your Honour, no; they are nibbling us away.'

'They?'

'Your Honour, them dreadful rats. Dust and hollowness where solid oak ought to be! Rats nibbling a grave for every man on board! Oh! Does your Honour love your Lady and your pretty children?'

'Yes, my man, to be sure.'

'Then for God's sake, make for the nearest shore, for at this present moment the rats are all stopping in their work, and are all looking straight towards you with bare teeth, and are all saying to one another that you shall never, never, never, never see your Lady and your children more.'

'My poor fellow, you are a case for the doctor. Sentry, take care of this man!'

So, he was bled and he was blistered, and he was this and that, for six whole days and nights. So, then he again asked leave to speak to the Admiral. The Admiral giv' leave. He went down on his knees in the Great State Cabin. 'Now, Admiral, you must die! You took no warning; you must die! The rats are never wrong in their calculations, and they make out that they'll be through at twelve to-night. So, you must die!—With me and all the rest!' And so at twelve o'clock there was a great leak reported in the ship, and a torrent of water rushed in, and nothing could stop it, and they all went down, every living soul. And what the rats—being water-rats—left of Chips at last floated to shore, and sitting on him was an immense overgrown rat, laughing, that dived when the corpse touched the beach, and never came up. And there was a deal of seaweed on the remains. And if you get thirteen bits of seaweed, and dry them, and burn them in the fire, they will go off like in these thirteen words as plain as plain can be:

'A Lemon has pips,
And a Yard has ships,
And *I*'ll have Chips!'

The same female bard—descended, possibly, from those terrible old scalds who seem to have existed for the express purpose of addling the brains of mankind when they begin to investigate languages—made a standing pretence which greatly assisted in forcing me back to a number of hideous places that I would by all means have avoided. This pretence was, that all her ghost stories had occurred to her own relations. Politeness towards a meritorious family, therefore, forbade my doubting them, and they acquired an air of authentication that impaired my digestive powers for life. There was a narrative concerning an unearthly animal foreboding death, which appeared in the open street to a parlour-maid who 'went to fetch the beer' for supper: first (as I now recall it) assuming the likeness of a black dog, and gradually rising on its hind-legs, and swelling into the semblance of some quadruped greatly surpassing a hippopotamus: which apparition—not because I deemed it in the least improbable, but because I felt it to be really too large to bear—I feebly endeavoured to explain away. But, on Mercy's retorting with wounded dignity that the parlour-maid was her own sister-in-law, I perceived there was no hope, and resigned myself to this zoological phenomenon as one of my many pursuers. There was another narrative describing the apparition of a young woman who came out of a glass case, and haunted another young woman until the other young woman questioned it, and elicited that its bones (Lord! To think of its being so particular about its bones!) were buried under the glass case, whereas she required them to be interred, with every Undertaking solemnity up to twenty-four pound ten, in another particular place. This narrative I considered I had a personal interest in disproving, because we had cases at home, and how, otherwise, was I to be guaranteed from the intrusion of young women requiring *me* to bury them up to twenty-four pound ten, when I had only twopence a week? But my remorseless nurse cut the ground from under my tender feet, by informing me that She was the other young woman; and I couldn't say, 'I don't believe you;' it was not possible.

Such are a few of the uncommercial journeys that I was forced to make, against my will, when I was very young and unreasoning. And really, as to the latter part of them, it is not so very long ago—now I come to think of it—that I was asked to undertake them once again with a steady countenance.

THE LAWYER AND THE GHOST

I knew a man—let me see—forty years ago now—who took an old, damp, rotten set of chambers, in one of the most ancient Inns, that had been shut up and empty for years and years before. There were lots of old women's stories about the place, and it certainly was very far from being a cheerful one; but he was poor, and the rooms were cheap, and that would have been quite a sufficient reason for him, if they had been ten times worse than they really were.

The man was obliged to take some mouldering fixtures that were on the place, and, among the rest, was a great lumbering wooden press for papers, with large glass doors, and a green curtain inside; a pretty useless thing for him, for he had no papers to put in it; and as to his clothes, he carried them about with him, and that wasn't very hard work, either.

Well, he had moved in all his furniture—it wasn't quite a truck-full—and had sprinkled it about the room, so as to make the four chairs look as much like a dozen as possible, and was sitting down before the fire at night, drinking the first glass of two gallons of whiskey he had ordered on credit, wondering whether it would ever be paid for, and if so, in how many years' time, when his eyes encountered the glass doors of the wooden press.

'Ah,' says he. 'If I hadn't been obliged to take that ugly article at the old broker's valuation, I might have got something comfortable for the money. I'll tell you what it is, old fellow,' he said, speaking aloud to the press, having nothing else to speak to; 'If it wouldn't cost more to break up your old carcase, than it would ever be worth afterwards, I'd have a fire out of you in less than no time.'

He had hardly spoken the words, when a sound resembling a faint groan, appeared to issue from the interior of the case. It startled him at first, but thinking, on a moment's reflection, that it must be some young fellow in the next chamber, who had been dining out, he put his feet on the fender, and raised the poker to stir the fire.

At that moment, the sound was repeated: and one of the glass doors slowly opening, disclosed a pale and emaciated figure in soiled and worn apparel, standing erect in the press. The figure was tall and thin, and the countenance expressive of care and anxiety; but there was something in the hue of the skin, and gaunt and unearthly appearance of the whole form, which no being of this world was ever seen to wear.

'Who are you?' said the new tenant, turning very pale; poising the poker in his hand, however, and taking a very decent aim at the countenance of the figure. 'Who are you?'

'Don't throw that poker at me,' replied the form: 'If you hurled it with ever so sure an aim, it would pass through me, without resistance, and expend its force on the wood behind. I am a spirit!'

'And, pray, what do you want here?' faltered the tenant.

'In this room,' replied the apparition, 'my worldly ruin was worked, and I and my children beggared. In this press, the papers in a long, long suit, which accumulated for years, were deposited. In this room, when I had died of grief, and long-deferred hope, two wily harpies divided the wealth for which I had contested during a wretched existence, and of which, at last, not one farthing was left for my unhappy descendants. I terrified them from the spot, and since that day have prowled by night—the only period at which I can re-visit the earth—about the scenes of my long-protracted misery. This apartment is mine: leave it to me!'

'If you insist upon making your appearance here,' said the tenant, who had had time to collect his presence of mind during this prosy statement of the ghost's, 'I shall give up possession with the greatest pleasure, but I should like to ask you one question, if you will allow me.'

'Say on,' said the apparition, sternly.

'Well,' said the tenant, 'I don't apply the observation personally to you, because it is equally applicable to most of the ghosts I ever heard of; but it does appear to me somewhat inconsistent, that when you have an opportunity of visiting the fairest spots of earth—for I suppose space is nothing to you—you should always return exactly to the very places where you have been most miserable.'

'Egad, that's very true; I never thought of that before,' said the ghost.

'You see, sir,' pursued the tenant, 'this is a very uncomfortable room. From the appearance of that press, I should be disposed to say that it is not wholly free from bugs; and I really think you might find more comfortable quarters: to say nothing of the climate of London, which is extremely disagreeable.'

'You are very right, sir,' said the ghost politely, 'it never struck me till now; I'll try a change of air directly.'

In fact, he began to vanish as he spoke: his legs, indeed, had quite disappeared!

'And if, sir,' said the tenant, calling after him, 'if you *would* have the goodness to suggest to the other ladies and gentlemen who are now engaged in haunting old empty houses, that they might be much more comfortable elsewhere, you will confer a very great benefit on society.'

'I will,' replied the ghost, 'we must be dull fellows, very dull fellows, indeed; I can't imagine how we can have been so stupid.'

With these words, the spirit disappeared, and what is rather remarkable, he never came back again.

THE QUEER CHAIR

The Bagman's Story

One winter's evening, about five o'clock, just as it began to grow dusk, a man in a gig might have been seen urging his tired horse along the road which leads across Marlborough Downs, in the direction of Bristol. I say he might have been seen, and I have no doubt he would have been, if anybody but a blind man had happened to pass that way; but the weather was so bad, and the night so cold and wet, that nothing was out but the water, and so the traveller jogged along in the middle of the road, lonesome and dreary enough. If any bagman of that day could have caught sight of the little neck-or-nothing sort of gig, with a clay-coloured body and red wheels, and the vixenish ill-tempered, fast-going bay mare, that looked like a cross between a butcher's horse and a two-penny post-office pony, he would have known at once, that this traveller could have been no other than Tom Smart, of the great house of Bilson and Slum, Cateaton Street, City. However, as there was no bagman to look on, nobody knew anything at all about the matter; and so Tom Smart and his clay-coloured gig with the red wheels, and the vixenish mare with the fast pace, went on together, keeping the secret among them: and nobody was a bit the wiser.

There are many pleasanter places even in this dreary world, than Marlborough Downs when it blows hard; and if you throw in beside, a gloomy winter's evening, a miry and sloppy road, and a pelting fall of heavy rain, and try the effect, by way of experiment, in your own proper person, you will experience the full force of this observation.

The wind blew—not up the road or down it, though that's bad enough, but sheer across it, sending the rain slanting down like the lines they used to rule in the copy-books at school, to make the boys slope well. For a moment it would die away, and the traveller would begin to delude himself into the belief that, exhausted with its previous fury, it had quietly lain itself down to rest, when, whoo! he would hear it growling and whistling in the distance, and on it would come rushing over the hill-tops, and sweeping along the plain, gathering sound and strength as it drew nearer, until it dashed with a heavy gust against horse and man, driving the sharp rain into their ears, and its cold damp breath into their very bones; and past them it would scour, far, far away, with a stunning roar, as if in ridicule of their weakness, and triumphant in the consciousness of its own strength and power.

The bay mare splashed away, through the mud and water, with drooping ears; now and then tossing her head as if to express her disgust at this very ungentlemanly behaviour of the elements, but keeping a good pace notwithstanding, until a gust of wind, more furious than any that had yet assailed them, caused her to stop suddenly and plant her four feet firmly against the ground, to prevent her being blown over. It's a special mercy that she did this, for if she *had* been blown over, the vixenish mare was so light, and the gig was so light, and Tom Smart such a light weight into the bargain, that they must infallibly have all gone rolling over and over together, until they reached the confines of earth, or until the wind fell; and in either case the probability is, that neither the vixenish mare, nor the clay-coloured gig with the red wheels, nor Tom Smart, would ever have been fit for service again.

'Well, damn my straps and whiskers,' says Tom Smart, (Tom sometimes had an unpleasant knack of swearing), 'Damn my straps and whiskers,' says Tom, 'if this ain't pleasant, blow me!'

You'll very likely ask me why, as Tom Smart had been pretty well blown already, he expressed this wish to be submitted to the same process again. I can't say—all I know is, that Tom Smart said so—or at least he always told my uncle he said so, and it's just the same thing.

'Blow me,' says Tom Smart; and the mare neighed as if she were precisely of the same opinion.

'Cheer up, old girl,' said Tom, patting the bay mare on the neck with the end of his whip. 'It won't do pushing on, such a night as this; the first house we come to we'll put up at, so the faster you go the sooner it's over. Soho, old girl—gently—gently.'

Whether the vixenish mare was sufficiently well acquainted with the tones of Tom's voice to comprehend his meaning, or whether she found it colder standing still than moving on, of course I can't say. But I can say that Tom had no sooner finished speaking, than she pricked up her ears, and started forward at a speed which made the clay-coloured gig rattle till you would have supposed every one of the red spokes were going to fly out on the turf of Marlborough Downs; and even Tom, whip as he was, couldn't stop or check her pace, until she drew up, of her own accord, before a road-side inn on the right-hand side of the way, about half a quarter of a mile from the end of the Downs.

Tom cast a hasty glance at the upper part of the house as he threw the reins to the hostler, and stuck the whip in the box. It was a strange old place, built of a kind of shingle, inlaid, as it were, with cross-beams, with gabled-topped windows projecting completely over the pathway, and a low door with a dark porch, and a couple of steep steps leading down into the house, instead of the modern fashion of half a dozen shallow ones leading up to it. It was a comfortable-looking place though, for there was a strong cheerful light in the bar-window, which shed a bright ray across the road, and even lighted up the hedge on the other side; and there was a red flickering light in the opposite window, one moment but faintly discernible, and the next gleaming strongly through the drawn curtains, which intimated that a rousing fire was blazing within. Marking these little evidences with the eye of an experienced traveller, Tom dismounted with as much agility as his half-frozen limbs would permit, and entered the house.

In less than five minutes' time, Tom was ensconced in the

room opposite the bar—the very room where he had imagined the fire blazing—before a substantial matter-of-fact roaring fire, composed of something short of a bushel of coals, and wood enough to make half a dozen decent gooseberry bushes, piled half way up the chimney, and roaring and crackling with a sound that of itself would have warmed the heart of any reasonable man. This was comfortable, but this was not all, for a smartly-dressed girl, with a bright eye and a neat ankle, was laying a very clean white cloth on the table; and as Tom sat with his slippered feet on the fender, and his back to the open door, he saw a charming prospect of the bar reflected in the glass over the chimney-piece, with delightful rows of green bottles and gold labels, together with jars of pickles and preserves, and cheeses and boiled hams, and rounds of beef, arranged on shelves in the most tempting and delicious array. Well, this was comfortable too; but even this was not all—for in the bar, seated at tea at the nicest possible little table, drawn close up before the brightest possible little fire, was a buxom widow of somewhere about eight-and-forty or thereabouts, with a face as comfortable as the bar, who was evidently the landlady of the house, and the supreme ruler over all these agreeable possessions. There was only one drawback to the beauty of the whole picture, and that was a tall man—a very tall man—in a brown coat and bright basket buttons, and black whiskers, and wavy black hair, who was seated at tea with the widow, and who it required no great penetration to discover was in a fair way of persuading her to be a widow no longer, but to confer upon him the privilege of sitting down in that bar, for and during the whole remainder of the term of his natural life.

Tom Smart was by no means of an irritable or envious disposition, but somehow or other the tall man with the brown coat and the bright basket buttons did rouse what little gall he had in his composition, and did make him feel extremely idignant: the more especially as he could now and then observe, from his seat before the glass, certain little affectionate familiarities passing between the tall man and the widow, which sufficiently denoted that the tall man was as high in favour as he was in size. Tom was fond of hot punch—I may venture to say he was *very* fond of hot punch—and after he had seen the vixenish mare well fed and well littered down, and had eaten every bit of the nice little hot dinner which the widow tossed up for him with her own hands, he just ordered a tumbler of it, by way of experiment. Now, if there was one thing in the whole range of domestic art, which the widow could manufacture better than another, it was this identical article; and the first tumbler was adapted to Tom Smart's taste with such peculiar nicety, that he ordered a second with the least possible delay. Hot punch is a pleasant thing, gentlemen—an extremely pleasant thing under any circumstances—but in that snug old parlour, before the roaring fire, with the wind blowing outside till every timber in the old house creaked again, Tom Smart found it perfectly delightful. He ordered another tumbler, and then another—I am not quite certain whether he didn't order another after that—but the more he drank of the hot punch, the more he thought of the tall man.

'Confound his impudence!' said Tom to himself, 'what business has he in that snug bar? Such an ugly villain too!' said Tom. 'If the widow had any taste, she might surely pick up some better fellow than that.' Here Tom's eye wandered from the glass on the chimney-piece, to the glass on the table; and as he felt himself become gradually sentimental, he emptied the fourth tumbler of punch and ordered a fifth.

Tom Smart, gentlemen, had always been very much attached to the public line. It had long been his ambition to stand in a bar of his own, in a green coat, knee-cords, and tops. He had a great notion of taking the chair at convivial dinners, and he had often thought how well he could preside in a room of his own in the talking way, and what a capital example he could set to his customers in the drinking compartment. All these things passed rapidly through Tom's mind as he sat drinking the hot punch by the roaring fire, and he felt very justly and properly indignant that the tall man should be in a fair way of keeping such an excellent house, while he, Tom Smart, was as far from it as ever. So, after deliberating over the last two tumblers, whether he hadn't a perfect right to pick a quarrel with the tall man for having contrived to get into the good graces of the buxom widow, Tom Smart at last arrived at the satisfactory conclusion that he was a very ill-used and persecuted individual, and had better go to bed.

Up a wide and ancient staircase the smart girl preceded Tom, shading the chamber candle with her hand, to protect it from the currents of air which in such a rambling old place might have found plenty of room to disport themselves in, without blowing the candle out, but which did blow it out nevertheless; thus affording Tom's enemies an opportunity of asserting that it was he, and not the wind, who extinguished the candle, and that while he pretended to be blowing it alight again, he was in fact kissing the girl. Be this as it may, another light was obtained, and Tom was conducted through a maze of rooms, and a labyrinth of passages, to the apartment which had been prepared for his reception, where the girl bade him good night, and left him alone.

It was a good large room with big closets, and a bed which might have served for a whole boarding-school, to say nothing of a couple of oaken presses that would have held the baggage of a small army; but what struck Tom's fancy most was a strange, grim-looking high-backed chair, carved in the most fantastic manner, with a flowered damask cushion, and the round knobs at the bottom of the legs carefully tied up in red cloth, as if it had got the gout in its toes. Of any other queer chair, Tom would only have thought it *was* a queer chair, and there would have been an end of the matter; but there was something about this particular chair, and yet he couldn't tell what it was, so odd and so unlike any other piece of furniture he had ever seen, that it seemed to fascinate him. He sat down before the fire, and stared at the old chair for half an hour;—Deuce take the chair, it was such a strange old thing, he couldn't take his eyes off it.

'Well,' said, Tom, slowly undressing himself, and staring at the old chair all the while, which stood with a mysterious aspect by the bedside, 'I never saw such a rum concern as that in my days. Very odd,' said Tom, who had got rather sage with the hot punch, 'Very odd.' Tom shook his head with an air of profound wisdom, and looked at the chair again. He couldn't make anything of it though, so he got into bed, covered himself up warm, and fell asleep.

In about half an hour, Tom woke up, with a start, from a confused dream of tall men and tumblers of punch: and the first object that presented itself to his waking imagination was the queer chair.

'I won't look at it any more,' said Tom to himself, and he squeezed his eyelids together, and tried to persuade himself he was going to sleep again. No use; nothing but queer chairs danced before his eyes, kicking up their legs, jumping over each other's backs, and playing all kinds of antics.

'I may as well see one real chair, as two or three complete sets of false ones,' said Tom, bringing out his head from under the bed-clothes. There it was, plainly discernible by the light of the fire, looking as provoking as ever.

Tom gazed at the chair; and, suddenly as he looked at it, a most extraordinary change seemed to come over it. The carving of the back gradually assumed the lineaments and expression of an old shrivelled human face; the damask cushion became an antique, flapped waistcoat; the round knobs grew into a couple of feet, encased in red cloth slippers; and the old chair looked like a very ugly old man of the previous century, with his arms a-kimbo. Tom sat up in bed, and rubbed his eyes to dispel the illusion. No. The chair was an ugly old gentleman; and what was more, he was winking at Tom Smart.

Tom was naturally a headlong, careless sort of dog, and he had had five tumblers of hot punch into the bargain; so, although he was a little startled at first, he began to grow rather indignant when he saw the old gentleman winking and leering at him with such an impudent air. At length he resolved he wouldn't stand it; and as the old face still kept winking away as fast as ever, Tom said, in a very angry tone: 'What the devil are you winking at me for?'

'Because I like it, Tom Smart,' said the chair; or the old

gentleman, whichever you like to call him. He stopped winking though, when Tom spoke, and began grinning like a superannuated monkey.

'How do you know my name, old nut-cracker face!' inquired Tom Smart, rather staggered;—though he pretended to carry it off so well.

'Come, come, Tom,' said the old gentleman, 'that's not the way to address solid Spanish Mahogany. Dam'me, you couldn't treat me with less respect if I was veneered.' When the old gentleman said this, he looked so fierce that Tom began to be frightened.

'I didn't mean to treat you with any disrespect, sir,' said Tom; in a much humbler tone than he had spoken in at first.

'Well, well,' said the old fellow, 'perhaps not—perhaps not. Tom—'

'Sir—'

'I know everything about you, Tom; everything. You're very poor, Tom.'

'I certainly am,' said Tom Smart. 'But how came you to know that?'

'Never mind that,' said the old gentleman; 'you're much too fond of punch, Tom.'

Tom Smart was just on the point of protesting that he hadn't tasted a drop since his last birthday, but when his eye encountered that of the old gentleman, he looked so knowing that Tom blushed, and was silent.

'Tom,' said the old gentleman, 'the widow's a fine woman – remarkably fine woman – eh, Tom?' Here the old fellow screwed up his eyes, cocked up one of his wasted little legs, and looked altogether so unpleasantly amorous, that Tom was quite disgusted with the levity of his behaviour – at his time of life, too!

'I am her guardian, Tom,' said the old gentleman.

'Are you?' inquired Tom Smart.

'I knew her mother, Tom,' said the old fellow; 'and her grandmother. She was very fond of me—made me this waistcoat, Tom.'

'Did she?' said Tom Smart.

'And these shoes,' said the old fellow, lifting up one of

the red-cloth mufflers; 'but, don't mention it, Tom. I shouldn't like to have it known that she was so much attached to me. It might occasion some unpleasantness in the family.' When the old rascal said this, he looked so extremely impertinent, that, as Tom Smart afterwards declared, he could have sat upon him without remorse.

'I have been a great favourite among the women in my time, Tom,' said the profligate old debauchee; 'hundreds of fine women have sat in my lap for hours together. What do you think of that, you dog, eh!' The old gentleman was proceeding to recount some other exploits of his youth, when he was seized with such a violent fit of creaking that he was unable to proceed.

'Just serves you right, old boy,' thought Tom Smart; but he didn't say anything.

'Ah!' said the old fellow, 'I am a good deal troubled with this now. I am getting old, Tom, and have lost nearly all my rails. I have had an operation performed, too – a small piece let into my back – and I found it a severe trial, Tom.'

'I dare say you did, sir,' said Tom Smart.

'However,' said the old gentleman, 'that's not the point. Tom! I want you to marry the widow.'

'Me, sir!' said Tom.

'You,' said the old gentleman.

'Bless your reverend locks,' said Tom (he had a few scattered horse-hairs left), 'bless your reverend locks, she wouldn't have me.' And Tom sighed involuntarily, as he thought of the bar.

'Wouldn't she?' said the old gentleman, firmly.

'No, no,' said Tom; 'there's somebody else in the wind. A tall man – a confoundedly tall man – with black whiskers.'

'Tom,' said the old gentleman; 'she will never have him.'

'Won't she?' said Tom. 'If you stood in the bar, old gentleman, you'd tell another story.'

'Pooh, pooh,' said the old gentleman. 'I know all about that.'

'About what?' said Tom.

'The kissing behind the door, and all that sort of thing, Tom,' said the old gentleman. And here he gave another impudent look, which made Tom very wroth, because as you all know, gentlemen, to hear an old fellow, who ought to know better, talking about these things, is very unpleasant – nothing more so.

'I know all about that, Tom,' said the old gentleman. 'I have seen it done very often in my time, Tom, between more people than I should like to mention to you; but it never came to anything after all.'

'You must have seen some queer things,' said Tom, with an inquisitive look.

'You may say that, now,' replied the old fellow, with a very complicated wink. 'I am the last of my family, Tom,' said the old gentleman, with a melancholy sigh.

'Was it a large one?' inquired Tom Smart.

'There were twelve of us, Tom,' said the old gentleman; 'fine straight-backed, handsome fellows as you'd wish to see. None of your modern abortions – all with arms, and with a degree of polish, though I say it that should not, which would have done your heart good to behold.'

'And what's become of the others, sir?' asked Tom Smart.

The old gentleman applied his elbow to his eye as he replied, 'Gone, Tom, gone. We had hard service, Tom, and they hadn't all my constitution. They got rheumatic about the legs and arms, and went into kitchens and other hospitals; and one of 'em, with long service and hard usage, positively lost his senses: he got so crazy that he was obliged to be burnt. Shocking thing that, Tom.'

'Dreadful!' said Tom Smart.

The old fellow paused for a few minutes, apparently struggling with his feelings of emotion, and then said: 'However, Tom, I am wandering from the point. This tall man, Tom, is a rascally adventurer. The moment he married the widow, he would sell off all the furniture, and run away. What would be the consequence? She would be deserted and reduced to ruin, and I should catch my death of cold in some broker's shop.'

'Yes, but—'

'Don't interrupt me,' said the old gentleman. 'Of you, Tom, I entertain a very different opinion; for I well know that if you once settled yourself in a public-house, you would never leave it, as long as there was anything to drink within its walls.'

'I am very much obliged to you for your good opinion, sir,' said Tom Smart.

'Therefore,' resumed the old gentleman, in a dictatorial tone; 'you shall have her, and he shall not.'

'What is to prevent it?' said Tom Smart, eagerly.

'This disclosure,' replied the old gentleman; 'he is already married.'

'How can I prove it?' said Tom, starting half out of bed.

The old gentleman untucked his arm from his side, and having pointed to one of the oaken presses, immediately replaced it in its old position.

'He little thinks,' said the old gentleman, 'that in the right-hand pocket of a pair of trousers in that press, he has left a letter, entreating him to return to his disconsolate wife, with six – mark me, Tom – six babes, and all of them small ones.'

As the old gentleman solemnly uttered these words, his features grew less and less distinct, and his figure more shadowy. A film came over Tom Smart's eyes. The old man seemed gradually blending into the chair, the damask waistcoat to resolve into a cushion, the red slippers to shrink into little red cloth bags. The light faded gently away, and Tom Smart fell back on his pillow, and dropped asleep.

Morning aroused Tom from the lethargic slumber, into which he had fallen on the disappearance of the old man. He sat up in bed, and for some minutes vainly endeavoured to recall the events of the preceding night. Suddenly they rushed upon him. He looked at the chair; it was a fantastic grim-looking piece of furniture, certainly, but it must have been a remarkably ingenious and lively imagination, that could have discovered any resemblance between it and an old man.

'How are you, old boy?' said Tom. He was bolder in the daylight – most men are.

The chair remained motionless, and spoke not a word.

'Miserable morning,' said Tom. No. The chair would not be drawn into conversation.

'Which press did you point to?—can you tell me that,' said Tom. Devil a word, gentlemen, the chair would say.

'It's not much trouble to open it anyhow,' said Tom, getting out of bed very deliberately. He walked up to one of the presses. The key was in the lock; he turned it, and opened the door. There *was* a pair of trousers there. He put his hand into the pocket, and drew forth the identical letter the old gentleman had described!

'Queer sort of thing, this,' said Tom Smart; looking first at the chair and then at the press, and then at the letter, and then at the chair again. 'Very queer,' said Tom. But, as there was nothing in either, to lessen the queerness, he thought he might as well dress himself, and settle the tall man's business at once—just to put him out of his misery.

Tom surveyed the rooms he passed through, on his way downstairs, with the scrutinising eye of a landlord; thinking it not impossible, that before long, they and their contents would be his property. The tall man was standing in the snug little bar, with his hands behind him, quite at home. He grinned vacantly at Tom. A casual observer might have supposed he did it, only to show his white teeth; but Tom Smart thought that a consciousness of triumph was passing through the place where the tall man's mind would have been, if he had had any. Tom laughed in his face; and summoned the landlady.

'Good morning, ma'am,' said Tom Smart, closing the door of the little parlour as the widow entered.

'Good morning, sir,' said the widow. 'What will you take for breakfast, sir?'

Tom was thinking how he should open the case, so he made no answer.

'There's a very nice ham,' said the widow, 'and a beautiful cold larded fowl. Shall I send 'em in, sir?'

These words roused Tom from his reflections. His

admiration of the widow increased as she spoke. Thoughtful creature! Comfortable provider!

'Who is that gentleman in the bar, ma'am?' inquired Tom.

'His name is Jinkins, sir,' said the widow, slightly blushing.

'He's a tall man,' said Tom.

'He is a very fine man,' replied the widow, 'and a very nice gentleman.'

'Ah!' said Tom.

'Is there anything more you want, sir?' inquired the widow, rather puzzled by Tom's manner.

'Why, yes,' said Tom. 'My dear ma'am, will you have the kindness to sit down for one moment?'

The widow looked much amazed but she sat down, and Tom sat down too, close beside her. I don't know how it happened, gentlemen – indeed my uncle used to tell me that Tom Smart said *he* didn't know how it happened either – but somehow or other the palm of Tom's hand fell upon the back of the widow's hand, and remained there while he spoke.

'My dear ma'am,' said Tom Smart – he had always a great notion of committing the amiable – 'My dear ma'am, you deserve a very excellent husband; you do indeed.'

'Lor, sir!' said the widow – as well she might: Tom's mode of commencing the conversation being rather unusual, not to say startling; the fact of his never having set eyes upon her before the previous night, being taken into consideration. 'Lor, sir!'

'I scorn to flatter, my dear ma'am,' said Tom Smart. 'You deserve a very admirable husband, and whoever he is, he'll be a very lucky man.' As Tom said this his eye involuntarily wandered from the widow's face, to the comforts around him.

The widow looked more puzzled than ever, and made an effort to rise. Tom gently pressed her hand, as if to detain her, and she kept her seat. Widows, gentlemen, are not usually timorous, as my uncle used to say.

'I am sure I am very much obliged to you, sir, for your

good opinion,' said the buxom landlady, half laughing; 'and if ever I marry again'—

'*If*,' said Tom Smart, looking very shrewdly out of the right-hand corner of his left eye. '*If*—'

'Well,' said the widow, laughing outright this time. '*When* I do, I hope I shall have as good a husband as you describe.'

'Jinkins to wit,' said Tom.

'Lor, sir!' exclaimed the widow.

'Oh, don't tell me,' said Tom, 'I know him.'

'I am sure nobody who knows him, knows anything bad of him,' said the widow, bridling up at the mysterious air with which Tom had spoken.

'Hem!' said Tom Smart.

The widow began to think it was high time to cry, so she took out her handkerchief, and inquired whether Tom wished to insult her: whether he thought it like a gentleman to take away the character of another gentleman behind his back: why, if he had got anything to say, he didn't say it to the man, like a man, instead of terrifying a poor weak woman in that way; and so forth.

'I'll say it to him fast enough,' said Tom, 'only I want you to hear it first.'

'What is it?' inquired the widow, looking intently in Tom's countenance.

'I'll astonish you,' said Tom, putting his hand in his pocket.

'If it is that he wants money,' said the widow, 'I know that already, and you needn't trouble yourself.'

'Pooh, nonsense, that's nothing,' said Tom Smart. '*I* want money. 'Tan't that.'

'Oh, dear, what can it be?' exclaimed the poor widow.

'Don't be frightened,' said Tom Smart. He slowly drew forth the letter, and unfolded it. 'You won't scream?' said Tom, doubtfully.

'No, no,' replied the widow; 'let me see it.'

'You won't go fainting away, or any of that nonsense?' said Tom.

'No, no,' returned the widow, hastily.

'And don't run out, and blow him up,' said Tom, 'because I'll do all that for you; you had better not exert yourself.'

'Well, well,' said the widow, 'let me see it.'

'I will,' replied Tom Smart; and, with these words, he placed the letter in the widow's hand.

Gentlemen, I have heard my uncle say, that Tom Smart said the widow's lamentations when she heard the disclosure would have pierced a heart of stone. Tom was certainly very tender-hearted, but they pierced his, to the very core. The widow rocked herself to and fro, and wrung her hands.

'Oh, the deception and villainy of man!' said the widow.

'Frightful, my dear ma'am; but compose yourself,' said Tom Smart.

'Oh, I can't compose myself,' shrieked the widow. 'I shall never find any one else I can love so much!'

'Oh yes, you will, my dear soul,' said Tom Smart, letting fall a shower of the largest sized tears, in pity for the widow's misfortunes. Tom Smart, in the energy of his compassion, had put his arm round the widow's waist; and the widow, in a passion of grief, had clasped Tom's hand. She looked up in Tom's face, and smiled through her tears. Tom looked down in hers, and smiled through his.

I never could find out, gentlemen, whether Tom did or did not kiss the widow at that particular moment. He used to tell my uncle he didn't, but I have my doubts about it. Between ourselves, gentlemen, I rather think he did.

At all events, Tom kicked the very tall man out at the front door half an hour after, and married the widow a month after. And he used to drive about the country, with the clay-coloured gig with red wheels, and the vixenish mare with the fast pace, till he gave up business many years afterwards, and went to France with his wife; and then the old house was pulled down.

THE GHOSTS OF THE MAIL

The Story of the Bagman's Uncle

'My uncle, gentlemen,' said the bagman, 'was one of the merriest, pleasantest, cleverest fellows that ever lived. I wish you had known him, gentlemen. On second thoughts, gentlemen, I *don't* wish you had known him, for if you had, you would have been all, by this time, in the ordinary course of nature, if not dead, at all events so near it, as to have taken to stopping at home and giving up company: which would have deprived me of the inestimable pleasure of addressing you at this moment. Gentlemen, I wish your fathers and mothers had known my uncle. They would have been amazingly fond of him, especially your respectable mothers; I know they would. If any two of his numerous virtues predominated over the many that adored his character, I should say they were his mixed punch and his after supper song. Excuse my dwelling on these melancholy recollections of departed worth; you won't see a man like my uncle every day in the week.'

I have always considered it a great point in my uncle's character, gentlemen, that he was the intimate friend and companion of Tom Smart, of the great house of Bilson and Slum, Cateaton Street, City. My uncle collected for Tiggin and Welps, but for a long time he went pretty near the same journey as Tom; and the very first night they met, my uncle took a fancy for Tom, and Tom took a fancy for my uncle. They made a bet of a new hat before they had known each other half an hour, who should brew the best quart of punch and drink it the quickest. My uncle was judged to have won the making, but Tom Smart beat him in the drinking by about half a salt-spoon-full. They took another quart a-piece to drink each other's health in, and were staunch friends ever afterwards. There's a destiny in these things, gentlemen; we can't help it.

In the personal appearance, my uncle was a trifle shorter than the middle size; he was a thought stouter too, than the ordinary run of people, and perhaps his face might be a shade redder. He had the jolliest face you ever saw, gentlemen: something like Punch, with a handsomer nose and chin; his eyes were always twinkling and sparkling with good humour; and a smile—not one of your unmeaning wooden grins, but a real, merry, hearty, good-tempered smile—was perpetually on his countenance. He was pitched out of his gig once, and knocked, head first, against a mile-stone. There he lay, stunned, and so cut about the face with some gravel which had been heaped up alongside it, that, to use my uncle's own strong expression, if his mother could have revisited the earth, she wouldn't have known him. Indeed, when I come to think of the matter, gentlemen, I feel pretty sure she wouldn't, for she died when my uncle was two years and seven months old, and I think it's very likely that, even without the gravel, his top-boots would have puzzled the good lady not a little: to say nothing of his jolly red face. However, there he lay, and I have heard my uncle say, many a time, that the man said who picked him up that he was smiling as merrily as if he had tumbled out for a treat, and that after they had bled him, the first faint glimmerings of returning animation, were, his jumping up in bed, bursting out into a loud laugh, kissing the young woman who held the basin, and demanding a mutton chop and a pickled walnut. He was very fond of pickled walnuts, gentlemen. He said he always found that, taken without vinegar, they relished the beer.

My uncle's great journey was in the fall of the leaf, at which time he collected debts, and took orders, in the north: going from London to Edinburgh, from Edinburgh to Glasgow, from Glasgow back to Edinburgh, and thence to London by the smack. You are to understand that his second visit to Edinburgh was for his own pleasure. He used to go back for a week, just to look up his old friends;

and what with breakfasting with this one, lunching with that, dining with a third, and supping with another, a pretty tight week he used to make of it. I don't know whether any of you, gentlemen, ever partook of a real substantial hospitable Scotch breakfast, and then went out to a slight lunch of a bushel of oysters, a dozen or so of bottled ale, and a noggin or two of whiskey to close up with. If you ever did, you will agree with me that it requires a pretty strong head to go out to dinner and supper afterwards.

But, bless your hearts and eye-brows, all this sort of thing was nothing to my uncle! He was so well seasoned, that it was mere child's play. I have heard him say that he could see the Dundee people out, any day, and walk home afterwards without staggering; and yet the Dundee people have as strong heads and as strong punch, gentlemen, as you are likely to meet with, between the poles. I have heard of a Glasgow man and a Dundee man drinking against each other for fifteen hours at a sitting. They were both suffocated, as nearly as could be ascertained, at the same moment, but with this trifling exception, gentlemen, they were not a bit the worse for it.

One night, within four-and-twenty hours of the time when he had settled to take shipping for London, my uncle supped at the house of a very old friend of his, a Baillie Mac something and four syllables after it, who lived in the old town of Edinburgh. There were the baillie's wife, and the baillie's three daughters, and the baillie's grown-up son, and three or four stout, bushy eye-browed, canny old Scotch fellows, that the baillie had got together to do honour to my uncle, and help to make merry. It was a glorious supper. There were kippered Salmon, and Finnan haddocks, and a lamb's head, and a haggis – a celebrated Scotch dish, gentlemen, which my uncle used to say always looked to him, when it came to table, very much like a cupid's stomach – and a great many other things besides, that I forget the names of, but very good things notwithstanding. The lassies were pretty and agreeable; the baillie's wife was one of the best creatures that ever lived; and my uncle was in thoroughly good cue. The consequence of which was, that the young ladies tittered and giggled, and the old lady laughed out loud, and the baillie and the other old fellows roared till they were red in the face, the whole mortal time. I don't quite recollect how many tumblers of whiskey toddy each man drank after supper; but this I know, that about one o'clock in the morning, the baillie's grown-up son became insensible while attempting the first verse of 'Willie brewed a peck o'maut;' and he having been, for half an hour before, the only other man visible above the mahogany, it occurred to my uncle that it was almost time to think about going: especially as drinking had set in at seven o'clock, in order that he might get home at a decent hour. But, thinking it might not be quite polite to go just then, my uncle voted himself into the chair, mixed another glass, rose to propose his own health, addressed himself in a neat and complimentary speech, and drank the toast with great enthusiasm. Still nobody woke; so my uncle took a little drop more – neat this time, to prevent the toddy from disagreeing with him – and, laying violent hands on his hat, sallied forth into the street.

It was a wild gusty night when my uncle closed the baillie's door, and settling his hat firmly on his head, to prevent the wind from taking it, thrust his hands into his pockets, and looking upward, took a short survey of the state of the weather. The clouds were drifting over the moon at their giddiest speed: at one time wholly obscuring her: at another, suffering her to burst forth in full splendour and shed her light on all the objects around: anon, driving over her again, with increased velocity, and shrouding everything in darkness. 'Really, this won't do,' said my uncle, addressing himself to the weather, as if he felt himself personally offended. 'This is not at all the kind of thing for my voyage. It will not do, at any price,' said my uncle very impressively. Having repeated this, several times, he recovered his balance with some difficulty – for he was rather giddy with looking up into the sky so long – and walked merrily on.

The baillie's house was in the Canongate, and my uncle was going to the other end of Leith Walk, rather better than a mile's journey. On either side of him, there shot up against the dark sky, tall gaunt straggling houses, with time-stained fronts, and windows that seemed to have shared the lot of eyes in mortals, and to have grown dim and sunken with age. Six, seven, eight stories high, were the houses; story piled above story, as children build with cards – throwing their dark shadows over the roughly paved road, and making the dark night darker. A few oil lamps were scattered at long distances, but they only served to mark the dirty entrance to some narrow close, or to show where a common stair communicated, by steep and intricate windings, with the air of a man who had seen them too often before, to think them worthy of much notice now, my uncle walked up the middle of the street, with a thumb in each waistcoat pocket, indulging from time to time in various snatches of song, chanted forth with such good will and spirit, that the quiet honest folk started from their first sleep and lay trembling in bed till the sound died away in the distance; when, satisfying themselves that it was only some drunken ne'er-do-weel finding his way home, they covered themselves up warm and fell asleep again.

I am particular in describing how my uncle walked up the middle of the street, with his thumbs in his waistcoat pockets, gentlemen, because as he often used to say (and with great reason too) there is nothing at all extraordinary in this story, unless you distinctly understand at the beginning that he was not by any means of a marvellous or romantic turn.

Gentlemen, my uncle walked on with his thumbs in his waistcoat pockets, taking the middle of the street to himself, and singing, now a verse of a love song, and then a verse of a drinking one, and when he was tired of both, whistling melodiously, until he reached the North Bridge, which, at this point, connects the old and new towns of Edinburgh. Here he stopped for a minute, to look at the strange irregular clusters of lights piled one above the other, and twinkling afar off so high, that they looked like stars, gleaming from the castle walls on the one side and the Calton Hill on the other, as if they illuminated veritable castles in the air; while the old picturesque town slept heavily on, in gloom and darkness below: its palace and chapel of Holyrood, guarded day and night, as a friend of my uncle's used to say, by old Arthur's Seat, towering, surly and dark, like some gruff genius over the ancient city he has watched so long. I say, gentlemen, my uncle stopped here, for a minute, to look about him; and then, paying a compliment to the weather which had a little cleared up, though the moon was sinking, walked on again, as royally as before; keeping the middle of the road with great dignity, and looking as if he would very much like to meet with somebody who would dispute possession of it with him. There was nobody at all disposed to contest the point, as it happened; and so, on he went, with his thumbs in his waistcoat pockets, like a lamb.

When my uncle reached the end of Leith Walk, he had to cross a pretty large piece of waste ground which separated him from a short street which he had to turn down, to go direct to his lodging. Now, in this piece of waste ground, there was, at that time, an enclosure belonging to some wheelwright who contracted with the Post-office for the purchase of old worn-out mail coaches; and my uncle, being very fond of coaches, old, young, or middle-aged, all at once took it into his head to step out of his road for no other purpose than to peep between the palings at these mails – about a dozen of which, he remembered to have seen, crowded together in a very forlorn and dismantled state, inside. My uncle was a very enthusiastic, emphatic sort of person, gentlemen; so, finding that he could not obtain a good peep between the palings, he got over them, and sitting himself quietly down on an old axletree, began to contemplate the mail coaches with a deal of gravity.

There might be a dozen of them, or there might be more – my uncle was never quite certain on this point, and being a man of scrupulous veracity about numbers, didn't like to say – but there they stood, all huddled together in the most desolate condition imaginable. The doors had been torn from their hinges and removed; the linings had been stripped off: only a shred hanging here and there by a rusty nail;

the lamps were gone, the poles had long since vanished, the iron-work was rusty, the paint was worn away; the wind whistled through the chinks in the bare wood work; and the rain, which had collected on the roofs, fell drop by drop, into the insides with a hollow and melancholy sound. They were the decaying skeletons of departed mails, and in that lonely place, at that time of night, they looked chill and dismal.

My uncle rested his head upon his hands, and thought of the busy bustling people who had rattled about, years before, in the old coaches, and were now as silent and changed; he thought of the numbers of people to whom one of those crazy mouldering vehicles had borne, night after night, for many years, and through all weathers, the anxiously expected intelligence, the eagerly looked-for remittance, the promised assurance of health and safety, the sudden announcement of sickness and death. The merchant, the lover, the wife, the widow, the mother, the schoolboy, the very child who tottered to the door at the postman's knock—how had they all looked forward to the arrival of the old coach. And where were they all now!

Gentlemen, my uncle used to say that he thought all this at the time, but I rather suspect he learnt it out of some book afterwards, for he distinctly stated that he fell into a kind of doze, as he sat on the old axletree looking at the decayed mail coaches, and that he was suddenly awakened by some deep church-bell striking two. Now, my uncle was never a fast thinker, and if he had thought all these things, I am quite certain it would have taken him till full half-past two o'clock, at the very least. I am, therefore, decidedly of opinion, gentlemen, that my uncle fell into a kind of doze, without having thought about any thing at all.

Be this as it may, a church bell struck two. My uncle woke, rubbed his eyes, and jumped up in astonishment.

In one instant after the clock struck two, the whole of this deserted and quiet spot had become a scene of most extraordinary life and animation. The mail coach doors were on their hinges, the lining was replaced, the iron-work was as good as new, the paint was restored, the lamps were alight, cushions and great coats were on every coach box, porters were thrusting parcels into every boot, guards were stowing away letter bags, hostlers were dashing pails of water against the renovated wheels; numbers of men were rushing about, fixing poles into every coach; passengers arrived, portmanteaus were handed up, horses were put to; in short, it was perfectly clear that every mail there was to be off directly. Gentlemen, my uncle opened his eyes so wide at all this, that, to the very last moment of his life, he used to wonder how it fell out that he had ever been able to shut 'em again.

'Now then!' said a voice, as my uncle felt a hand on his shoulder, 'You're booked for one inside. You'd better get in.'

'*I* booked!' said my uncle, turning round.

'Yes, certainly.'

My uncle, gentlemen, could say nothing; he was so very much astonished. The queerest thing of all, was, that although there was such a crowd of persons, and although fresh faces were pouring in, every moment, there was no telling where they came from. They seemed to start up, in some strange manner, from the ground, or the air, and disappear in the same way. When a porter had put his luggage in the coach, and received his fare, he turned round and was gone; and before my uncle had well begun to wonder what had become of him, half-a-dozen fresh ones started up, and staggered along under the weight of the parcels which seemed big enough to crush them. The passengers were all dressed so oddly too! Large, broad-skirted laced coats with great cuffs and no collars; and wigs, gentlemen, – great formal wigs with a tie behind. My uncle could make nothing of it.

'Now, *are* you going to get in?' said the person who had addressed my uncle before. He was dressed as a mail guard, with a wig on his head and most enormous cuffs to his coat, and had a lantern in one hand, and a huge blunderbuss in the other, which he was going to stow away in his little arm-chest. '*Are* you going to get in, Jack Martin?' said the guard, holding the lantern to my uncle's face.

'Hallo!' said my uncle, falling back a step or two. 'That's familiar!'

'It's so on the way-bill,' replied the guard.

'Isn't there a "Mister" before it?' said my uncle. For he felt, gentlemen, that for a guard he didn't know, to call him Jack Martin, was a liberty which the Post-office wouldn't have sanctioned if they had known it.

'No, there is not,' rejoined the guard coolly.

'Is the fare paid?' inquired my uncle.

'Of course it is,' rejoined the guard.

'It is, is it?' said my uncle. 'Then here goes! Which coach?'

'This,' said the guard, pointing to an old-fashioned Edinburgh and London Mail, which had the steps down, and the door open. 'Stop! Here are the other passengers. Let them get in first.'

As the guard spoke, there all at once appeared, right in front of my uncle, a young gentleman in a powdered wig, and a sky-blue coat trimmed with silver, made very full and broad in the skirts, which were lined with buckram. Tiggin and Welps were in the printed calico and waistcoat piece line, gentlemen, so my uncle knew all the materials at once. He wore knee breeches, and a kind of leggings rolled up over his silk stockings, and shoes with buckles; he had ruffles at his wrists, a three-cornered hat on his head, and a long taper sword by his side. The flaps of his waistcoat came half way down his thighs, and the ends of his cravat reached to his waist. He stalked gravely to the coach-door, pulled off his hat, and held it above his head at arm's length: cocking his little finger in the air at the same time, as some affected people do, when they take a cup of tea. Then he drew his feet together, and made a low grave bow, and then put out his left hand. My uncle was just going to step forward, and shake it heartily, when he perceived that these attentions were directed, not towards him, but to a young lady who just then appeared at the foot of the steps, attired in an old-fashioned green velvet dress with a long waist and stomacher. She had no bonnet on her head, gentlemen, which was muffled in a black silk hood, but she looked round for an instant as she prepared to get into the coach, and such a beautiful face as she disclosed, my uncle had never seen – not even in a picture. She got into the coach, holding up her dress with one hand; and, as my uncle always said with a round oath, when he told the story, he wouldn't have believed it possible that legs and feet could have been brought to such a state of perfection unless he had seen them with his own eyes.

But, in this one glimpse of the beautiful face, my uncle saw that the young lady cast an imploring look upon him, and that she appeared terrified and distressed. He noticed, too, that the young fellow in the powdered wig, notwithstanding his show of gallantry, which was all very fine and grand, clasped her tight by the wrist when she got in, and followed himself immediately afterwards. An uncommonly ill-looking fellow, in a close brown wig and a plum-coloured suit, wearing a very large sword, and boots up to his hips, belonged to the party; and when he sat himself down next to the young lady, who shrunk into a corner at his approach, my uncle was confirmed in his original impression that something dark and mysterious was going forward, or, as he always said to himself, that 'there was a screw loose somewhere'. It's quite surprising how quickly he made up his mind to help the lady at any peril, if she needed help.

'Death and lightning!' exclaimed the young gentleman, laying his hand upon his sword as my uncle entered the coach.

'Blood and thunder!' roared the other gentleman. With this, he whipped his sword out, and made a lunge at my uncle without further ceremony. My uncle had no weapon about him, but with great dexterity he snatched the ill-looking gentleman's three-cornered hat from his head, and, receiving the point of his sword right through the crown, squeezed the sides together, and held it tight.

'Pink him behind!' cried the ill-looking gentleman to his companion, as he struggled to regain his sword.

'He had better not,' cried my uncle, displaying the heel of one of his shoes, in a threatening manner. 'I'll kick his brains out, if he has any, or fracture his skull if he hasn't.' Exerting all his strength, at this moment, my uncle wrenched the ill-looking man's sword from his grasp, and flung it clean out of the coach-window: upon which the younger gentleman vociferated 'Death and lightning!' again, and laid his hand upon the hilt of his sword, in a very fierce manner, but didn't draw it. Perhaps, gentlemen, as my uncle used to say with a smile, perhaps he was afraid of alarming the lady.

'Now, gentlemen,' said my uncle, taking his seat deliberately, 'I don't want to have any death, with or without lightning, in a lady's presence, and we have had quite blood and thundering enough for one journey; so, if you please, we'll sit in our places like quiet insides. Here, guard, pick up that gentleman's carving-knife.'

As quickly as my uncle said the words, the guard appeared at the coach-window, with the gentleman's sword in his hand. He held up his lantern, and looked earnestly in my uncle's face, as he handed it in; when, by its light, my uncle saw, to his great surprise, that an immense crowd of mail coach guards swarmed round the window, every one of whom had his eyes earnestly fixed upon him too. He had never seen such a sea of white faces, red bodies, and earnest eyes, in all his born days.

This is the strangest sort of thing I ever had anything to do with,' thought my uncle; 'allow me to return you your hat, sir.'

'The ill-looking gentleman received his three-cornered hat in silence, looked at the hole in the middle with an inquiring air, and finally stuck it on the top of his wig with a solemnity the effect of which was a trifle impaired by his sneezing violently at the moment, and jerking it off again.

'All right!' cried the guard with the lantern, mounting into his little seat behind. Away they went. My uncle peeped out of the coach-window as they emerged from the yard, and observed that the other mails, with coachmen, guards, horses, and passengers, complete, were driving round and round in circles, at a slow trot of about five miles an hour. My uncle burnt with indignation, gentlemen. As a commercial man, he felt that the mail bags were not to be trifled with, and he resolved to memorialise the Post-office on the subject, the very instant he reached London.

At present, however, his thoughts were occupied with the young lady who sat in the farthest corner of the coach, with her face muffled closely in her hood; the gentleman with the sky-blue coat sitting opposite her; the other man in the plum-coloured suit, by her side, the both watching her intently. If she so much as rustled the folds of her hood, he could hear the ill-looking man clap his hand upon his sword, and could tell by the other's breathing (it was so dark he couldn't see his face) that he was looking as big as if he were going to devour her at a mouthful. This roused my uncle more and more, and he resolved, come what come might, to see the end of it. He had a great admiration for bright eyes, and sweet faces, and pretty legs and feet; in short, he was fond of the whole sex. It runs in our family, gentlemen – so am I.

Many were the devices which my uncle practised, to attract the lady's attention, or at all events, to engage the mysterious gentlemen in conversation. They were all in vain; the gentlemen wouldn't talk, and the lady didn't dare. He thrust his head out of the coach-window at intervals, and bawled out to know why they didn't go faster? But he called till he was hoarse; nobody paid the least attention to him. He leant back in the coach, and thought of the beautiful face, and the feet and legs. This answered better; it whiled away the time, and kept him from wondering where he was going, and how it was that he found himself in such an odd situation. Not that this would have worried him much, anyway—he was a mighty free and easy, roving, devil-may-care sort of person, was my uncle, gentlemen.

All of a sudden the coach stopped. 'Hallo!' said my uncle, 'What's in the wind now?'

'Alight here,' said the guard, letting down the steps.

'Here!' cried my uncle.

'Here,' rejoined the guard.

'I'll do nothing of the sort,' said my uncle.

'Very well, then stop where you are,' said the guard.

'I will,' said my uncle.

'Do,' said the guard.

The other passengers had regarded this colloquy with great attention, and, finding that my uncle was determined not to alight, the younger man squeezed past him, to hand the lady out. At this moment, the ill-looking man was inspecting the hole in the crown of his three-cornered hat. As the young lady brushed past, she dropped one of her gloves into my uncle's hand, and softly whispered, with her lips so close to his face that he felt her warm breath on his nose, the single word 'Help!' Gentlemen, my uncle leaped out of the coach at once, with such violence that it rocked on the springs again.

'Oh! You've thought better of it, have you?' said the guard when he saw my uncle standing on the ground.

My uncle looked at the guard for a few seconds, in some doubt whether it wouldn't be better to wrench his blunderbuss from him, fire it in the face of the man with the big sword, knock the rest of the company over the head with the stock, snatch up the young lady, and go off in the smoke. On second thoughts, however, he abandoned this plan, as being a shade too melodramatic in the execution, and followed the two mysterious men, who, keeping the lady between them, were now entering an old house in front of which the coach had stopped. They turned into the passage, and my uncle followed.

Of all the ruinous and desolate places my uncle had ever beheld, this was the most so. It looked as if it had once been a large house of entertainment; but the roof had fallen in, in many places, and the stairs were steep, rugged, and broken. There was a huge fire-place in the room into which they walked, and the chimney was blackened with smoke; but no warm blaze lighted it up now. The white feathery dust of burnt wood was still strewed over the hearth, but the stove was cold, and all was dark and gloomy.

'Well,' said my uncle, as he looked about him, 'A mail travelling at the rate of six miles and a half an hour, and stopping for an indefinite time at such a hole as this, is rather an irregular sort of proceeding, I fancy. This shall be made known. I'll write to the papers.'

My uncle said this in a pretty loud voice, and in an open unreserved sort of manner, with the view of engaging the two strangers in conversation if he could. But, neither of them took any more notice of him than whispering to each other, and scowling at him as they did so. The lady was at the farther end of the room, and once she ventured to wave her hand, as if beseeching my uncle's assistance.

At length the two strangers advanced a little, and the conversation began in earnest.

'You don't know this is a private room, I suppose, fellow?' said the gentleman in sky-blue.

'No, I do not, fellow,' rejoined my uncle. 'Only if this is a private room specially ordered for the occasion, I should think the public room must be a *very* comfortable one;' with this my uncle sat himself down in a high-backed chair, and took such an accurate measure of the gentleman, with his eyes, that Tiggin and Welps could have supplied him with printed calico for a suit, and not an inch too much or too little, from the estimate alone.

'Quit this room,' said both the men together, grasping their swords.

'Eh?' said my uncle, not at all appearing to comprehend their meaning.

'Quit the room, or you are a dead man,' said the ill-looking fellow with the large sword, drawing it at the same time and flourishing it in the air.

'Down with him!' cried the gentleman in sky-blue, drawing his sword also, and falling back two or three yards. 'Down with him!' The lady gave a loud scream.

Now, my uncle was always remarkable for great boldness, and great presence of mind. All the time that he had appeared so indifferent to what was going on, he had been looking slyly about, for some missile or weapon of defence, and at the very instant when the swords were drawn, he espied, standing in the chimney corner, an old basket-hilted rapier, in a rusty scabbard. At one bound, my uncle caught it in his hand, drew it, flourished it gallantly above his head, called aloud to the lady to keep out of the way, hurled the chair at the man in sky-blue, and the scabbard at the man in plum-colour, and taking advantage of the confusion, fell upon them both, pell-mell.

Gentlemen, there is an old story – none the worse for being true – regarding a fine young Irish gentleman, who being asked if he could play the fiddle, replied he had no doubt he could, but he couldn't exactly say, for certain, because he had never tried. This is not inapplicable to my uncle and his fencing. He had never had a sword in his hand before, except once when he played Richard the Third at a private theatre: upon which occasion it was arranged with Richmond that he was to be run through, from behind, without showing fight at all. But here he was, cutting and slashing with two experienced swordsmen: thrusting and guarding and poking and slicing, and acquitting himself in the most manful and dexterous manner possible, although up to that time he had never been aware that he had the least notion of the science. It only shows how true the old saying is, that a man never knows what he can do, till he tries, gentlemen.

The noise of the combat was terrific; each of the three combatants swearing like troopers, and their swords clashing with as much noise as if all the knives and steels in Newport market were rattling together, at the same time. When it was at its very height, the lady (to encourage my uncle most probably) withdrew her hood entirely from her face, and disclosed a countenance of such dazzling beauty, that he would have fought against fifty men, to win one smile from it, and die. He had done wonders before, but now he began to powder away like a raving mad giant.

At this very moment, the gentleman in sky-blue turning round, and seeing the young lady with her face uncovered, vented an exclamation of rage and jealousy, and, turning his weapon against her beautiful bosom, pointed a thrust at her heart, which caused my uncle to utter a cry of apprehension that made the building ring. The lady stepped lightly aside, and snatching the young man's sword from his hand, before he had recovered his balance, drove him to the wall, and running it through him, and the panelling, up to the very hilt, pinned him there, hard and fast. It was a splendid example. My uncle, with a loud shout of triumph, and a strength that was irresistible, made his adversary retreat in the same direction, and plunging the old rapier into the very centre of a large red flower in the pattern of his waistcoat, nailed him beside his friend; there they both stood, gentlemen, jerking their arms and legs about, in agony, like the toy-shop figures that are moved by a piece of packthread. My uncle always said, afterwards, that this was one of the surest means he knew of, for disposing of an enemy; but it was liable to one objection on the ground of expense, inasmuch as it involved the loss of a sword for every man disabled.

'The mail, the mail!' cried the lady, running up to my uncle and throwing her beautiful arms round his neck; 'we may yet escape.'

'*May!*' cried my uncle; 'why, my dear, there's nobody else to kill, is there?' My uncle was rather disappointed, gentlemen, for he thought a little quiet bit of love-making would be agreeable after the slaughtering, if it were only to change the subject.

'We have not an instant to lose here,' said the young lady. 'He (pointing to the young gentleman in sky-blue) is the only son of the powerful Marquess of Filletoville.'

'Well, then, my dear, I'm afraid he'll never come to the title,' said my uncle, looking coolly at the young gentleman as he stood fixed up against the wall, in the cockchafer fashion I have described. You have cut off the entail, my love.'

'I have been torn from my home and friends by these villains,' said the young lady, her features glowing with indignation. 'That wretch would have married me by violence in another hour.'

'Confound his impudence!' said my uncle, bestowing a very contemptuous look on the dying heir of Filletoville.

'As you may guess from what you have seen,' said the young lady, 'the party were prepared to murder me if I appealed to anyone for assistance. If their accomplices find us here, we are lost. Two minutes hence may be too late. The mail!' With these words, overpowered by her feelings, and the exertion of sticking the young Marquess of Filletoville, she sunk into my uncle's arms. My uncle caught her up, and bore her to the house-door. There stood the mail, with four long-tailed, flowing-maned, black horses, ready harnessed; but no coachman, no guard, no hostler even, at the horses' heads.

Gentlemen, I hope I do no injustice to my uncle's memory, when I express my opinion, that although he was a bachelor, he *had* held some ladies in his arms, before this time; I believe indeed, that he had rather a habit of kissing barmaids; and I know, that in one or two instances, he had been seen by credible witnesses, to hug a landlady in a very perceptible manner. I mention the circumstance, to show what a very uncommon sort of person this beautiful young lady must have been, to have affected my uncle in the way she did; he used to say, that as her long dark hair trailed over his arm, and her beautiful dark eyes fixed themselves upon his face when she recovered, he felt so strange and nervous that his legs trembled beneath him. But, who can look in a sweet soft pair of dark eyes, without feeling queer? *I* can't, gentlemen. I am afraid to look at some eyes I know, and that's the truth of it.

'You will never leave me,' murmured the young lady.

'Never,' said my uncle. And he meant it too.

'My dear preserver!' exclaimed the young lady. 'My dear, kind, brave preserver!'

'Don't,' said my uncle, interrupting her.

'Why?' inquired the young lady.

'Because your mouth looks so beautiful when you speak,' rejoined my uncle, 'that I'm afraid I shall be rude enough to kiss it.'

The young lady put up her hand as if to caution my uncle not to do so, and said – no, she didn't say anything – she smiled. When you are looking at a pair of the most delicious lips in the world, and see them gently break into a roguish smile – if you are very near them, and nobody else by – you cannot better testify your admiration of their beautiful form and colour than by kissing them at once. My uncle did so, and I honour him for it.

'Hark!' cried the young lady, starting. 'The noise of wheels and horses!'

'So it is,' said my uncle, listening. He had a good ear for wheels, and the trampling of hoofs; but there appeared to be so many horses and carriages rattling towards them, from a distance, that it was impossible to form a guess at their number. The sound was like that of fifty breaks, with six blood cattle in each.

'We are pursued!' cried the young lady, clasping her hands. 'We are pursued. I have no hope but in you!'

There was such an expression of terror in her beautiful face, that my uncle made up his mind at once. He lifted her into the coach, told her not to be frightened, pressed his lips to hers once more, and then advising her to draw up the window to keep the cold air out, mounted to the box.

'Stay, love,' cried the young lady.

'What's the matter?' said my uncle, from the coach-box.

'I want to speak to you,' said the young lady; 'only a word. Only one word, dearest.'

'Must I get down?' inquired my uncle. The lady made no answer, but she smiled again. Such a smile, gentlemen! It beat the other one, all to nothing. My uncle descended from his perch in a twinkling.

'What is it, my dear?' said my uncle, looking in at the coach-window. The lady happened to bend forward at the same time, and my uncle thought she looked more beautiful than she had done yet. He was very close to her just then, gentlemen, so he really ought to know.

'What is it, my dear?' said my uncle.

'Will you never love anyone but me; never marry anyone beside?' said the young lady.

My uncle swore a great oath that he never would marry anybody else, and the young lady drew in her head, and pulled up the window. He jumped upon the box, squared his elbows, adjusted the ribands, seized the whip which lay on the roof, gave one flick to the off leader, and away went the four long-tailed flowing-maned black horses, at fifteen good English miles an hour, with the old mail coach behind them. Whew! How they tore along!

The noise behind grew louder. The faster the old mail went, the faster came the pursuers—men, horses, dogs, were leagued in the pursuit. The noise was frightful, but, above all, rose the voice of the young lady, urging my uncle on, and shrieking, 'Faster! Faster!'

They whirled past the dark trees, as feathers would be swept before a hurricane. Houses, gates, churches, haystacks, objects of every kind they shot by, with a velocity and noise like roaring waters suddenly let loose. Still the noise of pursuit grew louder, and still my uncle could hear the young lady wildly screaming, 'Faster! Faster!'

My uncle plied whip and rein, and the horses flew onward till they were white with foam; and yet the noise behind increased; and yet the young lady cried 'Faster! Faster!' My uncle gave a loud stamp on the boot in the energy of the moment, and—found that it was grey morning, and he was sitting in the wheelwright's yard, on the box of an old Edinburgh mail, shivering with the cold and wet and stamping his feet to warm them! He got down, and looked eagerly inside for the beautiful young lady. Alas! There was neither door nor seat to the coach. It was a mere shell.

Of course, my uncle knew very well that there was some mystery in the matter, and that everything had passed exactly as he used to relate it. He remained staunch to the great oath he had sworn to the beautiful young lady: refusing several eligible landladies on her account, and dying a bachelor at last. He always said, what a curious thing it was that he should have found out, by such a mere accident as his climbing over the palings, that the ghosts of mail coaches and horses, guards, coachmen, and passengers, were in the habit of making journeys regularly every night. He used to add, that he believed he was the only living person who had ever been taken as a passenger on one of these excursions. And I think he was right, gentlemen—at least I never heard of any other.

'I wonder what these ghosts of mail coaches carry in their bags,' said the landlord, who had listened to the whole story with profound attention.

'The dead letters, of course,' said the Bagman.

'Oh, ah! To be sure,' rejoined the landlord. 'I never thought of that.'

A MADMAN'S MANUSCRIPT

Yes!—a madman's! How that word would have struck to my heart, many years ago! How it would have roused the terror that used to come upon me sometimes; sending the blood hissing and tingling through my veins, till the cold dew of fear stood in large drops upon my skin, and my knees knocked together with fright! I like it now though. It's a fine name. Shew me the monarch whose angry frown was ever feared like the glare of a madman's eye – whose cord and axe were ever half so sure as a madman's grip. Ho! Ho! It's a grand thing to be mad! to be peeped at like a wild lion through the iron bars – to gnash one's teeth and howl, through the long still night, to the merry ring of a heavy chain – and to roll and twine among the straw, transported with such brave music. Hurrah for the madhouse! Oh, it's a rare place!

I remember days when I was *afraid* of being mad; when I used to start from my sleep, and fall upon my knees, and pray to be spared from the curse of my race; when I rushed from the sight of merriment or happiness, to hide myself in some lonely place, and spend the weary hours in watching the progress of the fever that was to consume my brain. I knew that madness was mixed up with my very blood, and the marrow of my bones; that one generation had passed away without the pestilence appearing among them, and that I was the first in whom it would revive. I knew it *must* be so: that so it always had been, and so it ever would be: and when I cowered in some obscure corner of a crowded room, and saw men whisper, and point, and turn their eyes towards me, I knew they were telling each other of the doomed madman; and I slunk away again to mope in solitude.

I did this for years; long, long years they were. The nights here are long sometimes—very long; but they are nothing to the restless nights, and dreadful dreams I had at that time. It makes me cold to remember them. Large dusky forms with sly and jeering faces crouched in the corners of the room, and bent over my bed at night, tempting me to madness. They told me in low whispers, that the floor of the old house in which my father's father died, was stained with his own blood, shed by his own hand in raging madness. I drove my fingers into my ears, but they screamed into my head till the room rang with it, that in one generation before him the madness slumbered, but that his grandfather had lived for years with his hands fettered to the ground, to prevent his tearing himself to pieces. I knew they told the truth – I knew it well. I had found it out years before, though they had tried to keep it from me. Ha! ha! I was too cunning for them, madman as they thought me.

At last it came upon me, and I wondered how I could ever have feared it. I could go into the world now, and laugh and shout with the best among them. I knew I was mad, but they did not even suspect it. How I used to hug myself with delight, when I thought of the fine trick I was playing them after their old pointing and leering, when I was not mad, but only dreading that I might one day become so! And how I used to laugh for joy, when I was alone, and thought how well I kept my secret, and how quickly my kind friends would have fallen from me, if they had known the truth. I could have screamed with ecstasy when I dined alone with some fine roaring fellow, to think how pale he would have turned, and how fast he would have run, if he had known that the dear friend who sat close to him, sharpening a bright glittering knife, was a madman with all the power, and half the will, to plunge it in his heart. Oh, it was a merry life!

Riches became mine, wealth poured in upon me, and I rioted in pleasures enhanced a thousandfold to me by the consciousness of my well-kept secret. I inherited an estate. The law – the eagle-eyed law itself – had been deceived, and had handed over disputed thousands to a madman's hands. Where was the wit of the sharp-sighted men of sound mind? Where was the dexterity of the lawyers, eager to discover a flaw? The madman's cunning had over-reached them all.

I had money. How I was courted! I spent it profusely. How I was praised! How those three proud overbearing brothers humbled themselves before me! The old white-headed father, too – such deference, such respect, such devoted friendship – he worshipped me! The old man had a daughter, and the young men a sister; and all the five were poor. I was rich; and when I married the girl, I saw a smile of triumph play upon the faces of her needy relatives, as they thought of their well-planned scheme, and their fine prize. It was for me to smile. To smile! To laugh outright, and tear my hair, and roll upon the ground with shrieks of merriment. They little thought they had married her to a madman.

Stay. If they had known it, would they have saved her? A sister's happiness against her husband's gold. The lightest feather I blow into the air, against the gay chain that ornaments my body!

In one thing I was deceived with all my cunning. If I had not been mad – for though we madmen are sharp-witted enough, we get bewildered sometimes – I should have known that the girl would rather have been placed, stiff and cold in a dull leaden coffin, then borne an envied bride to my rich, glittering house. I should have known that her heart was with the dark-eyed boy whose name I once heard her breathe in her troubled sleep; and that she had been sacrificed to me, to relieve the poverty of the old white-headed man, and the haughty brothers.

I don't remember forms or faces now, but I know the girl was beautiful. I *know* she was; for in the bright moon-light nights, when I start up from my sleep, and all is quiet about me, I see, standing still and motionless in one corner of this cell, a slight and wasted figure with long black hair, which streaming down her back, stirs with no earthly wind, and eyes that fix their gaze on me, and never wink or close. Hush! the blood chills at my heart as I write it down – that form is *her*'s; the face is very pale, and the eyes are glassy bright; but I know them well. That figure never moves; it never frowns and mouths as others do, that fill this place sometimes; but it is much more dreadful to me, even than the spirits that tempted me many years ago – it comes fresh from the grave; and is so very death-like.

For nearly a year I saw that face grow paler; for nearly a year I saw the tears steal down the mournful cheeks, and never knew the cause. I found it out at last though. They could not keep it from me long. She had never liked me; I had never thought she did: she despised my wealth, and hated the splendour in which she lived; I had not expected that. She loved another. This I had never thought of. Strange feelings came over me, and thoughts, forced upon me by some secret power, whirled round and round my brain. I did not hate her, though I hated the boy she still wept for. I pitied – yes, I pitied – the wretched life to which her cold and selfish relations had doomed her. I knew that she could not live long, but the thought that before her death she might give birth to some ill-fated being, destined to hand-down madness to its offspring, determined me. I resolved to kill her.

For many weeks I thought of poison, and then of drowning, and then of fire. A fine sight the grand house in flames, and the madman's wife smouldering away to cinders. Think of the jest of a large reward, too, and of some sane man swinging in the wind for a deed he never did, and all through a madman's cunning! I thought often of this, but I gave it up at last. Oh! the pleasure of stropping the razor day after day, feeling the sharp edge, and thinking of the gash one stroke of its thin bright edge would make!

At last the old spirits who had been with me so often before whispered in my ear that the time was come, and thrust the open razor into my hand. I grasped it firmly, rose softly from the bed, and leaned over my sleeping wife. Her face was buried in her hands. I withdrew them softly, and they fell listlessly on her bosom. She had been weeping; for the traces of the tears were still wet upon her cheek. Her face was calm and placid; and even as I looked upon it, a tranquil smile lighted up her pale features. I laid my hand softly on her shoulder. She started – it was only a passing dream. I leant forward again. She screamed, and woke.

One motion of my hand, and she would never again have uttered cry or sound. But I was startled, and drew back. Her eyes were fixed on mine. I know not how it was, but they cowed and frightened me; and I quailed beneath them. She rose from the bed, still gazing fixedly and steadily on me. I trembled; the razor was in my hand, but I could not move. She made towards the door. As she neared it, she turned, and withdrew her eyes from my face. The spell was broken. I bounded forward, and clutched her by the arm. Uttering shriek upon shriek, she sunk upon the ground.

Now I could have killed her without a struggle; but the house was alarmed. I heard the tread of footsteps on the stairs. I replaced the razor in its usual drawer, unfastened the door, and called loudly for assistance.

They came, and raised her, and placed her on the bed. She lay bereft of animation for hours; and when life, look and speech returned, her senses had deserted her, and she raved wildly and furiously.

Doctors were called in – great men who rolled up to my door in easy carriages, with fine horses and gaudy servants. They were at her bedside for weeks. They had a great meeting, and consulted together in low and solemn voices in another room. One, the cleverest and most celebrated among them, took me aside, and bidding me prepare for the worst, told me – me, the madman! – that my wife was mad. He stood close beside me at an open window, his eyes looking in my face, and his hand laid upon my arm. With one effort, I could have hurled him into the street beneath. It would have been rare sport to have done it; but my secret was at stake, and I let him go. A few days after, they told me I must place her under some restraint: I must provide a keeper for her. I! I went into the open fields where none could hear me, and laughed till the air resounded with my shouts!

She died next day. The white-headed old man followed her to the grave, and the proud brothers dropped a tear over the insensible corpse of whose sufferings they had regarded in her lifetime with muscles of iron. All this was food for my secret mirth, and I laughed behind the white handkerchief which I held up to my face, as we rode home, 'till the tears came into my eyes.

But though I had carried my object and killed her, I was restless and disturbed, and I felt that before long my secret must be known. I could not hide the wild mirth and joy which boiled within me, and made me when I was alone, at home, jump up and beat my hands together, and dance round and round, and roar aloud. When I went out, and saw the busy crowds hurrying about the streets; or to the theatre, and heard the sound of music, and beheld the people dancing, I felt such glee, that I could have rushed among them, and torn them to pieces limb from limb, and howled in transport. But I ground my teeth, and struck my feet upon the floor, and drove my sharp nails into my hands. I kept it down; and no one knew I was a madman yet.

I remember – though it's one of the last things I *can* remember: for now I mix up realities with my dreams, and having so much to do, and being always hurried here, have no time to separate the two, from some strange confusion in which they get involved—I remember how I let it out at last. Ha! ha! I think I see their frightened looks now, and feel the ease with which I flung them from me, and dashed my clenched fist into their white faces, and then flew like the wind, and left them screaming and shouting far behind. The strength of a giant comes upon me when I think of it. There – see how this iron bar bends beneath my furious wrench. I could snap it like a twig, only there are long galleries here with many doors – I don't think I could find my way along them; and even if I could, I know there are iron gates below which they keep locked and barred. They know what a clever madman I have been, and they are proud to have me here, to show.

'Let me see; yes, I had been out. It was late at night when I reached home, and found the proudest of the three proud brothers waiting to see me – urgent business he said: I recollect it well. I hated that man with all a madman's hate. Many and many a time had my fingers longed to tear him. They told me he was there. I ran swiftly upstairs. He had a word to say to me. I dismissed the servants. It was late, and we were alone together – *for the first time*.

I kept my eyes carefully from him at first, for I knew what he little thought – and I gloried in the knowledge – that the light of madness gleamed from them like fire. We sat in silence for a few minutes. He spoke at last. My recent dissipation, and strange remarks, made so soon after his sister's death, were an insult to her memory. Coupling together many circumstances which had at first escaped his observation, he thought I had not treated her well. He wished to know whether he was right in inferring that I meant to cast reproach upon her memory, and a disrespect upon her family. It was due to the uniform he wore, to demand this explanation.

This man had a commission in the army – a commission, purchased with my money, and his sister's misery! This was the man who had been foremost in the plot to ensnare me, and grasp my wealth. This was the man who had been the main instrument in forcing his sister to wed me; well knowing that her heart was given to that puling boy. Due to *his* uniform! The livery of his degradation! I turned my eyes upon him – I could not help it – but I spoke not a word.

I saw the sudden change that came upon him beneath my gaze. He was a bold man, but the colour faded from his face, and he drew back his chair. I dragged mine nearer to him; and as I laughed – I was very merry then – I saw him shudder. I felt the madness rising within me. He was afraid of me.

'You were very fond of your sister when she was alive' – I said – 'Very.'

He looked uneasily round him, and I saw his hand grasp the back of his chair: but he said nothing.

'You villain,' said I, 'I found you out; I discovered your hellish plots against me; I know her heart was fixed on someone else before you compelled her to marry me. I know it – I know it.'

He jumped suddenly from his chair, brandished it aloft, and bid me stand back – for I took care to be getting closer to him all the time I spoke.

I screamed rather than talked, for I felt tumultuous passions eddying through my veins, and the old spirits whispering and taunting me to tear his heart out.

'Damn you,' said I, starting up, and rushing upon him; 'I killed her. I am a madman. Down with you. Blood, blood! I will have it!'

I turned aside with one blow the chair he hurled at me in his terror, and closed with him; and with a heavy crash we rolled upon the floor together.

It was a fine struggle that; for he was a tall strong man, fighting for his life; and I, a powerful madman, thirsting to destroy him. I knew no strength could equal mine, and I was right. Right again, though a madman! His struggles grew fainter. I knelt upon his chest, and clasped his brawny throat firmly with both hands. His face grew purple; his eyes were starting from his head, and with protruded tongue, he seemed to mock me. I squeezed the tighter.

The door was suddenly burst open with a loud noise, and a crowd of people rushed forward, crying aloud to each other to secure the madman.

My secret was out; and my only struggle now was for liberty and freedom. I gained my feet before a hand was on me, threw myself among my assailants, and cleared my way with my strong arm, as if I bore a hatchet in my hand, and hewed them down before me. I gained the door, dropped over the bannisters, and in an instant was in the street.

Straight and swift I ran, and no one dared to stop me. I heard the noise of feet behind, and redoubled my speed. It grew fainter and fainter in the distance, and at length died away altogether: but on I bounded, through marsh and rivulet, over fence and wall, with a wild shout which was taken up by the strange beings that flocked around me on every side, and swelled the sound, till it pierced the air. I was borne upon the arms of demons who swept along upon the wind, and bore down bank and hedge before them, and spun me round and round with a rustle and a speed that made my head swim, until at last they threw me from them with a violent shock, and I fell heavily upon the earth. When I woke I found myself here – here in this gray cell where the sun-light seldom comes, and the moon steals in, in rays which only serve to show the dark shadows about me, and that silent figure in its old corner. When I lie awake, I can sometimes hear strange shrieks and cries from distant parts of this large place. What they are, I know not; but they neither come from that pale form, nor does it regard them. For from the first shades of dusk 'till the earliest light of the morning, it still stands motionless in the same place, listening to the music of my iron chain, and watching my gambols on my straw bed.

At the end of the manuscript was written, in another hand this note: [The unhappy man whose ravings are recorded above, was a melancholy instance of the baneful results of energies misdirected in early life, and excesses prolonged until their consequences could never be repaired. The thoughtless riot, dissipation, and debauchery of his younger days, produced fever and delirium. The first effects of the latter was the strange delusion, founded upon a well-known medical theory, strongly contended for by some, and as strongly contested by others, that an hereditary madness existed in his family. This produced a settled gloom, which in time developed a morbid insanity, and finally terminated in raving madness. There is every reason to believe that the events he detailed, though distorted in the description by his diseased imagination, really happened. It is only matter of wonder to those who were acquainted with the vices of his early career, that his passions, when no longer controlled by reason, did not lead him to the commission of still more frightful deeds.]

THE STORY OF THE GOBLINS WHO STOLE A SEXTON

In an old Abbey town, down in this part of the country, a long, long, while ago – so long, that the story must be a true one, because our great-grandfathers implicitly believed it – there officiated as sexton and grave-digger in the church-yard, one Gabriel Grub. It by no means follows that because a man is a sexton, and constantly surrounded by the emblems of mortality, therefore he should be a morose and melancholy man; your undertakers are the merriest fellows in the world; and I once had the honour of being on intimate terms with a mute, who in private life, and off duty, was as comical and jocose a little fellow as ever chirped out a devil-may-care song, without a hitch in his memory, or drained off the contents of a good stiff glass without stopping for breath. But, notwithstanding these precedents to the contrary, Gabriel Grub was an ill-conditioned, cross-grained, surly fellow – a morose and lonely man, who consorted with nobody but himself, and an old wicker bottle which fitted into his large deep waist-coat pocket – and who eyed each merry face, as it passed him by, with such a deep scowl of malice and ill-humour, as it was difficult to meet, without feeling something the worse for.

A little before twilight, one Christmas Eve, Gabriel shouldered his spade, lighted his lantern, and betook him-self towards the old churchyard; for he had got a grave to finish by next morning, and, feeling very low, he thought it might raise his spirits, perhaps, if he went on with his work at once. As he went his way, up the ancient street, he saw the cheerful light of the blazing fires gleam through the old casements, and heard the loud laugh and the cheerful shouts of those who were assembled around them; he marked the bustling preparations for next day's cheer, and smelt the numerous savoury odours consequent thereupon, as they steamed up from the kitchen windows in clouds. All this was gall and wormwood to the heart of Gabriel Grub; and when groups of children bounded out of the houses, tripped across the road, and were met, before they could knock at the opposite door, by half a dozen curly-headed little rascals who crowded round them as they flocked upstairs to spend the evening in their Christmas games, Gabriel smiled grimly, and clutched the handle of his spade with a firmer grasp, as he thought of measles, scarlet-fever, thrush, whooping-cough, and a good many other sources of consolation besides.

In this happy frame of mind, Gabriel strode along: returning a short, sullen growl to the good-humoured greetings of such of his neighbours as now and then passed him: until he turned into the dark lane which led to the churchyard. Now, Gabriel had been looking forward to reaching the dark lane, because it was, generally speaking, a nice, gloomy, mournful place, into which the towns-people did not much care to go, except in broad daylight, and when the sun was shining; consequently, he was not a little indignant to hear a young urchin roaring out some jolly song about a merry Christmas, in this very sanctuary, which had been called Coffin Lane ever since the days of the old abbey, and the time of the shaven-headed monks. As Gabriel walked on, and the voice drew nearer, he found it proceeded from a small boy, who was hurrying along, to join one of the little parties in the old street, and who, partly to keep himself company, and partly to prepare himself for the occasion, was shouting out the song at the highest pitch of his lungs. So Gabriel waited until the boy came up, and then dodged him into a corner, and rapped him over the head with his lantern five or six times, to teach him to modulate his voice. And as the boy hurried away with his hand to his head, singing quite a different sort of tune, Gabriel Grub chuckled very heartily to himself, and entered the churchyard, locking the gate behind him.

He took off his coat, put down his lantern, and getting

into the unfinished grave, worked at it for an hour or so, with right good will. But the earth was hardened with the frost, and it was no very easy matter to break it up, and shovel it out; and although there was a moon, it was a very young one, and shed little light upon the grave, which was in the shadow of the church. At any other time, these obstacles would have made Gabriel Grub very moody and miserable, but he was so well pleased with having stopped the small boy's singing, that he took little heed of the scanty progress he had made, and looked down into the grave, when he had finished work for the night, with grim satisfaction: murmuring as he gathered up his things:

'Brave lodgings for one, brave lodgings for one,
A few feet of cold earth, when life is done;
A stone at the head, a stone at the feet,
A rich, juicy meal for the worms to eat;
Rank grass over head, and damp clay around,
Brave lodgings for one, these, in holy ground!'

'Ho! Ho!' laughed Gabriel Grub, as he sat himself down on a flat tombstone which was a favourite resting-place of his; and drew forth his wicker bottle. 'A coffin at Christmas! A Christmas Box. Ho! ho! ho!'

'Ho! ho! ho!' repeated a voice which sounded close behind him.

Gabriel paused, in some alarm, in the act of raising the wicker bottle to his lips: and looked round. The bottom of the oldest grave about him, was not more still and quiet, than the churchyard in the pale moonlight. The cold hoar frost glistened on the tombstones, and sparkled like rows of gems, among the stone carvings of the old church. The snow lay hard and crisp upon the ground; and spread over the thickly-strewn mounds of earth so white and smooth a cover that it seemed as if corpses lay there, hidden only by their winding sheets. Not the faintest rustle broke the profound tranquillity of the solemn scene. Sound itself appeared to be frozen up, all was so cold and still.

'It was the echoes,' said Gabriel Grub, raising the bottle to his lips again.

'It was *not*,' said a deep voice.

Gabriel started up, and stood rooted to the spot with astonishment and terror; for his eyes rested on a form that made his blood run cold.

Seated on an upright tombstone, close to him, was a strange unearthly figure, whom Gabriel felt at once, was no being of this world. His long fantastic legs which might have reached the ground, were cocked up, and crossed after a quaint, fantastic fashion; his sinewy arms were bare; and his hands rested on his knees. On his short round body, he wore a close covering, ornamented with small slashes; a short cloak dangled at his back; the collar was cut into curious peaks, which served the goblin in lieu of ruff or neckerchief; and his shoes curled at his toes into long points. On his head, he wore a broad-brimmed sugar-loaf hat, garnished with a single feather. The hat was covered with the white frost; and the goblin looked as if he had sat on the same tombstone very comfortably, for two or three hundred years. He was sitting perfectly still; his tongue was put out, as if in derision; and he was grinning at Gabriel Grub with such a grin as only a goblin could call up.

'It was *not* the echoes,' said the goblin.

Gabriel Grub was paralysed, and could make no reply.

'What do you do here on Christmas Eve?' said the goblin sternly.

'I came to dig a grave, sir,' stammered Gabriel Grub.

'What man wanders among graves and churchyards on such a night as this?' cried the goblin.

'Gabriel Grub! Gabriel Grub!' screamed a wild chorus of voices that seemed to fill the churchyard. Gabriel looked fearfully round – nothing was to be seen.

'What have you got in that bottle?' said the goblin.

'Hollands, sir,' replied the sexton, trembling more than ever; for he had bought it of the smugglers, and he thought that perhaps his questioner might be in the excise department of the goblins.

'Who drinks Hollands alone, and in a churchyard, on such a night as this?' said the goblin.

'Gabriel Grub! Gabriel Grub!' exclaimed the wild voices again.

The goblin leered maliciously at the terrified sexton, and then raising his voice, exclaimed: 'And who, then, is our fair and lawful prize?'

To this inquiry the invisible chorus replied, in a strain that sounded like the voices of many choristers singing to the mighty swell of the old church organ – a strain that seemed borne to the sexton's ears upon a wild wind, and to die away as it passed onward; but the burden of the reply was still the same, 'Gabriel Grub! Gabriel Grub!'

The goblin grinned a broader grin than before, as he said, 'Well Gabriel, what do you say to this?'

The sexton gasped for breath.

'What do you think of this, Gabriel?' said the goblin, kicking up his feet in the air on either side of the tombstone, and looking at the turned-up points with as much complacency as if he had been contemplating the most fashionable pair of Wellingtons in all Bond Street.

'It's – it's – very curious sir,' replied the sexton, half dead with fright; 'very curious, and very pretty, but I think I'll go back and finish my work, sir, if you please.'

'Work!' said the goblin, 'what work?'

'The grave, sir; making the grave,' stammered the sexton.

'Oh, the grave, eh?' said the goblin. 'Who makes graves at a time when all other men are merry, and takes a pleasure in it?'

Again the mysterious voices replied, 'Gabriel Grub! Gabriel Grub!'

'I'm afraid my friends want you, Gabriel,' said the goblin, thrusting his tongue further into his cheek than ever – and a most astonishing tongue it was – 'I'm afraid my friends want you, Gabriel,' said the goblin.

'Under favour, sir,' replied the horror-stricken sexton, 'I don't think they can, sir; they don't know me, sir; I don't think the gentlemen have ever seen me, sir.'

'Oh yes they have,' replied the goblin; 'we know the man with the sulky face and grim scowl, that came down the street tonight, throwing his evil looks at the children, and grasping his burying spade the tighter. We know the man who struck the boy in the envious malice of his heart, because the boy could be merry, and he could not. We know him, we know him.'

Here, the goblin gave a loud shrill laugh, which the echoes returned twenty-fold: and throwing his legs up in the air, stood upon his head, or rather upon the very point of his sugar-loaf hat, on the narrow edge of the tombstone: whence he threw a somerset with extraordinary agility, right to the sexton's feet, at which he planted himself in the attitude in which tailors generally sit upon the shop-board.

'I – I – am afraid I must leave you, sir,' said the sexton, making an effort to move.

'Leave us!' said the goblin, 'Gabriel Grub going to leave us. Ho! ho! ho!'

As the goblin laughed, the sexton observed, for one instant, a brilliant illumination within the windows of the church, as if the whole building were lighted up; it disappeared, the organ pealed forth a lively air, and whole troops of goblins, the very counterpart of the first one, poured into the churchyard, and began playing at leap-frog with the tombstones: never stopping for an instant to take breath, but 'overing' the highest among them, one after the other, with the most marvellous dexterity. The first goblin was a most astonishing leaper, and none of the others could come near him; even in the extremity of his terror the sexton could not help observing, that while his friends were content to leap over the common-sized gravestones, the first one took the family vaults, iron railings and all, with as much ease as if they had been so many street-posts.

At last the game reached to a most exciting pitch; the organ played quicker and quicker; and the goblins leaped faster and faster: coiling themselves up, rolling head over heels upon the ground, and bounding over the tombstones like footballs. The sexton's brain whirled round with the rapidity of the motion he beheld, and his legs reeled beneath him, as the spirits flew before his eyes: when the goblin king, suddenly darting towards him, laid his hand upon his collar, and sank with him through the earth.

When Gabriel Grub had had time to fetch his breath, which the rapidity of his descent had for the moment taken away, he found himself in what appeared to be a large cavern, surrounded on all sides by crowds of goblins, ugly and grim; in the centre of the room, on an elevated seat, was stationed his friend of the churchyard; and close beside him stood Gabriel Grub himself, without power of motion.

'Cold tonight,' said the king of the goblins, 'very cold. A glass of something warm, here!'

At this command, half a dozen officious goblins, with a perpetual smile upon their faces, whom Gabriel Grub imagined to be courtiers, on that account, hastily disappeared, and presently returned with a goblet of liquid fire, which they presented to the king.

'Ah!' cried the goblin, whose cheeks and throat were transparent, as he tossed down the flame, 'This warms one, indeed! Bring a bumper of the same, for Mr Grub.'

It was in vain for the unfortunate sexton to protest that he was not in the habit of taking anything warm at night; one of the goblins held him while another poured the blazing liquid down his throat; the whole assembly screeched with laughter as he coughed and choked, and wiped away the tears which gushed plentifully from his eyes, after swallowing the burning draught.

'And now,' said the king, fantastically poking the taper corner of his sugar-loaf hat into the sexton's eye, and thereby occasioning him the most exquisite pain: 'And now, show the man of misery and gloom, a few of the pictures from our own great storehouse!'

As the goblin said this, a thick cloud which obscured the remoter end of the cavern, rolled gradually away, and disclosed, apparently at a great distance, a small and scantily furnished, but neat and clean apartment. A crowd of little children were gathered round a bright fire, clinging to their mother's gown, and gambolling around her chair. The mother occasionally rose, and drew aside the window-curtain, as if to look for some expected object: a frugal meal was placed near the fire. A knock was heard at the door: the mother opened it, and the children crowded round her, and clapped their hands for joy, as their father entered. He was wet and weary, and shook the snow from his garments, as the children crowded round him, and seizing his cloak, hat, stick and gloves, with busy zeal, ran with them from the room. Then, as he sat down to his meal before the fire, the children climbed about his knee, and the mother sat by his side, and all seemed happiness and comfort.

But a change came upon the view, almost imperceptibly. The scene was altered to a small bedroom, where the fairest and youngest child lay dying; the roses had fled from his cheek, and the light from his eye; and even as the sexton looked upon him with an interest he had never felt or known before, he died. His young brothers and sisters crowded round his little bed, and seized his tiny hand, so cold and heavy; but they shrunk back from its touch, and looked with awe on his infant face; for calm and tranquil as it was, and sleeping in rest and peace as the beautiful child seemed to be, they saw that he was dead, and they knew that he was an Angel looking down upon, and blessing them, from a bright and happy Heaven.

Again the light cloud passed across the picture, and again the subject changed. The father and mother were old and helpless now, and the number of those about them was diminished more than half; but content and cheerfulness sat on every face, and beamed in every eye, as they crowded round the fireside, and told and listened to old stories of earlier and bygone days. Slowly and peacefully, the father sank into the grave, and soon after, the sharer of all his cares and troubles followed him to a place of rest. The few, who yet survived them, knelt by their tomb, and watered the green turf which covered it, with their tears; then rose, and turned away: sadly and mournfully, but not with bitter cries, or despairing lamentations, for they knew that they should one day meet again; and once more they mixed with the busy world, and their content and cheerfulness was restored. The cloud settled upon the picture and concealed it from the sexton's view.

'What do you think of *that*?' said the goblin, turning his large face towards Gabriel Grub.

Gabriel murmured out something about its being very pretty, and looked somewhat ashamed, as the goblin bent his fiery eyes upon him.

'*You* a miserable man!' said the goblin, in a tone of excessive contempt. 'You!' He appeared disposed to add more, but indignation choked his utterance, so he lifted up one of his very pliable legs, and flourishing it above his head a little, to insure his aim, administered a good sound kick to Gabriel Grub; immediately after which, all the goblins in waiting, crowded round the wretched sexton, and kicked him without mercy: according to the established and invariable custom of courtiers upon earth, who kick whom royalty kicks, and hugs whom royalty hugs.

'Show him some more!' said the king of the goblins.

At these words, the cloud was dispelled, and a rich and beautiful landscape was disclosed to view – there is just such another, to this day, within half a mile of the old abbey town. The sun shone from out the clear blue sky, the water sparkled beneath his rays, and the trees looked greener, and the flowers more gay, beneath his cheering influence. The water rippled on, with a pleasant sound; the trees rustled in the light wind that murmured among their leaves; the birds sang upon the boughs; and the lark carolled on high her welcome to the morning. Yes, it was morning; the bright, balmy morning of summer; the minutest leaf, the smallest blade of grass, was instinct with life. The ant crept forth to her daily toil, the butterfly fluttered and basked in the warm rays of the sun; myriads of insects spread their transparent wings, and revelled in their brief but happy existence. Man walked forth, elated with the scene; and all was brightness and splendour.

'*You* a miserable man!' said the king of the goblins, in a more contemptuous tone than before. And again the king of the goblins gave his leg a flourish; again it descended on the shoulders of the sexton; and again the attendant goblins imitated the example of their chief.

Many a time the cloud went and came, and many a lesson it taught to Gabriel Grub, who, although his shoulders smarted with pain from the frequent applications of the goblins' feet, looked on with an interest that nothing could diminish. He saw that men who worked hard, and earned their scanty bread with lives of labour, were cheerful and happy; and that to the most ignorant, the sweet face of nature was a never-failing source of cheerfulness and joy. He saw those who had been delicately nurtured, and tenderly brought up, cheerful under privations, and superior to suffering that would have crushed many of a rougher grain, because they bore within their own bosoms the materials of happiness, contentment, and peace. He saw that women, the tenderest and most fragile of all God's creatures, were the oftenest superior to sorrow, adversity, and distress; and he saw that it was because they bore, in their own hearts, an inexhaustible well-spring of affection and devotion. Above all, he saw that men like himself, who snarled at the mirth and cheerfulness of others, were the foulest weeds on the fair surface of the earth; and setting all the good of the world against the evil, he came to the conclusion that it was a very decent and respectable sort of world after all. No sooner had he formed it, than the cloud which closed over the last picture, seemed to settle on his senses, and lull him to repose. One by one, the goblins faded from his sight; and as the last one disappeared, he sunk to sleep.

The day had broken when Gabriel Grub awoke, and found himself lying, at full length on the flat gravestone in the churchyard, with the wicker bottle lying empty by his side, and his coat, spade, and lantern, all well whitened by the last night's frost, scattered on the ground. The stone on which he had first seen the goblin seated, stood bolt upright before him, and the grave at which he had worked, the night before, was not far off. At first, he began to doubt the reality of his adventures, but the acute pain in his shoulders when he attempted to rise, assured him that the kicking of the goblins was certainly not ideal. He was staggered again, by observing no traces of footsteps in the snow on which the goblins had played at leap-frog with the gravestones, but he speedily accounted for this circumstance when he remembered that, being spirits, they would leave no visible impression behind them. So, Gabriel Grub got on his feet as well as he could, for the pain in his back; and brushing the frost off his coat, put it on, and turned his face towards the town.

But he was an altered man, and he could not bear the thought of returning to a place where his repentance would be scoffed at, and his reformation disbelieved. He hesitated for a few moments; and then turned away to wander where he might, and seek his bread elsewhere.

The lantern, the spade, and the wicker bottle, were found, that day, in the churchyard. There were a great many speculations about the sexton's fate, at first, but it was speedily determined that he had been carried away by the goblins; and there were not wanting some very credible witnesses who had distinctly seen him whisked through the air on the back of a chestnut horse blind of one eye, with the hind-quarters of a lion, and the tail of a bear. At length all this was devoutly believed; and the new sexton used to exhibit to the curious, for a trifling emolument, a good-sized piece of the church weathercock which had been accidentally picked up by himself in the churchyard, a year or two afterwards.

Unfortunately, these stories were somewhat disturbed by the unlooked-for re-appearance of Gabriel Grub himself, some ten years afterwards, a ragged, contented, rheumatic old man. He told his story to the clergyman, and also to the mayor; and in course of time it began to be received, as a matter of history, in which form it has continued down to this very day. The believers in the weathercock tale, having misplaced their confidence once, were not easily prevailed upon to part with it again, so they looked as wise as they could, shrugged their shoulders, touched their foreheads, and murmured something about Gabriel Grub having drunk all the Hollands, and then fallen asleep on the flat tombstone; and they affected to explain what he supposed he had witnessed in the goblin's cavern, by saying that he had seen the world, and grown wiser. But this opinion, which was by no means a popular one at any time, gradually died off; and be the matter how it may, as Gabriel Grub was afflicted with rheumatism to the end of his days, this story has at least one moral, if it teach no better one—and that is, that if a man turn sulky and drink by himself at Christmas time, he may make up his mind to be not a bit the better for it: let the spirits be never so good, or let them be even as many degrees beyond proof, as those which Gabriel Grub saw in the goblin's cavern.

BARON KOËLDWETHOUT'S APPARITION

The Baron Von Koëldwethout, of Grogzwig in Germany, was as likely a young baron as you would wish to see. I needn't say that he lived in a castle, because that's of course; neither need I say that he lived in an old castle, for what German baron ever lived in a new one? There were many strange circumstances connected with this venerable building, among which not the least startling and mysterious were, that when the wind blew, it rumbled in the chimneys, or even howled among the trees in the neighbouring forest; and that when the moon shone, she found her way through certain small loopholes in the wall, and actually made some parts of the wide halls and galleries quite light, while she left others in gloomy shadow. I believe that one of the baron's ancestors, being short of money, had inserted a dagger in a gentleman who called one night to ask his way, and it *was* supposed that these miraculous occurrences took place in consequence. And yet I hardly know how that could have been, either, because the baron's ancestor, who was an amiable man, felt very sorry afterwards for having been so rash, and laying violent hands upon a quantity of stone and timber which belonged to a weaker baron, built a chapel as an apology, and so took a receipt from Heaven in full of all demands.

Talking of the baron's ancestor puts me in mind of the baron's great claims to respect on the score of his pedigree. I am afraid to say, I am sure, how many ancestors the baron had; but I know that he had a great many more than any other man of his time, and I only wish that he had lived in these latter days that he might have had more. It is a very hard thing upon the great men of past centuries, that they should have come into the world so soon, because a man who was born three or four hundred years ago, cannot reasonably be expected to have had as many relations before him as a man who is born now. The last man, whoever he is – and he may be a cobbler or some low vulgar dog for aught we know – will have a longer pedigree than the greatest nobleman now alive: and I contend that this is not fair.

Well, but the Baron Von Koëldwethout of Grogzwig – he was a fine swarthy fellow, with dark hair and large moustachios, who rode a-hunting in clothes of Lincoln green, with russet boots on his feet, and a bugle slung over his shoulder like the guard of a long stage. When he blew this bugle, four-and-twenty other gentlemen of inferior rank, in Lincoln green a little coarser, and russet boots with a little thicker soles, turned out directly, and away galloped the whole train, with spears in their hands like lackered area railings, to hunt down the boars, or perhaps encounter a bear, in which latter case the baron killed him first and greased his whiskers with him afterwards.

This was a merry life for the Baron of Grogzwig, and a merrier still for the baron's retainers, who drank Rhine wine every night till they fell under the table, and then had the bottles on the floor, and called for pipes. Never were such jolly, roystering, rollicking, merry-making blades, as the jovial crew of Grogzwig.

But the pleasures of the table, or the pleasures of under the table, require a little variety; especially when the same five-and-twenty people sit daily down to the same board, to discuss the same subjects, and tell the same stories. The baron grew weary, and wanted excitement. He took to quarrelling with his gentlemen, and tried kicking two or three of them every day after dinner. This was a pleasant change at first; but it became monotonous after a week or so, and the baron fell quite out of sorts, and cast about in despair for some new amusement.

One night, after a day's sport in which he had outdone Nimrod or Gillingwater, and slaughtered 'another fine bear' and brought him home in triumph, the Baron Von Koëldwethout sat moodily at the head of his table, eyeing the smoky roof of the hall with a discontented aspect. He swallowed huge bumpers of wine, but the more he swallowed, the more he frowned: the gentlemen who had been honoured with the dangerous distinction of sitting on his right and left, imitated him to a miracle in the drinking, and frowned at each other.

'I will!' cried the baron suddenly, smiting the table with his right hand, and twirling his moustache with his left. 'Fill to the Lady of Grogzwig.'

The four-and-twenty Lincoln greens turned pale, with the exception of their four-and-twenty noses, which were unchangeable.

'I said to the Lady of Grogzwig,' repeated the baron, looking round the board.

'To the Lady of Grogzwig!' shouted the Lincoln greens; and down their four-and-twenty throats went four-and-twenty imperial pints of such rare old hock, that they smacked their eight-and-forty lips, and winked again.

'The fair daughter of the Baron Von Swillenhausen,' said Koëldwethout, condescending to explain. 'We will demand her in marriage of her father, ere the sun goes down tomorrow. If he refuse our suit, we will cut off his nose.'

A hoarse murmur arose from the company, and every man touched, first the hilt of his sword, and then the tip of his nose, with appalling significance.

What a pleasant thing filial piety is to contemplate! If the daughter of the Baron Von Swillenhausen had pleaded a pre-occupied heart, or fallen at her father's feet and corned them in tears, or only fainted away, and complimented the old gentleman in frantic ejaculations, the odds are a hundred to one, but Swillenhausen castle would have been turned out at window, or rather the baron turned out at window, and the castle demolished. The damsel held her peace however when an early messenger bore the request of Von Koëldwethout next morning, and modestly retired to her chamber, from the casement of which she watched the coming of the suitor and his retinue. She was no sooner assured that the horseman with the large moustachios was her proffered husband, than she hastened to her father's presence, and expressed her readiness to sacrifice herself to secure his peace. The venerable baron caught his child to his arms, and shed a wink of joy.

There was great feasting at the castle that day. The four-and-twenty Lincoln greens of Von Koëldwethout exchanged vows of eternal friendship with twelve Lincoln greens of Von Swillenhausen, and promised the old baron that they would drink his wine 'Till all was blue' – meaning probably until their whole countenances had acquired the same tint as their noses. Everybody slapped everybody else's back when the time for parting came; and the Baron Von Koëldwethout and his followers rode gaily home.

For six mortal weeks the bears and boars had a holiday. The houses of Koëldwethout and Swillenhausen were united; the spears rusted and the baron's bugle grew hoarse for lack of blowing.

These were great times for the four-and-twenty; but, alas! their high and palmy days had taken boots to themselves, and were already walking off.

'My dear,' said the baroness.

'My love,' said the baron.

'Those coarse, noisy men—'

'Which, ma'am?' said the baron starting.

'The baroness pointed from the window at which they stood, to the court-yard beneath, where the unconscious Lincoln greens were taking a copious stirrup-cup preparatory to issuing forth after a boar or two.

'My hunting train, ma'am,' said the baron.

'Disband them, love,' murmured the baroness.

'Disband them!' cried the baron, in amazement.

'To please me, love,' replied the baroness.

'To please the devil, ma'am,' answered the baron.

Whereupon the baroness uttered a great cry, and swooned away at the baron's feet.

What could the baron do? He called for the lady's maid, and roared for the doctor; and then rushing into the yard, kicked the two Lincoln greens who were the most used to it, and cursing the others all round, bade them go – but never mind where. I don't know the German for it, or I would put it delicately that way.

It is not for me to say by what means or by what degrees, some wives manage to keep down some husbands as they do, although I may have my private opinion on the subject, and may think that no Member of Parliament ought to be married, inasmuch as three married members out of every four, must vote according to their wives' consciences (if there be such things), and not according to their own. All I need say just now is, that the Baroness Von Koëldwethout somehow or other acquired great control over the Baron Von Koëldwethout, and that little by little, and bit by bit, and day by day, and year by year, the baron got the worst of some disputed question, or was slily unhorsed from some old hobby; and that by the time he was a fat hearty fellow of forty-eight or thereabouts, he had no feasting, no revelry, no hunting train, and no hunting—nothing in short that he liked, or used to have; and that although he was as fierce as a lion and as bold as brass, he was decidedly snubbed and put down by his own lady, in his own castle of Grogzwig.

Nor was this the whole extent of the baron's misfortunes. About a year after his nuptials there came into the world a lusty young baron, in whose honour a great many fireworks were let off, and a great many dozens of wine drunk; but next year there came a young baroness, and next year another young baron, and so on every year either a baron or baroness (and one year both together), until the baron found himself the father of a small family of twelve. Upon every one of these anniversaries the venerable Baroness Von Swillenhausen was nervously sensitive for the well-being of her child the Baroness Von Koëldwethout, and although it was not found that the good lady ever did anything material towards contributing to her child's recovery, still she made it a point of duty to be as nervous as possible at the castle of Grogzwig, and to divide her time between moral observations on the baron's housekeeping, and bewailing the hard lot of her unhappy daughter. And if the Baron of Grogzwig, a little hurt and irritated at this, took heart and ventured to suggest that his wife was at least no worse off than the wives of other barons, the Baroness Von Swillenhausen begged all persons to take notice, that nobody but she sympathised with her dear daughter's sufferings; upon which her relations and friends remarked, that to be sure she did cry a great deal more than her son-in-law, and that if there was a hard-hearted brute alive, it was that Baron of Grogzwig.

The poor baron bore it all as long as he could, and when he could bear it no longer lost his appetite and his spirits, and sat himself gloomily and dejectedly down. But there were worse troubles yet in store for him, and as they came on, his melancholy and sadness increased. Times changed. He got into debt. The Grogzwig coffers ran low, though the Swillenhausen family had looked upon them as inexhaustible, and just when the baroness was on the point of making a thirteenth addition to the family pedigree, Von Koëldwethout discovered that he had no means of replenishing them.

'I don't see what is to be done,' said the Baron. 'I think I'll kill myself.'

This was a bright idea. The baron took an old hunting-knife from a cupboard hard by, and having sharpened it on his boot, made what boys call 'an offer' at his throat.

'Hem!' said the Baron, stopping short. 'Perhaps it's not sharp enough.'

The baron sharpened it again, and made another offer, when his hand was arrested by a loud screaming among the young barons and baronesses, who had a nursery in an upstairs tower with iron bars outside the window, to prevent their tumbling out into the moat.

'If I had been a bachelor,' said the baron sighing; 'I might have done it fifty times over, without being interrupted. Hallo. Put a flask of wine and the largest pipe in the little vaulted room behind the hall.'

One of the domestics in a very kind manner executed the baron's order in the course of half an hour or so, and Von Koëldwethout being apprised thereof, strode to the vaulted room, the walls of which being of dark shining wood gleamed in the light of the blazing logs which were piled upon the hearth. The bottle and pipe were ready, and upon the whole the place looked very comfortable.

'Leave the lamp,' said the baron.

'Anything else, my lord?' inquired the domestic.

'The room,' replied the baron. The domestic obeyed, and the baron locked the door.

'I'll smoke a last pipe,' said the baron, 'and then I'll be off.' So, putting the knife upon the table till he wanted it, and tossing off a goodly measure of wine, the Lord of Grogzwig threw himself back in his chair, stretched his legs out before the fire, and puffed away.

He thought about a great many things – about his present troubles and past days of bachelorship, and about the Lincoln greens long since dispersed up and down the country no one knew whither, with the exception of two who had been unfortunately beheaded, and four who had killed themselves with drinking. His mind was running upon bears and boars, when in the process of draining his glass to the bottom he raised his eyes, and saw for the first time and with unbounded astonishment, that he was not alone.

No, he was not; for on the opposite side of the fire there sat with folded arms a wrinkled hideous figure, with deeply sunk and bloodshot eyes, and an immensely long cadaverous face, shadowed by jagged and matted locks of coarse black hair. He wore a kind of tunic of a dull bluish colour, which the baron observed on regarding it attentively, was clasped or ornamented down the front with coffin handles. His legs too, were encased in coffin plates as though in armour, and over his left shoulder he wore a short dusky cloak, which seemed made of a remnant of some pall. He took no notice of the baron, but was intently eyeing the fire.

'Halloa!' said the baron, stamping his foot to attract attention.

'Halloa!' replied the stranger, moving his eyes towards the baron, but not his face or himself. 'What now?'

'What now!' replied the baron, nothing daunted by his hollow voice and lustreless eyes, '*I* should ask that question. How did you get here?'

'Through the door,' replied the figure.

'What are you?' says the baron.

'A man,' replied the figure.

'I don't believe it,' says the baron.

'Disbelieve it then,' says the figure.

'I will,' rejoined the baron.

The figure looked at the bold Baron of Grogzwig for some time, and then said familiarly, 'There's no coming over you, I see. I'm not a man!'

'What are you then?' asked the baron.

'A genius,' replied the figure.

'You don't look much like one,' returned the Baron scornfully.

'I am the Genius of Despair and Suicide,' said the apparition. 'Now you know me.'

With these words the apparition turned towards the baron as if composing himself for a talk – and what was very remarkable was, that he threw his cloak aside, and displaying a stake which was run through the centre of his body, pulled it out with a jerk, and laid it on the table as composedly as if it had been his walking-stick.

'Now,' said the figure, glancing at the hunting-knife, 'are you ready for me?'

'Not quite,' rejoined the baron; 'I must finish this pipe first.'

'Look sharp then,' said the figure.

'You seem in a hurry,' said the baron.

'Why, yes, I am,' answered the figure; 'they're doing a pretty brisk business in my way over in England and France just now, and my time is a good deal taken up.'

'Do you drink?' said the baron, touching the bottle with the bowl of his pipe.

'Nine times out of ten, and then very hard,' rejoined the figure, drily.

'Never in moderation?' asked the baron.

'Never,' replied the figure, with a shudder, 'that breeds cheerfulness.'

The baron took another look at his new friend, whom he thought an uncommonly queer customer, and at length enquired whether he took any active part in such little proceedings as that which he had in contemplation.

'No,' replied the figure, evasively; 'but I am always present.'

'Just to see fair, I suppose,' said the baron.

'Just that,' replied the figure, playing with his stake, and examining the ferrule. 'Be as quick as you can, will you, for there's a young gentleman who is afflicted with too much money and leisure wanting me now, I find.'

'Going to kill himself because he has too much money!' exclaimed the baron, quite tickled; 'Ha! ha! that's a good one.' (This was the first time the baron had laughed for many a long day.)

'I say,' expostulated the figure, looking very much scared; 'don't do that again.'

'Why not?' demanded the baron.

'Because it gives me a pain all over,' replied the figure. 'Sigh as much as you please; that does me good.'

The baron sighed mechanically at the mention of the word, and the figure, brightening up again, handed him the hunting-knife with most winning politeness.

'It's not a bad idea though,' said the baron, feeling the edge of the weapon; 'a man killing himself because he has too much money.'

'Pooh!' said the apparition, petulantly, 'no better than a man's killing himself because he has got none or little.'

Whether the genius unintentionally committed himself in saying this, or whether he thought the baron's mind was so thoroughly made up that it didn't matter what he said, I have no means of knowing. I only know that the baron stopped his hand all of a sudden, opened his eyes wide, and looked as if quite a new light had come upon him for the first time.

'Why, certainly,' said Von Koëldwethout, 'nothing is too bad to be retrieved.'

'Except empty coffers,' cried the genius.

'Well; but they may be one day filled again,' said the baron.

'Scolding wives,' snarled the genius.

'Oh! They may be made quiet,' said the baron.

'Thirteen children,' shouted the genius.

'Can't all go wrong, surely,' said the baron.

The genius was evidently growing very savage with the baron for holding these opinions all at once, but he tried to laugh it off, and said if he would let him know when he had left off joking he should feel obliged to him.

'But I am not joking; I was never farther from it,' remonstrated the baron.

'Well, I am glad to hear that,' said the genius, looking very grim, 'because a joke, without any figure of speech, *is* the death of me. Come. Quit this dreary world at once.'

'I don't know,' said the baron, playing with the knife; 'it's a dreary one certainly, but I don't think yours is much better, for you have not the appearance of being particularly comfortable. That puts me in mind – what security have I that I shall be any the better for going out of the world after all!' he cried, starting up; 'I never thought of that.'

'Dispatch,' cried the figure, gnashing his teeth.

'Keep off,' said the baron. 'I'll brood over miseries no longer, but put a good face on the matter, and try the fresh air and the bears again; and if that don't do, I'll talk to the baroness soundly, and cut the Von Swillenhausens dead.' With this, the baron fell into his chair and laughed so loud and boisterously, that the room rang with it.

The figure fell back a pace or two, regarding the baron meanwhile with a look of intense terror, and when he had ceased, caught up the stake, plunged it violently into its body, uttered a frightful howl, and disappeared.

Von Koëldwethout never saw it again. Having once made up his mind to action, he soon brought the baroness and the Von Swillenhausens to reason, and died many years afterwards, not a rich man that I am aware of, but certainly a happy one: leaving behind him a numerous family, who had been carefully educated in bear and boar-hunting under his own personal eye. And my advice to all men is, that if ever they become hipped and melancholy from similar causes (as very manly men do), they look at both sides of the question, applying a magnifying glass to the best one; and if they still feel tempted to retire without leave, that they smoke a large pipe and drink a full bottle first, and profit by the laudable example of the Baron of Grogzwig.'

A CHRISTMAS CAROL

Being A Ghost Story of Christmas

MARLEY'S GHOST

Marley was dead, to begin with. There is no doubt whatever about that. The register of his burial was signed by the clergyman, the clerk, the undertaker, and the chief mourner. Scrooge signed it. And Scrooge's name was good upon 'Change for anything he chose to put his hand to. Old Marley was as dead as a door-nail.

Mind! I don't mean to say that I know, of my own knowledge, what there is particularly dead about a door-nail. I might have been inclined, myself, to regard a coffin-nail as the deadest piece of ironmongery in the trade. But the wisdom of our ancestors is in the simile; and my unhallowed hands shall not disturb it, or the Country's done for. You will, therefore, permit me to repeat, emphatically, that Marley was as dead as a door-nail.

Scrooge knew he was dead? Of course he did. How could it be otherwise? Scrooge and he were partners for I don't know how many years. Scrooge was his sole executor, his sole administrator, his sole assign, his sole residuary legatee, his sole friend, and sole mourner. And even Scrooge was not so dreadfully cut up by the sad event, but that he was an excellent man of business on the very day of the funeral, and solemnised it with an undoubted bargain.

The mention of Marley's funeral brings me back to the point I started from. There is no doubt that Marley was dead. This must be distinctly understood, or nothing wonderful can come of the story I am going to relate. If we were not perfectly convinced that Hamlet's Father died before the play began, there would be nothing more remarkable in his taking a stroll at night, in an easterly wind, upon his own ramparts, than there would be in any other middle-aged gentleman rashly turning out after dark in a breezy spot – say St Paul's Churchyard, for instance – literally to astonish his son's weak mind.

Scrooge never painted out Old Marley's name. There it stood, years afterwards, above the warehouse door: Scrooge and Marley. The firm was known as Scrooge and Marley. Sometimes people new to the business called Scrooge Scrooge, and sometimes Marley, but he answered to both names. It was all the same to him.

Oh! but he was a tight-fisted hand at the grindstone, Scrooge! a squeezing, wrenching, grasping, scraping, clutching, covetous, old sinner! Hard and sharp as flint, from which no steel had ever struck out generous fire; secret, and self-contained, and solitary as an oyster. The cold within him froze his old features, nipped his pointed nose, shrivelled his cheek, stiffened his gait; made his eyes red, his thin lips blue; and spoke out shrewdly in his grating voice. A frosty rime was on his head, and on his eyebrows, and his wiry chin. He carried his own low temperature always about with him; he iced his office in the dog-days; and didn't thaw it one degree at Christmas.

External heat and cold had little influence on Scrooge. No warmth could warm, no wintry weather chill him. No wind that blew was bitterer than he, no falling snow was more intent upon its purpose, no pelting rain less open to entreaty. Foul weather didn't know where to have him. The heaviest rain, and snow, and hail, and sleet could boast of the advantage over him in only one respect. They often 'came down' handsomely, and Scrooge never did.

Nobody ever stopped him in the street to say, with gladsome looks, 'My dear Scrooge, how are you? When will you come to see me?' No beggars implored him to bestow a trifle, no children asked him what it was o'clock, no man or woman ever once in all his life inquired the way to such and such a place, of Scrooge. Even the blind men's dogs appeared to know him; and, when they saw him coming on, would tug their owners into doorways and up courts; and then would wag their tails as though they said, 'No eye at all is better than an evil eye, dark master!'

But what did Scrooge care? It was the very thing he liked. To edge his way along the crowded paths of life, warning all human sympathy to keep its distance, was what the knowing ones call 'nuts' to Scrooge.

Once upon a time – of all the good days in the year, on Christmas Eve – old Scrooge sat busy in his counting-house. It was cold, bleak, biting weather: foggy withal: and he could hear the people in the court outside go wheezing up and down, beating their hands upon their breasts, and stamping their feet upon the pavement stones to warm them. The City clocks had only just gone three, but it was quite dark already – it had not been light all day – and candles were flaring in the windows of the neighbouring offices, like ruddy smears upon the palpable brown air. The fog came pouring in at every chink and keyhole, and was so dense without, that, although the court was of the narrowest, the houses opposite were mere phantoms. To see the dingy cloud come drooping down, obscuring everything, one might have thought that nature lived hard by, and was brewing on a large scale.

The door of Scrooge's counting-house was open, that he might keep his eye upon his clerk, who in a dismal little cell beyond, a sort of tank, was copying letters. Scrooge had a very small fire, but the clerk's fire was so very much smaller that it looked like one coal. But he couldn't replenish it, for Scrooge kept the coal-box in his own room; and so surely as the clerk came in with the shovel, the master predicted that it would be necessary for them to part. Wherefore the clerk put on his white comforter, and tried to warm himself at the candle; in which effort, not being a man of strong imagination, he failed.

'A merry Christmas, uncle! God save you!' cried a cheerful voice. It was the voice of Scrooge's nephew, who came upon him so quickly that this was the first intimation he had of his approach.

'Bah!' said Scrooge. 'Humbug!'

He had so heated himself with rapid walking in the fog

and frost, this nephew of Scrooge's, that he was all in a glow; his face was ruddy and handsome; his eyes sparkled, and his breath smoked again.

'Christmas a humbug, uncle!' said Scrooge's nephew. 'You don't mean that, I am sure?'

'I do,' said Scrooge. 'Merry Christmas! What right have you to be merry? What reason have you to be merry? You're poor enough.'

'Come, then,' returned the nephew gaily, 'What right have you to be dismal? What reason have you to be morose? You're rich enough.'

Scrooge, having no better answer ready on the spur of the moment, said, 'Bah!' again; and followed it up with 'Humbug!'

'Don't be cross, uncle!' said the nephew.

'What else can I be,' returned the uncle, 'when I live in such a world of fools as this? Merry Christmas! Out upon merry Christmas! What's Christmas-time to you but a time for paying bills without money; a time for finding yourself a year older, and not an hour richer; a time for balancing your books, and having every item in 'em through a round dozen of months presented dead against you? If I could work my will,' said Scrooge indignantly, 'every idiot who goes about with 'Merry Christmas' on his lips should be boiled with his own pudding, and buried with a stake of holly through his heart. He should!'

'Uncle!' pleaded the nephew.

'Nephew!' returned the uncle sternly, 'keep Christmas in your own way, and let me keep it in mine.'

'Keep it!' repeated Scrooge's nephew. 'But you don't keep it.'

'Let me leave it alone, then,' said Scrooge. 'Much good may it do you! Much good it has ever done you!'

'There are many things from which I might have derived good, by which I have not profited, I dare say,' returned the nephew; 'Christmas among the rest. But I am sure I have always thought of Christmas-time, when it has come round – apart from the veneration due to its sacred name and origin, if anything belonging to it can be apart from that – as a good time; a kind, forgiving, charitable, pleasant time; the only time I know of, in the long calendar of the year, when men and women seem by one consent to open their shut-up hearts freely, and to think of people below them as if they really were fellow-passengers to the grave, and not another race of creatures bound on other journeys. And therefore, uncle, though it has never put a scrap of gold or silver in my pocket, I believe that it *has* done me good, and *will* do me good; and I say, God bless it!'

The clerk in the tank involuntarily applauded. Becoming immediately sensible of the impropriety, he poked the fire, and extinguished the last frail spark for ever.

'Let me hear another sound from *you*,' said Scrooge, 'and you'll keep your Christmas by losing your situation! You're quite a powerful speaker, sir,' he added, turning to his nephew. 'I wonder you don't go into Parliament.'

'Don't be angry, uncle. Come! Dine with us tomorrow.'

Scrooge said that he would see him ——Yes, indeed he did. He went the whole length of the expression, and said that he would see him in that extremity first.

'But why?' cried Scrooge's nephew. 'Why?'

'Why did you get married?' said Scrooge.

'Because I fell in love.'

'Because you fell in love!' growled Scrooge, as if that were the only one thing in the world more ridiculous than a merry Christmas. 'Good afternoon!'

'Nay, uncle, but you never came to see me before that happened. Why give it as a reason for not coming now?'

'Good afternoon,' said Scrooge.

'I want nothing from you; I ask nothing of you; why cannot we be friends?'

'Good afternoon!' said Scrooge.

'I am sorry, with all my heart, to find you so resolute. We have never had any quarrel to which I have been a party. But I have made the trial in homage to Christmas, and I'll keep my Christmas humour to the last. So A Merry Christmas, uncle!'

'Good afternoon,' said Scrooge.

'And A Happy New Year!'

'Good afternoon!' said Scrooge.

His nephew left the room without an angry word, notwithstanding. He stopped at the outer door to bestow the greetings of the season on the clerk, who, cold as he was, was warmer than Scrooge; for he returned them cordially.

'There's another fellow,' muttered Scrooge, who overheard him: 'my clerk, with fifteen shillings a week, and a wife and family, talking about a merry Christmas. I'll retire to Bedlam.'

This lunatic, in letting Scrooge's nephew out, had let two other people in. They were portly gentlemen, pleasant to behold, and now stood, with their hats off, in Scrooge's office. They had books and papers in their hands, and bowed to him.

'Scrooge and Marley's, I believe,' said one of the gentlemen, referring to his list. 'Have I the pleasure of addressing Mr Scrooge, or Mr Marley?'

'Mr Marley has been dead these seven years,' Scrooge replied. 'He died seven years ago, this very night.'

'We have no doubt his liberality is well represented by his surviving partner,' said the gentleman, presenting his credentials.

It certainly was; for they had been two kindred spirits. At the ominous word 'liberality' Scrooge frowned, and shook his head, and handed the credentials back.

'At this festive season of the year, Mr Scrooge,' said the gentleman, taking up a pen, 'it is more than usually desirable that we should make some slight provision for the poor and destitute, who suffer greatly at the present time. Many thousands are in want of common necessaries; hundreds of thousands are in want of common comforts, sir.'

'Are there no prisons?' asked Scrooge.

'Plenty of prisons,' said the gentleman, laying down the pen again.

'And the Union workhouses?' demanded Scrooge. 'Are they still in operation?'

'They are. Still,' returned the gentleman, 'I wish I could say they were not.'

'The Treadmill and the Poor Law are in full vigour, then?' said Scrooge.

'Both very busy, sir.'

'Oh! I was afraid, from what you said at first, that something had occurred to stop them in their useful course,' said Scrooge. 'I am very glad to hear it.'

'Under the impression that they scarcely furnish Christian cheer of mind or body to the multitude,' returned the gentleman, 'a few of us are endeavouring to raise a fund to buy the poor some meat and drink, and means of warmth. We choose this time, because it is a time, of all others, when Want is keenly felt, and Abundance rejoices. What shall I put you down for?'

'Nothing!' Scrooge replied.

'You wish to be anonymous?'

'I wish to be left alone,' said Scrooge. 'Since you ask me what I wish, gentlemen, that is my answer. I don't make merry myself at Christmas, and I can't afford to make idle people merry. I help to support the establishments I have mentioned – they cost enough: and those who are badly off must go there.'

'Many can't go there; and many would rather die.'

'If they would rather die,' said Scrooge, 'they had better do it, and decrease the surplus population. Besides – excuse me – I don't know that.'

'But you might know it,' observed the gentleman.

'It's not my business,' Scrooge returned. 'It's enough for a man to understand his own business, and not to interfere with other people's. Mine occupies me constantly. Good afternoon, gentlemen!'

Seeing clearly that it would be useless to pursue their point, the gentlemen withdrew. Scrooge resumed his labours with an improved opinion of himself, and in a more facetious temper than was usual with him.

Meanwhile the fog and darkness thickened so, that people ran about with flaring links, proffering their services to go before horses in carriages, and conduct them on their way. The ancient tower of a church, whose gruff old bell was always peeping slily down at Scrooge out of a Gothic window in the wall, became invisible, and struck the hours and quarters in the clouds, with tremulous vibrations afterwards, as if its teeth were chattering in its frozen head up there. The cold became intense. In the main street, at the corner of the court, some labourers were repairing the gas-pipes, and had lighted a great fire in a brazier, round which a party of ragged men and boys were gathered: warming their hands and winking their eyes before the blaze in rapture. The water-plug being left in solitude, its overflowings suddenly congealed, and turned to misanthropic ice. The brightness of the shops, where holly sprigs and berries crackled in the lamp heat of the windows, made pale faces ruddy as they passed. Poulterers' and grocers' trades became a splendid joke: a glorious pageant, with which it was next to impossible to believe that such dull principles as bargain and sale had anything to do. The Lord Mayor, in the stronghold of the mighty Mansion House, gave orders to his fifty cooks and butlers to keep Christmas as a Lord Mayor's household should; and even the little tailor, whom he had fined five shillings on the previous Monday for being drunk and bloodthirsty in the streets, stirred up tomorrow's pudding in his garret, while his lean wife and the baby sallied out to buy the beef.

Foggier yet, and colder! Piercing, searching, biting cold. If the good St Dunstan had but nipped the Evil Spirit's nose with a touch of such weather as that, instead of using his familiar weapons, then indeed he would have roared to lusty purpose. The owner of one scant young nose, gnawed and mumbled by the hungry cold as bones are gnawed by dogs, stooped down at Scrooge's keyhole to regale him with a Christmas carol; but, at the first sound of 'God bless you, merry gentleman, May nothing you dismay!' Scrooge seized the ruler with such energy of action, that the singer fled in terror, leaving the keyhole to the fog, and even more congenial frost.

At length the hour of shutting up the counting-house arrived. With an ill-will Scrooge dismounted from his stool, and tacitly admitted the fact to the expectant clerk in the tank, who instantly snuffed his candle out, and put on his hat.

'You'll want all day tomorrow, I suppose?' said Scrooge.

'If quite convenient, sir.'

'It's not convenient,' said Scrooge, 'and it's not fair. If I was to stop half-a-crown for it, you'd think yourself ill used, I'll be bound?'

The clerk smiled faintly.

'And yet,' said Scrooge, 'you don't think *me* ill used when I pay a day's wages for no work.'

The clerk observed that it was only once a year.

'A poor excuse for picking a man's pocket every twenty-fifth of December!' said Scrooge, buttoning his great-coat to the chin. 'But I suppose you must have the whole day. Be here all the earlier next morning.'

The clerk promised that he would; and Scrooge walked out with a growl. The office was closed in a twinkling, and the clerk, with the long ends of his white comforter dangling below his waist (for he boasted no great-coat), went down a slide on Cornhill, at the end of a lane of boys, twenty times, in honour of its being Christmas-eve, and then ran home to Camden Town as hard as he could pelt, to play at blindman's buff.

Scrooge took his melancholy dinner in his usual melancholy tavern; and having read all the newspapers, and beguiled the rest of the evening with his banker's books, went home to bed. He lived in chambers which had once belonged to his deceased partner. They were a gloomy suite of rooms, in a lowering pile of building up a yard, where it had so little business to be, that one could scarcely help fancying it must have run there when it was a young house, playing at hide-and-seek with other houses, and have forgotten the way out again. It was old enough now, and dreary enough; for nobody lived in it but Scrooge, the other rooms being all let out as offices. The yard was so dark that even Scrooge, who knew its every stone, was fain to grope with his hands. The fog and frost so hung about the black old gateway of the house, that it seemed as if the Genius of the Weather sat in mournful meditation on the threshold.

Now, it is a fact that there was nothing at all particular about the knocker on the door, except that it was very large. It is also a fact that Scrooge had seen it, night and morning, during his whole residence in that place; also that Scrooge had as little of what is called fancy about him as any man in the City of London, even including – which is a bold word – the corporation, aldermen, and livery. Let it also be borne in mind that Scrooge had not bestowed one thought on Marley since his last mention of his seven-years'-dead partner that afternoon. And then let any man explain to me, if he can, how it happened that Scrooge, having his key in the lock of the door, saw in the knocker, without its undergoing any intermediate process of change – not a knocker, but Marley's face.

Marley's face. It was not in impenetrable shadow, as the other objects in the yard were, but had a dismal light about it, like a bad lobster in a dark cellar. It was not angry or ferocious, but looked at Scrooge as Marley used to look: with ghostly spectacles turned up on its ghostly forehead. The hair was curiously stirred, as if by breath or hot air; and, though the eyes were wide open, they were perfectly motionless. That, and its livid colour, made it horrible; but its horror seemed to be in spite of the face, and beyond its control, rather than a part of its own expression.

As Scrooge looked fixedly at this phenomenon, it was a knocker again.

To say that he was not startled, or that his blood was not conscious of a terrible sensation to which it had been a stranger from infancy, would be untrue. But he put his hand upon the key he had relinquished, turned it sturdily, walked in, and lighted his candle.

He *did* pause, with a moment's irresolution, before he shut the door; and he *did* look cautiously behind it first, as if he half expected to be terrified with the sight of Marley's pigtail sticking out into the hall. But there was nothing on the back of the door, except the screws and nuts that held the knocker on, so he said, 'Pooh, pooh!' and closed it with a bang.

The sound resounded through the house like thunder. Every room above, and every cask in the wine merchant's cellars below, appeared to have a separate peal of echoes of its own. Scrooge was not a man to be frightened by echoes. He fastened the door, and walked across the hall, and up the stairs: slowly, too: trimming his candle as he went.

You may talk vaguely about driving a coach and six up a good old flight of stairs, or through a bad young Act of Parliament; but I mean to say you might have got a hearse up that staircase, and taken it broadwise, with the splinter-bar towards the wall, and the door towards the balustrades: and done it easy. There was plenty of width for that, and room to spare; which is perhaps the reason why Scrooge thought he saw a locomotive hearse going on before him in the gloom. Half-a-dozen gas-lamps out of the street wouldn't have lighted the entry too well, so you may suppose that it was pretty dark with Scrooge's dip.

Up Scrooge went, not caring a button for that. Darkness is cheap, and Scrooge liked it. But, before he shut his heavy door, he walked through his rooms to see that all was right. He had just enough recollection of the face to desire to do that.

Sitting-room, bedroom, lumber-room. All as they should be. Nobody under the table, nobody under the sofa; a small fire in the grate; spoon and basin ready; and the little saucepan of gruel (Scrooge had a cold in his head) upon the hob. Nobody under the bed; nobody in the closet; nobody in his dressing-gown, which was hanging up in a suspicious attitude against the wall. Lumber-room as usual. Old fire-guard, old shoes, two fish baskets, washing-stand on three legs, and a poker.

Quite satisfied, he closed his door, and locked himself in; double locked himself in, which was not his custom. Thus secured against surprise, he took off his cravat; put on his dressing-gown and slippers, and his nightcap; and sat down before the fire to take his gruel.

It was a very low fire indeed; nothing on such a bitter night. He was obliged to sit close to it, and brood over it, before he could extract the least sensation of warmth from such a handful of fuel. The fire-place was an old one, built by some Dutch merchant long ago, and paved all round with quaint Dutch tiles, designed to illustrate the Scriptures. There were Cains and Abels, Pharaoh's daughters, Queens of Sheba, Angelic messengers descending through the air in clouds like feather beds, Abrahams, Belshazzars, Apostles putting off to sea in butter-boats, hundreds of figures to attract his thoughts; and yet that face of Marley, seven years dead, came like the ancient Prophet's rod, and swallowed up the whole. If each smooth tile had been a blank at first, with power to shape some picture on its surface from the disjointed fragments of his thoughts, there would have been a copy of old Marley's head on every one.

'Humbug!' said Scrooge; and walked across the room.

After several turns he sat down again. As he threw his head back in the chair, his glance happened to rest upon a bell, a disused bell, that hung in the room, and communicated, for some purpose now forgotten, with a chamber in the highest story of the building. It was with great astonishment, and with a strange, inexplicable dread, that, as he looked, he saw this bell begin to swing. It swung so softly in the outset that it scarcely made a sound; but soon it rang out loudly, and so did every bell in the house.

This might have lasted half a minute, or a minute, but it seemed an hour. The bells ceased, as they had begun, together. They were succeeded by a clanking noise, deep down below, as if some person were dragging a heavy chain over the casks in the wine merchant's cellar. Scrooge then remembered to have heard that ghosts in haunted houses were described as dragging chains.

The cellar door flew open with a booming sound, and then he heard the noise much louder on the floors below; then coming up the stairs; then coming straight towards his door.

'It's humbug still!' said Scrooge. 'I won't believe it.'

His colour changed, though, when, without a pause, it came in through the heavy door, and passed into the room before his eyes. Upon its coming in, the dying flame leaped up, as though it cried, 'I know him! Marley's Ghost!' and fell again.

The same face: the very same. Marley in his pigtail, usual waistcoat, tights and boots; the tassels on the latter bristling, like his pigtail, and his coat-skirts, and the hair upon his head. The chain he drew was clasped about his middle. It was long, and wound about him like a tail; and it was made (for Scrooge observed it closely) of cash-boxes, keys, padlocks, ledgers, deeds, and heavy purses wrought in steel. His body was transparent; so that Scrooge, observing him, and looking through his waistcoat, could see the two buttons on his coat behind.

Scrooge had often heard it said that Marley had no bowels, but he had never believed it until now.

No, nor did he believe it even now. Though he looked the phantom through and through, and saw it standing before him; though he felt the chilling influence of its death-cold eyes; and marked the very texture of the folded kerchief bound about its head and chin, which wrapper he had not observed before; he was still incredulous, and fought against his senses.

'How now!' said Scrooge, caustic and cold as ever. 'What do you want with me?'

'Much!' – Marley's voice, no doubt about it.

'Who are you?'

'Ask me who I *was*.'

'Who *were* you, then?' said Scrooge, raising his voice. 'You're particular for a shade.' He was going to say '*to* a shade,' but substituted this, as more appropriate.

'In life I was your partner, Jacob Marley.'

'Can you – can you sit down?' asked Scrooge, looking doubtfully at him.

'I can.'

'Do it then.'

Scrooge asked the question, because he didn't know whether a ghost so transparent might find himself in a condition to take a chair; and felt that, in the event of its being impossible, it might involve the necessity of an embarrassing explanation. But the Ghost sat down on the opposite side of the fire-place, as if he were quite used to it.

'You don't believe in me,' observed the Ghost.

'I don't,' said Scrooge.

'What evidence would you have of my reality beyond that of your own senses?'

'I don't know,' said Scrooge.

'Why do you doubt your senses?'

'Because,' said Scrooge, 'a little thing effects them. A slight disorder of the stomach makes them cheats. You may be an undigested bit of beef, a blot of mustard, a crumb of cheese, a fragment of an underdone potato. There's more of gravy than of grave about you, whatever you are!'

Scrooge was not much in the habit of cracking jokes, nor did he feel in his heart by any means waggish then. The truth is, that he tried to be smart, as a means of distracting his own attention, and keeping down his terror; for the spectre's voice disturbed the very marrow in his bones.

To sit staring at those fixed glazed eyes in silence, for a moment, would play, Scrooge felt, the very deuce with him. There was something very awful, too, in the spectre's being provided with an infernal atmosphere of his own. Scrooge could not feel it himself but this was clearly the case; for though the Ghost sat perfectly motionless, its hair, and skirts, and tassels were still agitated as by the hot vapour from an oven.

'You see this toothpick?' said Scrooge, returning quickly to the charge, for the reason just assigned; and wishing, though it were only for a second, to divert the vision's stony gaze from himself.

'I do,' replied the Ghost.

'You are not looking at it,' said Scrooge.

'But I see it,' said the Ghost, 'notwithstanding.'

'Well!' returned Scrooge, 'I have but to swallow this, and be for the rest of my days persecuted by a legion of goblins, all of my own creation. Humbug, I tell you; humbug!'

At this the spirit raised a frightful cry, and shook its chain with such a dismal and appalling noise, that Scrooge held on tight to his chair, to save himself from falling in a swoon. But how much greater was his horror when the phantom, taking off the bandage round his head, as if it were too warm to wear indoors, its lower jaw dropped down upon its breast!

Scrooge fell upon his knees, and clasped his hands before his face.

'Mercy!' he said. 'Dreadful apparition, why do you trouble me?'

'Man of the worldly mind!' replied the Ghost, 'do you believe in me or not?'

'I do,' said Scrooge. 'I must. But why do spirits walk the earth, and why do they come to me?'

'It is required of every man,' the Ghost returned, 'that the spirit within him should walk abroad among his fellow-men, and travel far and wide; and, if that spirit goes not forth in life, it is condemned to do so after death. It is doomed to wander through the world – oh, woe is me – and witness what it cannot share, but might have shared on earth, and turned to happiness!'

Again the spectre raised a cry; and shook its chain and wrung its shadowy hands.

'You are fettered,' said Scrooge, trembling. 'Tell me why?'

'I wear the chain I forged in life,' replied the Ghost. 'I made it link by link, and yard by yard; I girded it on of my own free-will, and of my own free-will I wore it. Is its pattern strange to *you*?'

Scrooge trembled more and more.

'Or would you know,' pursued the Ghost, 'the weight and length of the strong coil you bear yourself? It was full as heavy and as long as this, seven Christmas-eves ago. You have laboured on it since. It's a ponderous chain!'

Scrooge glanced about him on the floor, in the expectation of finding himself surrounded by some fifty or sixty fathoms of iron cable; but he could see nothing.

'Jacob!' he said imploringly. 'Old Jacob Marley, tell me more! Speak comfort to me, Jacob!'

'I have none to give,' the Ghost replied. 'It comes from other regions, Ebenezer Scrooge, and is conveyed by other ministers to other kinds of men. Nor can I tell you what I would. A very little more is all permitted to me. I cannot rest, I cannot stay, I cannot linger anywhere. My spirit never walked beyond our counting-house – mark me – in life my spirit never roved beyond the narrow limits of our money-changing hole; and weary journeys lie before me!'

It was a habit with Scrooge, whenever he became thoughtful, to put his hands in his breeches pockets. Pondering on what the Ghost had said, he did so now, but without lifting up his eyes, or getting off his knees.

'You must have been very slow about it, Jacob,' Scrooge observed in a business-like manner, though with humility and deference.

'Slow!' the Ghost repeated.

'Seven years dead,' mused Scrooge. 'And travelling all the time?'

'The whole time,' said the Ghost. 'No rest, no peace. Incessant torture of remorse.'

'You travel fast?' said Scrooge.

'On the wings of the wind,' replied the Ghost.

'You might have got over a great quantity of ground in seven years,' said Scrooge.

The Ghost, on hearing this, set up another cry, and clanked its chain so hideously in the dead silence of the night, that the Ward would have been justified in indicting it for a nuisance.

'Oh! captive, bound, and double-ironed,' cried the phantom, 'not to know that ages of incessant labour, by immortal creatures, for this earth must pass into eternity before the good of which it is susceptible is all developed! Not to know that any Christian spirit working kindly in its little sphere, whatever it may be, will find its mortal life too short for its vast means of usefulness! Not to know that no space of regret can make amends for one life's opportunities misused! Yet such was I! Oh, such was I!'

'But you were always a good man of business, Jacob,' faltered Scrooge, who now began to apply this to himself.

'Business!' cried the Ghost, wringing its hands again. 'Mankind was my business. The common welfare was my business; charity, mercy, forbearance, and benevolence were, all, my business. The dealings of my trade were but a drop of water in the comprehensive ocean of my business!'

It held up its chain at arm's length, as if that were the cause of all its unavailing grief, and flung it heavily upon the ground again.

'At this time of the rolling year,' the spectre said, 'I suffer most. Why did I walk through crowds of fellow-beings with my eyes turned down, and never raise them to that blessed Star which led the Wise Men to a poor abode? Were there no poor homes to which its light would have conducted *me*?'

Scrooge was very much dismayed to hear the spectre going on at this rate, and began to quake exceedingly.

'Hear me!' cried the Ghost. 'My time is nearly gone.'

'I will,' said Scrooge. 'But don't be hard upon me! Don't be flowery, Jacob! Pray!'

'How it is that I appear before you in a shape that you can see, I may not tell. I have sat invisible beside you many and many a day.'

It was not an agreeable idea. Scrooge shivered, and wiped the perspiration from his brow.

'That is no light part of my penance,' pursued the Ghost. 'I am here tonight to warn you that you have yet a chance and hope of escaping my fate. A chance and hope of my procuring, Ebenezer.'

'You were always a good friend to me,' said Scrooge. 'Thankee!'

'You will be haunted,' resumed the Ghost, 'by Three Spirits.'

Scrooge's countenance fell almost as low as the Ghost's had done.

'Is that the chance and hope you mentioned, Jacob?' he demanded in a faltering voice.

'It is.'

'I – I think I'd rather not,' said Scrooge.

'Without their visits,' said the Ghost, 'you cannot hope to shun the path I tread. Expect the first tomorrow when the bell tolls One.'

'Couldn't I take 'em all at once, and have it over, Jacob?' hinted Scrooge.

'Expect the second on the next night at the same hour. The third, upon the next night when the last stroke of Twelve has ceased to vibrate. Look to see me no more; and look that, for your own sake, you remember what has passed between us!'

When it had said these words, the spectre took its wrapper from the table, and bound it round its head as before. Scrooge knew this by the smart sound its teeth made when the jaws were brought together by the bandage. He ventured to raise his eyes again, and found his supernatural visitor confronting him in an erect attitude, with its chain wound over and about its arm.

The apparition walked backward from him; and, at every step it took, the window raised itself a little, so that, when the spectre reached it, it was wide open. It beckoned Scrooge to approach, which he did. When they were within two paces of each other, Marley's Ghost held up its hand, warning him to come no nearer. Scrooge stopped.

Not so much in obedience as in surprise and fear; for, on the raising of the hand, he became sensible of confused noises in the air; incoherent sounds of lamentation and regret; wailings inexpressibly sorrowful and self-accusatory. The spectre, after listening for a moment, joined the mournful dirge; and floated out upon the bleak, dark night.

Scrooge followed to the window: desperate in his curiosity. He looked out.

The air was filled with phantoms, wandering hither and thither in restless haste, and moaning as they went. Every one of them wore chains like Marley's Ghost; some few (they might be guilty governments) were linked together; none were free. Many had been personally known to Scrooge in their lives. He had been quite familiar with one old ghost in a white waistcoat, with a monstrous iron safe attached to its ankle, who cried piteously at being unable to assist a wretched woman with an infant, whom it saw below upon a doorstep. The misery with them all was, clearly, that they sought to interfere, for good, in human matters, and had lost the power for ever.

Whether these creatures faded into mist, or mist enshrouded them, he could not tell. But they and their spirit voices faded together; and the night became as it had been when he walked home.

Scrooge closed the window, and examined the door by which the Ghost had entered. It was double locked, as he had locked it with his own hands, and the bolts were undisturbed. He tried to say 'Humbug!' but stopped at the first syllable. And being, from the emotion he had undergone, or the fatigues of the day, or his glimpse of the Invisible World, or the dull conversation of the Ghost, or the lateness of the hour, much in need of repose, went straight to bed without undressing, and fell asleep upon the instant.

THE FIRST OF THE THREE SPIRITS

When Scrooge awoke it was so dark, that, looking out of bed, he could scarcely distinguish the transparent window from the opaque walls of his chamber. He was endeavouring to pierce the darkness with his ferret eyes, when the chimes of a neighbouring church struck the four quarters. So he listened for the hour.

To his great astonishment, the heavy bell went on from six to seven, and from seven to eight, and regularly up to twelve; then stopped. Twelve! It was past two when he went to bed. The clock was wrong. An icicle must have got into the works. Twelve!

He touched the spring of his repeater, to correct this most preposterous clock. Its rapid little pulse beat twelve, and stopped.

'Why, it isn't possible,' said Scrooge, 'that I can have slept through a whole day and far into another night. It isn't possible that anything has happened to the sun, and this is twelve at noon!'

The idea being an alarming one, he scrambled out of bed, and groped his way to the window. He was obliged to rub the frost off with the sleeve of his dressing-gown before he could see anything; and could see very little then. All he could make out was, that it was still very foggy and extremely cold, and that there was no noise of people running to and fro, and making a great stir, as there unquestionably would have been if night had beaten off bright day, and taken possession of the world. This was a great relief, because 'Three days after sight of this First of Exchange pay to Mr Ebenezer Scrooge or his order,' and so forth, would have become a mere United States security if there were no days to count by.

Scrooge went to bed again, and thought, and thought, and thought it over and over, and could make nothing of it. The more he thought, the more perplexed he was; and, the more he endeavoured not to think, the more he thought.

Marley's Ghost bothered him exceedingly. Every time he resolved within himself, after mature inquiry, that it was all a dream, his mind flew back again, like a strong spring released, to its first position, and presented the same problem to be worked all through, 'Was it a dream or not?'

Scrooge lay in this state until the chime had gone three quarters more, when he remembered, on a sudden, that the Ghost had warned him of a visitation when the bell tolled one. He resolved to lie awake until the hour was passed; and, considering that he could no more go to sleep than go to Heaven, this was, perhaps, the wisest resolution in his power.

The quarter was so long, that he was more than once convinced he must have sunk into a doze unconsciously, and missed the clock. At length it broke upon his listening ear.

'Ding, dong!'

'A quarter past,' said Scrooge, counting.

'Ding, dong!'

'Half past,' said Scrooge.

'Ding, dong!'

'A quarter to it,' said Scrooge.

'Ding, dong!'

'The hour itself,' said Scrooge triumphantly, 'and nothing else!'

He spoke before the hour bell sounded, which it now did with a deep, dull, hollow, melancholy ONE. Light flashed up in the room upon the instant, and the curtains of his bed were drawn.

The curtains of his bed were drawn aside, I tell you, by a hand. Not the curtains at his feet, nor the curtains at his back, but those to which his face was addressed. The curtains of his bed were drawn aside; and Scrooge, starting up into a half-recumbent attitude, found himself face to face with the unearthly visitor who drew them: as close to it as I am now to you, and I am standing in the spirit at your elbow.

It was a strange figure – like a child: yet not so like a child as like an old man, viewed through some supernatural medium, which gave him the appearance of having receded from the view, and being diminished to a child's proportions. Its hair, which hung about its neck and down its back, was white, as if with age; and yet the face had not a wrinkle in it, and the tenderest bloom was on the skin. The arms were very long and muscular; the hands the same, as if its hold were of uncommon strength. Its legs and feet, most delicately formed, were, like those upper members, bare. It wore a tunic of the purest white; and round its waist was bound a lustrous belt, the sheen of which was beautiful. It held a branch of fresh green holly in its hand; and, in singular contradiction of that wintry emblem, had its dress trimmed with summer flowers. But the strangest thing about it was, that from the crown of its head there sprung a bright clear jet of light, by which all this was visible; and which was doubtless the occasion of its using, in its duller moments, a great extinguisher for a cap, which it now held under its arm.

Even this, though, when Scrooge looked at it with increasing steadiness, was *not* its strangest quality. For, as its belt sparkled and glittered, now in one part and now in another, and what was light one instant at another time was dark, so the figure itself fluctuated in its distinctness: being now a thing with one arm, now with one leg, now with twenty legs, now a pair of legs without a head, now a head without a body: of which dissolving parts no outline would be visible in the dense gloom wherein they melted away.

And, in the very wonder of this, it would be itself again; distinct and clear as ever.

'Are you the Spirit, sir, whose coming was foretold to me?' asked Scrooge.

'I am!'

The voice was soft and gentle. Singularly low, as if, instead of being so close beside him, it were at a distance.

'Who and what are you?' Scrooge demanded.

'I am the Ghost of Christmas Past.'

'Long Past?' inquired Scrooge; observant of its dwarfish stature.

'No. Your past.'

'Perhaps Scrooge could not have told anybody why, if anybody could have asked him; but he had a special desire to see the Spirit in his cap; and begged him to be covered.

'What!' exclaimed the Ghost, 'would you so soon put out, with worldly hands, the light I give? Is it not enough that you are one of those whose passions made this cap, and force me through whole trains of years to wear it low upon my brow?'

Scrooge reverently disclaimed all intention to offend or any knowledge of having wilfully 'bonneted' the Spirit at any period of his life. He then made bold to inquire what business brought him there.

'Your welfare!' said the Ghost.

Scrooge expressed himself much obliged, but could not help thinking that a night of unbroken rest would have been more conducive to that end. The Spirit must have heard him thinking, for it said immediately:

'Your reclamation, then. Take heed!'

It put out its strong hand as it spoke, and clasped him gently by the arm.

'Rise! and walk with me!'

It would have been in vain for Scrooge to plead that the weather and the hour were not adapted to pedestrian purposes; that bed was warm, and the thermometer a long way below freezing; that he was clad but lightly in his slippers, dressing-gown, and nightcap; and that he had a cold upon him at that time. The grasp, though gentle as a woman's hand, was not to be resisted. He rose: but finding that the Spirit made towards the window, clasped its robe in supplication.

'I am a mortal,' Scrooge remonstrated, 'and liable to fall.'

'Bear but a touch of my hand *there*,' said the Spirit, laying it upon his heart, 'and you shall be upheld in more than this!'

As the words were spoken, they passed through the wall, and stood upon an open country road, with fields on either hand. The city had entirely vanished. Not a vestige of it was to be seen. The darkness and the mist had vanished with it, for it was a clear, cold, winter day, with snow upon the ground.

'Good Heaven!' said Scrooge, clasping his hands together, as he looked about him, 'I was bred in this place. I was a boy here!'

The Spirit gazed upon him mildly. Its gentle touch, though it had been light and instantaneous, appeared still present to the old man's sense of feeling. He was conscious of a thousand odours floating in the air, each one connected with a thousand thoughts, and hopes, and joys, and cares long, long forgotten!

'Your lip is trembling,' said the Ghost.

'And what is that upon your cheek?'

Scrooge muttered, with an unusual catching in his voice, that it was a pimple; and begged the Ghost to lead him where he would.

'You recollect the way?' inquired the Spirit.

'Remember it!' cried Scrooge with fervour; 'I could walk it blindfold.'

'Strange to have forgotten it for so many years!' observed the Ghost. 'Let us go on.'

They walked along the road, Scrooge recognising every gate, and post, and tree, until a little market-town appeared in the distance, with its bridge, its church, and winding river. Some shaggy ponies now were seen trotting towards them with boys upon their backs, who called to other boys in country gigs and carts, driven by farmers. All these boys were in great spirits, and shouted to each other, until the broad fields were so full of merry music, that the crisp air laughed to hear it.

'These are but shadows of the things that have been,' said the Ghost. 'They have no consciousness of us.'

The jocund travellers came on; and as they came, Scrooge knew and named them every one. Why was he rejoiced beyond all bounds to see them? Why did his cold eye glisten, and his heart leap up as they went past? Why was he filled with gladness when he heard them give each other Merry Christmas, as they parted at cross-roads and by-ways for their several homes? What was merry Christmas to Scrooge? Out upon merry Christmas! What good had it ever done to him?

'The school is not quite deserted,' said the Ghost. 'A solitary child, neglected by his friends, is left there still.'

Scrooge said he knew it. And he sobbed.

They left the high-road by a well-remembered lane, and soon approached a mansion of dull red brick, with a little weather-cock surmounted cupola on the roof, and a bell hanging in it. It was a large house, but one of broken fortunes: for the spacious offices were little used, their walls were damp and mossy, their windows broken, and their gates decayed. Fowls clucked and strutted in the stables; and the coach-houses and sheds were overrun with grass. Nor was it more retentive of its ancient state within; for, entering the dreary hall, and glancing through the open doors of many rooms, they found them poorly furnished, cold and vast. There was an earthy savour in the air, a chilly bareness in the place, which associated itself somehow with too much getting up by candle-light, and not too much to eat.

They went, the Ghost and Scrooge, across the hall, to a door at the back of the house. It opened before them, and disclosed a long, bare, melancholy room, made barer still by lines of plain deal forms and desks. At one of these a lonely boy was reading near a feeble fire; and Scrooge sat down upon a form, and wept to see his poor forgotten self as he had used to be.

Not a latent echo in the house, not a squeak and scuffle from the mice behind the panelling, not a drip from the half-thawed water-spout in the dull yard behind, not a sigh among the leafless boughs of one despondent poplar, not the idle swinging of an empty storehouse door, no, not a clicking in the fire, but fell upon the heart of Scrooge with softening influence, and gave a freer passage to his tears.

The Spirit touched him on the arm, and pointed to his younger self, intent upon his reading. Suddenly a man in foreign garments: wonderfully real and distinct to look at: stood outside the window, with an axe stuck in his belt, and leading by the bridle an ass laden with wood.

'Why, it's Ali Baba!' Scrooge exclaimed in ecstasy. 'It's dear old honest Ali Baba! Yes, yes, I know. One Christmas-time, when yonder solitary child was left here all alone, he *did* come, for the first time, just like that. Poor boy! And Valentine,' said Scrooge, 'and his wild brother, Orson; there they go! And what's his name, who was put down in his drawers, asleep, at the gate of Damascus; don't you see him? And the Sultan's Groom turned upside down by the Genii: there he is upon his head! Serve him right! I'm glad of it. What business had *he* to be married to the Princess?'

To hear Scrooge expending all the earnestness of his nature on such subjects, in a most extraordinary voice between laughing and crying; and to see his heightened and excited face; would have been a surprise to his business friends in the City, indeed.

'There's the Parrot!' cried Scrooge. 'Green body and yellow tail, with a thing like a lettuce growing out of the top of his head; there he is! Poor Robin Crusoe he called him, when he came home again after sailing round the island. "Poor Robin Crusoe, where have you been, Robin Crusoe?" The man thought he was dreaming, but he wasn't. It was the Parrot, you know. There goes Friday, running for his life to the little creek! Halloa! Hoop! Halloo!'

Then, with a rapidity of transition very foreign to his

usual character, he said, in pity for his former self, 'Poor boy!' and cried again.

'I wish,' Scrooge muttered, putting his hand in his pocket, and looking about him, after drying his eyes with his cuff: 'but it's too late now.'

'What is the matter?' asked the Spirit.

'Nothing,' said Scrooge. 'Nothing. There was a boy singing a Christmas Carol at my door last night. I should like to have given him something: that's all.'

The Ghost smiled thoughtfully, and waved its hand: saying, as it did so, 'Let us see another Christmas!'

Scrooge's former self grew larger at the words, and the room became a little darker and more dirty. The panels shrunk, the windows cracked; fragments of plaster fell out of the ceiling, and the naked laths were shown instead; but how all this was brought about Scrooge knew no more than you do. He only knew that it was quite correct: that everything had happened so; that there he was, alone again, when all the other boys had gone home for the jolly holidays.

He was not reading now, but walking up and down despairingly. Scrooge looked at the Ghost, and, with a mournful shaking of his head, glanced anxiously towards the door.

It opened; and a little girl, much younger than the boy, came darting in, and, putting her arms about his neck, and often kissing him, addressed him as her 'dear, dear brother.'

'I have come to bring you home, dear brother!' said the child, clapping her tiny hands, and bending down to laugh. 'To bring you home, home, home!'

'Home, little Fan?' returned the boy.

'Yes!' said the child, brimful of glee. 'Home for good and all. Home for ever and ever. Father is so much kinder than he used to be, that home's like Heaven! He spoke so gently to me one dear night when I was going to bed, that I was not afraid to ask him once more if you might come home; and he said Yes, you should; and sent me in a coach to bring you. And you're to be a man!' said the child, opening her eyes; 'and are never to come back here; but first we're to be together all the Christmas long, and have the merriest time in all the world.'

'You are quite a woman, little Fan!' exclaimed the boy.

She clapped her hands and laughed, and tried to touch his head; but, being too little, laughed again, and stood on tiptoe to embrace him. Then she began to drag him, in her childish eagerness, towards the door; and he, nothing loath to go, accompanied her.

A terrible voice in the hall cried, 'Bring down Master Scrooge's box, there!' and in the hall appeared the schoolmaster himself, who glared at Master Scrooge with a ferocious condescension, and threw him into a dreadful state of mind by shaking hands with him. He then conveyed him and his sister into the veriest old well of a shivering best parlour that ever was seen, where the maps upon the wall, and the celestial and terrestrial globes in the windows, were waxy with cold. Here he produced a decanter of curiously light wine, and a block of curiously heavy cake, and administered instalments of those dainties to the young people: at the same time sending out a meagre servant to offer a glass of 'something' to the postboy, who answered that he thanked the gentleman, but, if it was the same tap as he had tasted before, he had rather not. Master Scrooge's trunk being by this time tied on to the top of the chaise, the children bade the schoolmaster good-bye right willingly; and, getting into it, drove gaily down the garden sweep; the quick wheels dashing the hoar frost and snow from off the dark leaves of the evergreens like spray.

'Always a delicate creature, whom a breath might have withered,' said the Ghost. 'But she had a large heart!'

'So she had,' cried Scrooge. 'You're right. I will not gainsay it, Spirit. God forbid!'

'She died a woman,' said the Ghost, 'and had, as I think, children.'

'One child,' Scrooge returned.

'True,' said the Ghost. 'Your nephew!'

Scrooge seemed uneasy in his mind; and answered briefly, 'Yes.'

Although they had but that moment left the school behind them, they were now in the busy thoroughfares of the city, where shadowy passengers passed and repassed; where shadowy carts and coaches battled for the way, and all the strife and tumult of a real city were. It was made plain enough, by the dressing of the shops, that here, too, it was Christmas-time again; but it was evening, and the streets were lighted up.

The Ghost stopped at a certain warehouse door, and asked Scrooge if he knew it.

'Know it!' said Scrooge. 'Was I apprenticed here?'

They went in. At sight of an old gentleman in a Welsh wig, sitting behind such a high desk, that if he had been two inches taller, he must have knocked his head against the ceiling, Scrooge cried in great excitement: 'Why, it's old Fezziwig! Bless his heart, it's Fezziwig alive again!'

Old Fezziwig laid down his pen, and looked up at the clock, which pointed to the hour of seven. He rubbed his hands; adjusted his capacious waistcoat; laughed all over himself, from his shoes to his organ of benevolence; and called out, in a comfortable, oily, rich, fat, jovial voice:

'Yo ho, there! Ebenezer! Dick!'

Scrooge's former self, now grown a young man, came briskly in accompanied by his fellow-'prentice.

'Dick Wilkins, to be sure!' said Scrooge to the Ghost. 'Bless me, yes. There he is. He was very much attached to me, was Dick. Poor Dick! Dear, dear!'

'Yo ho, my boys!' said Fezziwig. 'No more work tonight. Christmas-eve, Dick. Christmas, Ebenezer! Let's have the shutters up,' cried old Fezziwig with a sharp clap of his hands, 'before a man can say Jack Robinson!'

You wouldn't believe how those two fellows went at it! They charged into the street with the shutters – one, two, three – had 'em up in their places – four, five, six – barred 'em and pinned 'em – seven, eight, nine – and came back before you could have got to twelve, panting like race-horses.

'Hilli-ho!' cried old Fezziwig, skipping down from the high desk with wonderful agility. 'Clear away, my lads, and let's have lots of room here! Hilli-ho, Dick! Chirrup, Ebenezer!'

Clear away! There was nothing they wouldn't have cleared away, or couldn't have cleared away, with old Fezziwig looking on. It was done in a minute. Every movable was packed off, as if it were dismissed from public life for evermore; the floor was swept and watered, the lamps were trimmed, fuel was heaped upon the fire; and the warehouse was as snug, and warm, and dry, and bright a ball-room as you would desire to see upon a winter's night.

In came a fiddler with a music-book, and went up to the lofty desk, and made an orchestra of it, and tuned like fifty stomachaches. In came Mrs Fezziwig, one vast substantial smile. In came the three Miss Fezziwigs, beaming and lovable. In came the six young followers whose hearts they broke. In came all the young men and women employed in the business. In came the housemaid, with her cousin the baker. In came the cook, with her brother's particular friend the milkman. In came the boy from over the way, who was suspected of not having board enough from his master; trying to hide himself behind the girl from next door but one, who was proved to have had her ears pulled by her mistress. In they all came, one after another; some shyly, some boldly, some gracefully, some awkwardly, some pushing, some pulling; in they all came, any how and every how. Away they all went, twenty couple at once; hands half round and back again the other way; down the middle and up again; round and round in various stages of affectionate grouping; old top couple always turning up in the wrong place; new top couple starting off again as soon as they got there; all top couples at last, and not a bottom one to help them! When this result was brought about, old Fezziwig, clapping his hands to stop the dance, cried out, 'Well done!' and the fiddler plunged his hot face into a pot of porter, especially provided for that purpose. But, scorning rest upon his reappearance, he instantly began again, though there were no dancers yet, as if the other fiddler had been carried home, exhausted, on a shutter, and he were a brand new man resolved to beat him out of sight, or perish.

There were more dances, and there were forfeits, and more dances, and there was cake, and there was negus, and there was a great piece of Cold Roast, and there was a great piece of Cold Boiled, and there were mince-pies, and plenty of beer. But the great effect of the evening came after the Roast and Boiled, when the fiddler (an artful dog, mind! The sort of man who knew his business better than you or I could have told it him!) struck up 'Sir Roger de Coverley.' Then old Fezziwig stood out to dance with Mrs Fezziwig. Top couple, too, with a good stiff piece of work cut out for them; three-or-four-and-twenty pair of partners; people who were not to be trifled with; people who *would* dance, and had no notion of walking.

But if they had been twice as many – ah! four times – old Fezziwig would have been a match for them, and so would Mrs Fezziwig. As to *her*, she was worthy to be his partner in every sense of the term. If that's not high praise, tell me higher, and I'll use it. A positive light appeared to issue from Fezziwig's calves. They shone in every part of the dance like moons. You couldn't have predicted, at any given time, what would become of them next. And when old Fezziwig and Mrs Fezziwig had gone all through the dance; advance and retire, both hands to your partner, bow and curtsy, cork-screw, thread-the-needle, and back again to your place; Fezziwig 'cut' – cut so deftly, that he appeared to wink with his legs, and came upon his feet again without a stagger.

When the clock struck eleven, this domestic ball broke up. Mr and Mrs Fezziwig took their stations, one on either side the door, and, shaking hands with every person individually as he or she went out, wished him or her a Merry Christmas. When everybody had retired but the two 'prentices, they did the same to them; and thus the cheerful voices died away, and the lads were left to their beds; which were under a counter in the back-shop.

During the whole of this time Scrooge had acted like a man out of his wits. His heart and soul were in the scene, and with his former self. He corroborated everything, remembered everything, enjoyed everything, and underwent the strangest agitation. It was not until now, when the bright faces of his former self and Dick were turned from them, that he remembered the Ghost, and became conscious that it was looking full upon him, while the light upon its head burnt very clear.

'A small matter,' said the Ghost, 'to make these silly folks so full of gratitude.'

'Small!' echoed Schrooge.

The Spirit signed to him to listen to the two apprentices, who were pouring out their hearts in praise of Fezziwig; and when he had done so, said: 'Why! Is it not? He has spent but a few pounds of your mortal money: three or four, perhaps. Is that so much that he deserves this praise?'

'It isn't that,' said Scrooge, heated by the remark, and speaking unconsciously like his former, not his latter self. 'It isn't that, Spirit. He has the power to render us happy or unhappy; to make our service light or burdensome; a pleasure or a toil. Say that his power lies in words and looks; in things so slight and insignificant that it is impossible to add and count 'em up: what then? The happiness he gives is quite as great as a fortune.'

He felt the Spirit's glance, and stopped.

'What is the matter?' asked the Ghost.

'Nothing particular,' said Scrooge.

'Something, I think?' the Ghost insisted.

'No,' said Scrooge, 'no. I should like to be able to say a word or two to my clerk just now. That's all.

His former self turned down the lamps as he gave utterance to the wish; and Scrooge and the Ghost again stood side by side in the open air.

'My time grows short,' observed the Spirit. 'Quick!'

This was not addressed to Scrooge, or to anyone whom he could see, but it produced an immediate effect. For again Scrooge saw himself. He was older now; a man in the prime of life. His face had not the harsh and rigid lines of later years; but it had begun to wear the signs of care and avarice. There was an eager, greedy, restless motion in the eye, which showed the passion that had taken root, and where the shadow of the growing tree would fall.

He was not alone, but sat by the side of a fair young girl in a mourning dress: in whose eyes there were tears, which sparkled in the light that shone out of the Ghost of Christmas Past.

'It matters little,' she said softly. 'To you, very little. Another idol has displaced me; and, if it can cheer and comfort you in time to come as I would have tried to do, I have no just cause to grieve.'

'What Idol has displaced you?' he rejoined.

'A golden one.'

'This is the even-handed dealing of the world!' he said. 'There is nothing on which it is so hard as poverty; and there is nothing it professes to condemn with such severity as the pursuit of wealth!'

'You fear the world too much,' she answered gently. 'All your other hopes have merged into the hope of being beyond the chance of its sordid reproach. I have seen your nobler aspirations fall off one by one, until the master passion, Gain, engrosses you. Have I not?'

'What then?' he retorted. 'Even if I have grown so much wiser, what then? I am not changed towards you.'

She shook her head.

'Am I?'

'Our contract is an old one. It was made when we were both poor, and content to be so, until, in good season, we could improve our worldly fortune by our patient industry. You *are* changed. When it was made you were another man.'

'I was a boy,' he said impatiently.

'Your own feeling tells you that you were not what you are,' she returned. 'I am. That which promised happiness when we were one in heart is fraught with misery now that we are two. How often and how keenly I have thought of this I will not say. It is enough that I *have* thought of it, and can release you.'

'Have I ever sought release?'

'In words. No. Never.'

'In what, then?'

'In a changed nature; in an altered spirit; in another

atmosphere of life; another Hope as its great end. In everything that made my love of any worth or value in your sight. If this had never been between us,' said the girl, looking mildly, but with steadiness, upon him; 'tell me, would you seek me out and try to win me now? Ah, no!'

He seemed to yield to the justice of this supposition in spite of himself. But he said, with a struggle, 'You think not.'

'I would gladly think otherwise if I could,' she answered. 'Heaven knows! When *I* have learned a Truth like this, I know how strong and irresistible it must be. But if you were free today, tomorrow, yesterday, can even I believe that you would choose a dowerless girl—you who, in your very confidence with her, weigh everything by Gain: or, choosing her, if for a moment you were false enough to your one guiding principle to do so, do I not know that your repentance and regret would surely follow? I do; and I release you. With a full heart, for the love of him you once were.'

He was about to speak; but, with her head turned from him, she resumed.

'You may – the memory of what is past half makes me hope you will – have pain in this. A very, very brief time, and you will dismiss the recollection of it gladly, as an unprofitable dream from which it happened well that you awoke. May you be happy in the life you have chosen!'

She left him, and they parted.

'Spirit!' said Scrooge, 'show me no more! Conduct me home. Why do you delight to torture me?'

'One shadow more!' exclaimed the Ghost.

'No more!' cried Scrooge. 'No more! I don't wish to see it. Show me no more!'

But the relentless Ghost pinioned him in both his arms, and forced him to observe what happened next.

They were in another scene and place; a room, not very large or handsome, but full of comfort. Near to the winter fire sat a beautiful young girl, so like the last that Scrooge believed it was the same, until he saw *her*, now a comely matron, sitting opposite her daughter. The noise in this room was perfectly tumultuous, for there were more children there than Scrooge in his agitated state of mind could count; and, unlike the celebrated herd in the poem, they were not forty children conducting themselves like one, but every child was conducting itself like forty. The consequences were uproarious beyond belief; but no one seemed to care; on the contrary, the mother and daughter laughed heartily, and enjoyed it very much; and the latter, soon beginning to mingle in the sports got pillaged by the young brigands most ruthlessly. What would I not have given to be one of them! Though I never could have been so rude, no, no! I wouldn't for the wealth of all the world have crushed that braided hair and torn it down; and, for the precious little shoe, I wouldn't have plucked it off, God bless my soul! to save my life. As to measuring her waist in sport, as they did, bold young brood, I couldn't have done it; I should have expected my arm to have grown round it for a punishment, and never come straight again. And yet I should have dearly liked, I own, to have touched her lips; to have questioned her, that she might have opened them; to have looked upon the lashes of her downcast eyes, and never raised a blush; to have let loose waves of hair, an inch of which would be a keepsake beyond price: in short, I should have liked, I do confess, to have had the lightest licence of a child, and yet to have been man enough to know its value.

But now a knocking at the door was heard, and such a rush immediately ensued that she, with laughing face and plundered dress, was borne towards it in the centre of a flushed and boisterous group, just in time to greet the father, who came home attended by a man laden with Christmas toys and presents. Then the shouting and the struggling, and the onslaught that was made on the defenceless porter! The scaling him, with chairs for ladders, to dive into his pockets, despoil him of brown-paper parcels, hold on tight by his cravat, hug him round the neck, pummel his back, and kick his legs in irrepressible affection! The shouts of wonder and delight with which the development of every package was received! The terrible announcement that the baby had been taken in the act of putting a doll's frying-pan into his mouth, and was more than suspected of having swallowed a fictitious turkey, glued on a wooden platter! The immense relief of finding this a false alarm! The joy, and gratitude, and ecstasy! They are all indescribable alike. It is enough that, by degrees, the children and their emotions got out of the parlour, and, by one stair at a time, up to the top of the house, where they went to bed, and so subsided.

And now Scrooge looked on more attentively than ever, when the master of the house, having his daughter leaning fondly on him, sat down with her and her mother at his own fireside; and when he thought that such another creature, quite as graceful and as full of promise, might have called him father, and been a spring-time in the haggard winter of his life, his sight grew very dim indeed.

'Belle,' said the husband, turning to his wife with a smile, 'I saw an old friend of yours this afternoon.'

'Who was it?'

'Guess!'

'How can I? Tut, don't I know?' she added in the same breath, laughing as he laughed. 'Mr Scrooge.'

'Mr Scrooge it was. I passed his office window; and as it was not shut up, and he had a candle inside, I could scarcely help seeing him. His partner lies upon the point of death, I hear; and there he sat alone. Quite alone in the world, I do believe.'

'Spirit!' said Scrooge in a broken voice, 'remove me from this place.'

'I told you these were shadows of the things that have been,' said the Ghost. 'That they are what they are, do not blame me!'

'Remove me!' Scrooge exclaimed. 'I cannot bear it!'

He turned upon the Ghost, and seeing that it looked upon him with a face in which in some strange way there were fragments of all the faces it had shown him, wrestled with it.

'Leave me! Take me back! Haunt me no longer!'

In the struggle – if that can be called a struggle in which the Ghost, with no visible resistance on its own part, was undisturbed by any effort of its adversary – Scrooge observed that its light was burning high and bright; and dimly connecting that with its influence over him, he seized the extinguisher cap, and by a sudden action pressed it down upon its head.

The Spirit dropped beneath it, so that the extinguisher covered the whole form; but, though Scrooge pressed it down with all his force, he could not hide the light, which streamed from under it in an unbroken flood upon the ground.

He was conscious of being exhausted, and overcome by an irresistible drowsiness; and, further of being in his own bedroom. He gave the cap a parting squeeze, in which his hand relaxed; and had barely time to reel to bed before he sank into a heavy sleep.

THE SECOND OF THE THREE SPIRITS

Awaking in the middle of a prodigiously tough snore, and sitting up in bed to get his thoughts together, Scrooge had no occasion to be told that the bell was again upon the stroke of One. He felt that he was restored to consciousness in the right nick of time, for the especial purpose of holding a conference with the second messenger dispatched to him through Jacob Marley's intervention. But, finding that he turned uncomfortably cold when he began to wonder which of his curtains this new spectre would draw back, he put them every one aside with his own hands, and, lying down again, established a sharp look-out all round the bed. For he wished to challenge the Spirit on the moment of its appearance, and did not wish to be taken by surprise and made nervous.

Gentlemen of the free-and-easy sort, who plume themselves on being acquainted with a move or two, and being usually equal to the time of day, express the wide range of their capacity for adventure by observing that they are good for anything from pitch-and-toss to manslaughter; between which opposite extremes, no doubt, there lies a tolerably wide and comprehensive range of subjects. Without venturing for Scrooge quite as hardily as this, I don't mind calling on you to believe that he was ready for a good broad field of strange appearances, and that nothing between a baby and a rhinoceros would have astonished him very much.

Now, being prepared for almost anything, he was not by any means prepared for nothing; and consequently, when the bell struck One, and no shape appeared, he was taken with a violent fit of trembling. Five minutes, ten minutes, a quarter of an hour went by, yet nothing came. All this time he lay upon his bed, the very core and centre of a blaze of ruddy light, which streamed upon it when the clock proclaimed the hour; and which, being only light, was more alarming than a dozen ghosts, as he was powerless to make out what it meant, or would be at; and was sometimes apprehensive that he might be at that very moment an interesting case of spontaneous combustion, without having the consolation of knowing it. At last, however, he began to think – as you or I would have thought at first; for it is always the person not in the predicament who knows what ought to have been done in it, and would unquestionably have done it too – at last, I say, he began to think that the source and secret of this ghostly light might be in the adjoining room, from whence, on further tracing it, it seemed to shine. This idea taking full possession of his mind, he got up softly, and shuffled in his slippers to the door.

The moment Scrooge's hand was on the lock, a strange voice called him by his name, and bade him enter. He obeyed.

It was his own room. There was no doubt about that. But it had undergone a surprising transformation. The walls and ceiling were so hung with living green, that it looked a perfect grove; from every part of which bright gleaming berries glistened. The crisp leaves of holly, mistletoe, and ivy reflected back the light, as if so many little mirrors had been scattered there; and such a mighty blaze went roaring up the chimney as that dull petrifaction of a hearth had never known in Scrooge's time, or Marley's, or for many and many a winter season gone. Heaped upon the floor, to form a kind of throne, were turkeys, geese, game, poultry, brawn, great joints of meat, sucking-pigs, long wreaths of sausages, mince-pies, plum-puddings, barrels of oysters, red-hot chestnuts, cherry-cheeked apples, juicy oranges, luscious pears, immense twelfth-cakes, and seething bowls of punch, that made the chamber dim with their delicious steam. In easy state upon this couch there sat a jolly Giant, glorious to see; who bore a glowing torch, in the shape not unlike Plenty's horn, and held it up, high up, to shed its light on Scrooge as he came peeping round the door.

'Come in!' exclaimed the Ghost. 'Come in! and know me better, man!'

Scrooge entered timidly, and hung his head before this Spirit. He was not the dogged Scrooge he had been; and, though the Spirit's eyes were clear and kind, he did not like to meet them.

'I am the Ghost of Christmas Present,' said the Spirit. 'Look upon me!'

Scrooge reverently did so. It was clothed in one simple deep green robe, or mantle, bordered with white fur. This garment hung so loosely on the figure, that its capacious breast was bare, as if disdaining to be warded or concealed by any artifice. Its feet, observable beneath the ample folds of the garment, were also bare; and on its head it wore no other covering than a holly wreath, set here and there with shining icicles. Its dark brown curls were long and free; free as its genial face, its sparkling eye, its open hand, its cheery voice, its unconstrained demeanour, and its joyful air. Girded round its middle was an antique scabbard; but no sword was in it, and the ancient sheath was eaten up with rust.

'You have never seen the like of me before!' exclaimed the Spirit.

'Never,' Scrooge made answer to it.

'Have never walked forth with the younger members of my family; meaning (for I am very young) my elder brothers born in these later years?' pursued the Phantom.

'I don't think I have,' said Scrooge. 'I am afraid I have not. Have you had many brothers, Spirit?'

'More than eighteen hundred,' said the Ghost.

'A tremendous family to provide for,' muttered Scrooge.

The Ghost of Christmas Present rose.

'Spirit,' said Scrooge submissively, 'conduct me where you will. I went forth last night on compulsion, and I learnt a lesson which is working now. Tonight, if you have aught to teach me, let me profit by it.'

'Touch my robe!'

Scrooge did as he was told, and held it fast.

Holly, mistletoe, red berries, ivy, turkeys, geese, game, poultry, brawn, meat, pigs, sausages, oysters, pies, puddings, fruit, and punch, all vanished instantly. So did the room, the fire, the ruddy glow, the hour of night, and they stood in the city streets on Christmas morning, where (for the weather was severe) the people made a rough, but brisk and not unpleasant kind of music, in scraping the snow from the pavement in front of their dwellings, and from the tops of their houses, whence it was mad delight to the boys to see it come plumping down into the road below, and splitting into artificial little snow-storms.

The house-fronts looked black enough, and the windows blacker, contrasting with the smooth white sheet of snow upon the roofs, and with the dirtier snow upon the ground; which last deposit had been ploughed up in deep furrows by the heavy wheels of carts and waggons; furrows that crossed and recrossed each other hundreds of times where the great streets branched off; and made intricate channels, hard to trace, in the thick yellow mud and icy water. The sky was gloomy, and the shortest streets were choked up with a dingy mist, half thawed, half frozen, whose heavier particles descended in a shower of sooty atoms, as if all the chimneys in Great Britain had, by one consent, caught fire, and were blazing away to their dear heart's content. There was nothing very cheerful in the climate or the town, and yet was there an air of cheerfulness abroad that the clearest summer air and brightest summer sun might have endeavoured to diffuse in vain.

For, the people who were shovelling away on the housetops were jovial and full of glee; calling out to one another from the parapets, and now and then exchanging a facetious snow-ball – better-natured missile far than many a wordy jest – laughing heartily if it went right, and not less heartily if it went wrong. The poulterers' shops were still half open, and the fruiterers' were radiant in their glory. There were great, round, pot-bellied baskets of chestnuts, shaped like the waistcoats of jolly old gentlemen, lolling at the doors and tumbling out into the street in their apoplectic opulence. There were ruddy, brown-faced, broad-girthed Spanish onions, shining in the fatness of their growth like Spanish Friars, and winking from their shelves in wanton slyness at the girls as they went by, and glanced demurely at the hung-up mistletoe. There were pears and apples clustered high in blooming pyramids; there were bunches of grapes, made, in the shopkeepers' benevolence, to dangle from conspicuous hooks that people's mouths might water gratis as they passed; there were piles of filberts, mossy and brown, recalling, in their fragrance, ancient walks among the woods, and pleasant shufflings ankle deep through withered leaves; there were Norfolk Biffins, squab and swarthy, setting off the yellow of the oranges and lemons, and, in the great compactness of their juicy persons, urgently entreating and beseeching to be carried home in paper bags, and eaten after dinner. The very gold and silver fish, set forth among these choice fruits in a bowl, though members of a dull and stagnant-blooded race, appeared to know that there was something going on; and, to a fish, went gasping round and round their little world in slow and passionless excitement.

The Grocer's! oh, the Grocers'! nearly closed, with perhaps two shutters down, or one; but through those gaps such glimpses! It was not alone that the scales descending on the counter made a merry sound, or that the twine and roller parted company so briskly, or that the canisters were rattled up and down like juggling tricks, or even that the blended scents of tea and coffee were so grateful to the nose, or even that the raisins were so plentiful and rare, the almonds so extremely white, the sticks of cinnamon so long and straight, the other spices so delicious, the candied fruits so caked and spotted with molten sugar as to make the coldest lookers-on feel faint, and subsequently bilious. Nor was it that the figs were moist and pulpy, or that the French plums blushed in modest tartness from their highly-decorated boxes, or that everything was good to eat and in its Christmas dress; but the customers were all so hurried and so eager in the hopeful promise of the day, that they tumbled up against each other at the door, crashing their wicker baskets wildly, and left their purchases upon the counter and came running back to fetch them, and committed hundreds of the like mistakes, in the best humour possible; while the Grocer and his people were so frank and fresh, that the polished hearts with which they fastened their aprons behind might have been their own, worn outside for general inspection, and for Christmas daws to peck at if they chose.

But soon the steeples called good people all to church and chapel, and away they came, flocking through the streets in their best clothes, and with their gayest faces. And at the same time there emerged, from scores of by-streets, lanes, and nameless turnings, innumerable people, carrying their dinners to the bakers' shops. The sight of these poor revellers appeared to interest the Spirit very much, for he stood with Scrooge beside him in a baker's doorway, and, taking off the covers as their bearers passed, sprinkled incense on their dinners from his torch. And it was a very uncommon kind of torch, for once or twice, when there were angry words between some dinner-carriers who had jostled each other, he shed a few drops of water on them from it, and their good-humour was restored directly. For they said, it was a shame to quarrel upon Christmas-day. And so it was! God love it, so it was!

In time the bells ceased, and the bakers were shut up; and yet there was a genial shadowing forth of all these dinners, and the progress of their cooking, in the thawed blotch of wet above each baker's oven; where the pavement smoked as if its stones were cooking too.

'Is there a peculiar flavour in what you sprinkle from your torch?' asked Scrooge.

'There is. My own.'

'Would it apply to any kind of dinner on this day?' asked Scrooge.

'To any kindly given. To a poor one most.'

'Why to a poor one most?' asked Scrooge.

'Because it needs it most.'

'Spirit!' said Scrooge after a moment's thought. 'I wonder you, of all the beings in the many worlds about us, should desire to cramp these people's opportunities of innocent enjoyment.'

'I!' cried the Spirit.

'You would deprive them of their means of dining every seventh day, often the only day on which they can be said to dine at all,' said Scrooge; 'wouldn't you?'

'I!' cried the Spirit.'

'You seek to close these places on the Seventh Day,' said Scrooge. 'And it comes to the same thing.'

'*I* seek!' exclaimed the Spirit.

'Forgive me if I am wrong. It has been done in your name, or at least in that of your family,' said Scrooge.

'There are some upon this earth of yours,' returned the Spirit, 'who lay claim to know us, and who do their deeds of passion, pride, ill-will, hatred, envy, bigotry, and selfishness in our name, who are as strange to us, and all our kith and kin, as if they had never lived. Remember that, and charge their doings on themselves, not us.'

Scrooge promised that he would; and they went on, invisible, as they had been before, into the suburbs of the town. It was a remarkable quality of the Ghost (which Scrooge had observed at the baker's), that, notwithstanding his gigantic size, he could accommodate himself to any place with ease; and that he stood beneath a low roof quite as gracefully and like a supernatural creature as it was possible he could have done in any lofty hall.

And perhaps it was the pleasure the good Spirit had in showing off this power of his, or else it was his own kind, generous, hearty nature, and his sympathy with all poor men, that led him straight to Scrooge's clerk's; for there he went, and took Scrooge with him, holding to his robe; and, on the threshold of the door, the Spirit smiled, and stopped to bless Bob Cratchit's dwelling with the sprinklings of his torch. Think of that! Bob had but fifteen 'Bob' a week himself; he pocketed on Saturdays but fifteen copies of his Christian name; and yet the Ghost of Christmas Present blessed his four-roomed house!

Then up rose Mrs Cratchit, Cratchit's wife, dressed out but poorly in a twice-turned gown, but brave in ribbons, which are cheap, and make a goodly show for sixpence; and she laid the cloth, assisted by Belinda Cratchit, second of her daughters, also brave in ribbons; while Master Peter Cratchit plunged a fork into the saucepan of potatoes, and, getting the corners of his monstrous shirt collar (Bob's private property, conferred upon his son and heir in honour of the day) into his mouth, rejoiced to find himself so gallantly attired, and yearned to show his linen in the fashionable Parks. And now two smaller Cratchits, boy and girl, came tearing in, screaming that outside the baker's they had smelt the goose, and known it for their own; and basking in luxurious thoughts of sage and onion, these young Cratchits danced about the table, and exalted Master Peter Cratchit to the skies, while he (not proud, although his collars nearly choked him) blew the fire until the slow potatoes bubbling up, knocked loudly at the saucepan lid to be let out and peeled.

'What has ever got your precious father, then?' said Mrs Cratchit. 'And your brother, Tiny Tim? And Martha warn't as late last Christmas-day by half an hour!'

'Here's Martha, mother!' said a girl, appearing as she spoke.

'Here's Martha, mother!' cried the two young Cratchits. 'Hurrah! There's *such* a goose, Martha!'

'Why, bless your heart alive, my dear, how late you are!' said Mrs Cratchit, kissing her a dozen times, and taking off her shawl and bonnet for her with officious zeal.

'We'd a deal of work to finish up last night,' replied the girl, 'and had to clear away this morning, mother!'

'Well! never mind so long as you are come,' said Mrs Cratchit. 'Sit ye down before the fire, my dear, and have a warm, Lord bless ye!'

'No, no! There's father coming,' cried the two young Cratchits, who were everywhere at once. 'Hide, Martha, hide!'

So Martha hid herself, and in came little Bob, the father, with at least three feet of comforter, exclusive of the fringe, hanging down before him; and his threadbare clothes darned up and brushed to look seasonable; and Tiny Tim upon his shoulder. Alas for Tiny Tim, he bore a little crutch, and had his limbs supported by an iron frame!

'Why, where's our Martha?' cried Bob Cratchit, looking round.

'Not coming,' said Mrs Cratchit.

'Not coming!' said Bob with a sudden declension in his high spirits; for he had been Tim's blood horse all the way from church, and had come home rampant. 'Not coming upon Christmas-day!'

Martha didn't like to see him disappointed, if it were only in joke; so she came out prematurely from behind the closet door, and ran into his arms, while the two young Cratchits hustled Tiny Tim, and bore him off into the wash-house, that he might hear the pudding singing in the copper.

'And how did little Tim behave?' asked Mrs Cratchit when she had rallied Bob on his credulity, and Bob had hugged his daughter to his heart's content.

'As good as gold,' said Bob, 'and better. Somehow, he gets thoughtful, sitting by himself so much, and thinks the strangest things you ever heard. He told me, coming home, that he hoped the people saw him in the church, because he was a cripple, and it might be pleasant to them to remember upon Christmas-day who made lame beggars walk and blind men see.'

Bob's voice was tremulous when he told them this, and trembled more when he said that Tiny Tim was growing strong and hearty.

His active little crutch was heard upon the floor, and back came Tiny Tim before another word was spoken, escorted by his brother and sister to his stool beside the fire; and while Bob, turning up his cuffs – as if, poor fellow, they were capable of being made more shabby – compounded some hot mixture in a jug with gin and lemons, and stirred it round and round, and put it on the hob to simmer, Master Peter and the two ubiquitous young Cratchits went to fetch the goose, with which they soon returned in high procession.

Such a bustle ensued that you might have thought a goose the rarest of all birds; a feathered phenomenon, to which a black swan was a matter of course – and, in truth, it was something very like it in that house. Mrs Cratchit made the gravy (ready beforehand in a little saucepan) hissing hot: Master Peter mashed the potatoes with incredible vigour; Miss Belinda sweetened up the apple sauce; Martha dusted the hot plates; Bob took Tiny Tim beside him in a tiny corner at the table; the two young Cratchits set chairs for everybody, not forgetting themselves, and, mounting guard upon their posts, crammed spoons into their mouths, lest they should shriek for goose before their turn came to be helped. At last the dishes were set on, and grace was said. It was succeeded by a breathless pause, as Mrs Cratchit, looking slowly all along the carving-knife, prepared to plunge it in the breast; but when she did, and when the long-expected gush of stuffing issued forth, one murmur of delight arose all round the board, and even Tiny Tim, excited by the two young Cratchits, beat on the table with the handle of his knife, and feebly cried Hurrah!

There never was such a goose. Bob said he didn't believe there ever was such a goose cooked. Its tenderness and flavour, size and cheapness, were the themes of universal admiration. Eked out by apple sauce and mashed potatoes, it was a sufficient dinner for the whole family; indeed, as Mrs Cratchit said with great delight (surveying one small atom of a bone upon the dish), they hadn't ate it all at last! Yet every one had had enough, and the youngest Cratchits, in particular, were steeped in sage and onion to the eyebrows! But now, the plates being changed by Miss Belinda,

Mrs Cratchit left the room alone – too nervous to bear witnesses – to take the pudding up, and bring it in.

Suppose it should not be done enough! Suppose it should break in turning out! Suppose somebody should have got over the wall of the back-yard and stolen it, while they were merry with the goose – a supposition at which the two young Cratchits became livid! All sorts of horrors were supposed.

Hallo! A great deal of steam! The pudding was out of the copper. A smell like a washing-day! That was the cloth. A smell like an eating-house and a pastrycook's next door to each other, with a laundress's next door to that! That was the pudding! In half a minute Mrs Cratchit entered – flushed, but smiling proudly – with the pudding, like a speckled cannon-ball, so hard and firm, blazing in half of half-a-quartern of ignited brandy, and bedight with Christmas holly stuck into the top.

Oh, a wonderful pudding! Bob Cratchit said, and calmly too, that he regarded it as the greatest success achieved by Mrs Cratchit since their marriage. Mrs Cratchit said that, now the weight was off her mind, she would confess she had her doubts about the quantity of flour. Everybody had something to say about it, but nobody said or thought it was at all a small pudding for a large family. It would have been flat heresy to do so. Any Cratchit would have blushed to hint at such a thing.

At last the dinner was all done, the cloth was cleared, the hearth swept, and the fire made up. The compound in the jug being tasted, and considered perfect, apples and oranges were put upon the table, and a shovel full of chestnuts on the fire. Then all the Cratchit family drew round the hearth in what Bob Cratchit called a circle, meaning half a one; and at Bob Cratchit's elbow stood the family display of glass. Two tumblers and a custard cup without a handle.

These held the hot stuff from the jug, however, as well as golden goblets would have done, and Bob served it out with beaming looks, while the chestnuts on the fire sputtered and cracked noisily. Then Bob proposed:

'A merry Christmas to us all, my dears. God bless us!'

Which all the family re-echoed.

'God bless us every one!' said Tiny Tim, the last of all.

He sat very close to his father's side, upon his little stool. Bob held his withered little hand in his, as if he loved the child, and wished to keep him by his side, and dreaded that he might be taken from him.

'Spirit,' said Scrooge with an interest he had never felt before, 'tell me if Tiny Tim will live.'

'I see a vacant seat,' replied the Ghost, 'in the poor chimney-corner, and a crutch without an owner, carefully preserved. If these shadows remain unaltered by the Future, the child will die.'

'No, no,' said Scrooge. 'Oh no, kind Spirit! say he will be spared.'

'If these shadows remain unaltered by the Future, none other of my race,' returned the Ghost, 'will find him here. What then? If he be like to die, he had better do it, and decrease the surplus population.'

Scrooge hung his head to hear his own words quoted by the Spirit, and was overcome with penitence and grief.

'Man,' said the Ghost, 'if man you be in heart, not adamant, forbear that wicked cant until you have discovered What the surplus is, and Where it is. Will you decide what men shall live, what men shall die? It may be that, in the sight of Heaven, you are more worthless and less fit to live than millions like this poor man's child. Oh God! to hear the Insect on the leaf pronouncing on the too much life among his hungry brothers in the dust!'

Scrooge bent before the Ghost's rebuke, and, trembling, cast his eyes upon the ground. But he raised them speedily on hearing his own name.

'Mr Scrooge!' said Bob. 'I'll give you Mr Scrooge, the Founder of the Feast!'

'The Founder of the Feast, indeed!' cried Mrs Cratchit, reddening. 'I wish I had him here. I'd give him a piece of my mind to feast upon, and I hope he'd have a good appetite for it.'

'My dear,' said Bob, 'the children! Christmas-day.'

'It should be Christmas-day, I am sure,' said she, 'on which one drinks the health of such an odious, stingy, hard, unfeeling man as Mr Scrooge. You know he is, Robert! Nobody knows it better than you do, poor fellow!'

'My dear!' was Bob's mild answer. 'Christmas-day.'

'I'll drink his health for your sake and the Day's,' said Mrs Cratchit, 'not for his. Long life to him! A merry Christmas and a happy New Year! He'll be very merry and very happy, I have no doubt!'

The children drank the toast after her. It was the first of their proceedings which had no heartiness in it. Tiny Tim drank it last of all, but he didn't care twopence for it. Scrooge was the Ogre of the family. The mention of his name cast a dark shadow on the party, which was not dispelled for full five minutes.

After it had passed away they were ten times merrier than before, from the mere relief of Scrooge the Baleful being done with. Bob Cratchit told them how he had a situation in his eye for Master Peter, which would bring in, if obtained, full five-and-sixpence weekly. The two young Cratchits laughed tremendously at the idea of Peter's being a man of business; and Peter himself looked thoughtfully at the fire from between his collars, as if he were deliberating what particular investments he should favour when he came into the receipt of that bewildering income. Martha, who was a poor apprentice at a milliner's, then told them what kind of work she had to do, and how many hours she worked at a stretch, and how she meant to lie abed tomorrow morning for a good long rest; tomorrow being a holiday she passed at home. Also how she had seen a countess and a lord some days before, and how the lord 'was much about as tall as Peter;' at which Peter pulled up his collars so high, that you couldn't have seen his head if you had been there. All this time the chestnuts and the jug went round and round; and by-and-by they had a song, about a lost child travelling in the snow, from Tiny Tim, who had a plaintive little voice, and sang it very well indeed.

There was nothing of high mark in this. They were not a handsome family; they were not well dressed; their shoes were far from being waterproof; their clothes were scanty; and Peter might have known, and very likely did, the inside of a pawnbroker's. But they were happy, grateful, pleased with one another, and contented with the time; and when they faded, and looked happier yet in the bright sprinklings of the Spirit's torch at parting, Scrooge had his eye upon them, and especially on Tiny Tim, until the last.

By this time it was getting dark, and snowing pretty heavily; and, as Scrooge and the Spirit went along the streets, the brightness of the roaring fires in the kitchens, parlours, and all sorts of rooms were wonderful. Here, the flickering of the blaze showed preparations for a cosy dinner, with hot plates baking through and through before the fire, and deep red curtains, ready to be drawn to shut out cold and darkness. There, all the children of the house were running out into the snow to meet their married sisters, brothers, cousins, uncles, aunts, and be the first to greet them. Here, again, were shadows on the window blinds of guests assembling; and there a group of handsome girls, all hooded and fur-booted, and all chattering at once, tripped lightly off to some near neighbour's house; where, woe upon the single man who saw them enter – artful witches, well they knew it – in a glow!

But, if you had judged from the numbers of people on their way to friendly gatherings, you might have thought that no one was at home to give them welcome when they got there, instead of every house expecting company, and piling up its fires half-chimney high. Blessings on it, how the Ghost exulted! How it bared its breadth of breast, and opened its capacious palm, and floated on, outpouring, with a generous hand, its bright and harmless mirth on everything within its reach! The very lamp-lighter, who ran on before, dotting the dusky streets with specks of light, and who was dressed to spend the evening somewhere, laughed out loudly as the Spirit passed, though little kenned the lamp-lighter that he had any company but Christmas.

And now, without a word of warning from the Ghost, they stood upon a bleak and desert moor, where monstrous masses of rude stone were cast about, as though it were the burial-place of giants; and water spread itself wheresoever it listed; or would have done so, but for the frost that held it prisoner; and nothing grew but moss and furze, and coarse, rank grass. Down in the west the setting sun had left a streak of fiery red, which glared upon the desolation for an instant, like a sullen eye, and, frowning lower, lower, lower yet, was lost in the thick gloom of darkest night.

'What place is this?' asked Scrooge.

'A place where miners live, who labour in the bowels of the earth,' returned the Spirit. 'But they know me. See!'

A light shone from the window of a hut, and swiftly they advanced towards it. Passing through the wall of mud and stone, they found a cheerful company assembled round a glowing fire. An old, old man and woman, with their children and their children's children, and another generation beyond that, all decked out gaily in their holiday attire. The old man, in a voice that seldom rose above the howling of the wind upon the barren waste, was singing them a Christmas song; it had been a very old song when he was a boy; and from time to time they all joined in the chorus. So surely as they raised their voices, the old man got quite blithe and loud; and, so surely as they stopped, his vigour sank again.

The Spirit did not tarry here, but bade Scrooge hold his robe, and, passing on above the moor, sped whither? Not to sea? To sea. To Scrooge's horror, looking back, he saw the last of the land, a frightful range of rocks, behind them; and his ears were deafened by the thundering of water, as it rolled and roared, and raged among the dreadful caverns it had worn, and fiercely tried to undermine the earth.

Built upon a dismal reef of sunken rocks, some league or so from shore, on which the waters chafed and dashed, the wild year through, there stood a solitary lighthouse. Great heaps of seaweed clung to its base, and storm-birds – born of the wind, one might suppose, as seaweed of the water – rose and fell about it, like the waves they skimmed.

But, even here, two men who watched the light, had made a fire, that through the loop-hole in the thick stone wall shed out a ray of brightness on the awful sea. Joining their horny hands over the rough table at which they sat, they wished each other Merry Christmas in their can of grog; and one of them: the elder too, with his face all damaged and scarred with hard weather, as the figure-head of an old ship might be: struck up a sturdy song that was like a gale in itself.

Again the Ghost sped on, above the black and heaving sea – on, on – until, being far away, as he told Scrooge, from any shore, they lighted on a ship. They stood beside the helmsman at the wheel, the look-out in the bow, the officers who had the watch; dark, ghostly figures in their several stations; but every man among them hummed a Christmas tune, or had a Christmas thought, or spoke below his breath to his companion of some bygone Christmas-day, with homeward hopes belonging to it. And every man on board, waking or sleeping, good or bad, had had a kinder word for one another on that day than on any day in the year; and had shared to some extent in its festivities; and had remembered those he cared for at a distance, and had known that they delighted to remember him.

It was a great surprise to Scrooge, while listening to the moaning of the wind, and thinking what a solemn thing it was to move on through the lonely darkness over an unknown abyss, whose depths were secrets as profound as death: it was a great surprise to Scrooge, while thus engaged, to hear a hearty laugh. It was a much greater surprise to Scrooge to recognise it as his own nephew's, and to find himself in a bright, dry, gleaming room, with the Spirit standing smiling by his side, and looking at that same nephew with approving affability!

'Ha, ha!' laughed Scrooge's nephew. 'Ha, ha, ha!'

If you should happen, by any unlikely chance, to know a man more blessed in a laugh than Scrooge's nephew, all I can say is, I should like to know him too. Introduce him to me, and I'll cultivate his acquaintance.

It is a fair, even-handed, noble adjustment of things, that, while there is infection in disease and sorrow, there is nothing in the world so irresistibly contagious as laughter and good-humour. When Scrooge's nephew laughed in this way: holding his sides, rolling his head, and twisting his face into the most extravagant contortions: Scrooge's niece, by marriage, laughed as heartily as he. And their assembled friends, being not a bit behindhand, roared out lustily.

'Ha, ha! Ha, ha, ha, ha!'

'He said that Christmas was a humbug, as I live!' cried Scrooge's nephew. 'He believed it, too!'

'More shame for him, Fred!' said Scrooge's niece indignantly. Bless those women! they never do anything by halves. They are always in earnest.

She was very pretty; exceedingly pretty. With a dimpled, surprised-looking, capital face; a ripe little mouth, that seemed made to be kissed – as no doubt it was; all kinds of good little dots about her chin, that melted into one another when she laughed; and the sunniest pair of eyes you ever saw in any little creature's head. Altogether she was what you would have called provoking, you know; but satisfactory, too. Oh, perfectly satisfactory!

'He's a comical old fellow,' said Scrooge's nephew, 'that's the truth; and not so pleasant as he might be. However, his offences carry their own punishment, and I have nothing to say against him.'

'I'm sure he is very rich, Fred,' hinted Scrooge's niece. 'At least, you always tell *me* so.'

'What of that, my dear?' said Scrooge's nephew. 'His wealth is of no use to him. He don't do any good with it. He don't make himself comfortable with it. He hasn't the satisfaction of thinking – ha, ha, ha! – that he is ever going to benefit Us with it.'

'I have no patience with him, observed Scrooge's niece. Scrooge's niece's sisters, and all the other ladies, expressed the same opinion.

'Oh I have!' said Scrooge's nephew. 'I am sorry for him; I couldn't be angry with him if I tried. Who suffers by his ill whims? Himself always. Here he takes it into his head to dislike us, and he won't come and dine with us. What's the consequence? He don't lose much of a dinner.'

'Indeed, I think he loses a very good dinner,' interrupted

Scrooge's niece. Everybody else said the same, and they must be allowed to have been competent judges, because they had just had dinner; and, with the dessert upon the table, were clustered round the fire, by lamp-light.

'Well! I am very glad to hear it,' said Scrooge's nephew, 'because I haven't any great faith in these young housekeepers. What do *you* say, Topper?'

Topper had clearly got his eye upon one of Scrooge's niece's sisters, for he answered that a bachelor was a wretched outcast, who had no right to express an opinion on the subject. Whereat Scrooge's niece's sister – the plump one with the lace tucker: not the one with the roses – blushed.

'Do go on, Fred,' said Scrooge's niece, clapping her hands. 'He never finishes what he begins to say! He is such a ridiculous fellow!'

Scrooge's nephew revelled in another laugh, and, as it was impossible to keep the infection off; though the plump sister tried hard to do it with aromatic vinegar; his example was unanimously followed.

'I was only going to say,' said Scrooge's nephew, 'that the consequence of his taking a dislike to us, and not making merry with us, is, as I think, that he loses some pleasant moments, which could do him no harm. I am sure he loses pleasanter companions than he can find in his own thoughts, either in his mouldy old office or his dusty chambers. I mean to give him the same chance every year, whether he likes it or not, for I pity him. He may rail at Christmas till he dies, but he can't help thinking better of it – I defy him – if he finds me going there, in good temper, year after year, and saying, 'Uncle Scrooge, how are you?' If it only puts him in the vein to leave his poor clerk fifty pounds *that*'s something; and I think I shook him yesterday.'

It was their turn to laugh, now, at the notion of his shaking Scrooge. But, being thoroughly good-natured, and not much caring what they laughed at, so that they laughed at any rate, he encouraged them in their merriment, and passed the bottle, joyously.

After tea they had some music. For they were a musical family, and knew what they were about when they sung a Glee or Catch, I can assure you: especially Topper, who could growl away in the bass like a good one, and never swell the large veins in his forehead, or get red in the face over it. Scrooge's niece played well upon the harp; and played, among other tunes, a simple little air (a mere nothing: you might learn to whistle it in two minutes), which had been familiar to the child who fetched Scrooge from the boarding-school, as he had been reminded by the Ghost of Christmas Past. When this strain of music sounded, all the things that Ghost had shown him came upon his mind; he softened more and more; and thought that if he could have listened to it often, years ago, he might have cultivated the kindnesses of life for his own happiness with his own hands, without resorting to the sexton's spade that buried Jacob Marley.

But they didn't devote the whole evening to music. After a while they played at forfeits; for it is good to be children sometimes, and never better than at Christmas, when its mighty Founder was a child himself. Stop! There was first a game at blind-man's buff. Of course there was. And I no more believe Topper was really blind than I believe he had eyes in his boots. My opinion is, that it was a done thing between him and Scrooge's nephew; and that the Ghost of Christmas Present knew it. The way he went after that plump sister in the lace tucker was an outrage on the credulity of human nature. Knocking down the fire-irons, tumbling over the chairs, bumping up against the piano, smothering himself amongst the curtains, wherever she went, there went he! He always knew where the plump sister was. He wouldn't catch anybody else. If you had fallen up against him (as some of them did) on purpose, he would have made a feint of endeavouring to seize you, which would have been an affront to your understanding, and would instantly have sidled off in the direction of the plump sister. She often cried out that it wasn't fair; and it really was not. But when, at last, he caught her; when, in spite of all her silken rustlings, and her rapid flutterings past him, he got her into a corner whence there was no escape; then his conduct was the most execrable. For his pretending not to know her, his pretending that it was necessary to touch her head-dress, and further to assure himself of her identity by pressing a certain ring upon her finger, and a certain chain about her neck; was vile, monstrous! No doubt she told him her opinion of it when, another blind man being in office, they were so very confidential together behind the curtains.

Scrooge's niece was not one of the blind-man's-buff party, but was made comfortable with a large chair and a footstool, in a snug corner where the Ghost and Scrooge were close behind her. But she joined in the forfeits, and loved her love to admiration with all the letters of the alphabet. Likewise at the game of How, When, and Where, she was very great, and, to the secret joy of Scrooge's nephew, beat her sisters hollow: though they were sharp girls too, as Topper could have told you. There might have been twenty people there, young and old, but they all played, and so did Scrooge; for, wholly forgetting, in the interest he had in what was going on, that his voice made no sound in their ears, he sometimes came out with his guess quite loud, and very often guessed right, too, for the sharpest needle, best Whitechapel, warranted not to cut in the eye, was not sharper than Scrooge; blunt as he took it in his head to be.

The Ghost was greatly pleased to find him in this mood, and looked upon him with such favour, that he begged like a boy to be allowed to stay until the guests departed. But this the Spirit said could not be done.

'Here is a new game,' said Scrooge. 'One half-hour, Spirit, only one!'

It was a game called Yes and No, where Scrooge's nephew had to think of something, and the rest must find out what; he only answering to their questions yes or no, as the case was. The brisk fire of questioning to which he was exposed elicited from him that he was thinking of an animal, a live animal, rather a disagreeable animal, a savage animal, an animal that growled and grunted sometimes, and talked sometimes, and lived in London, and walked about the streets, and wasn't made a show of, and wasn't led by anybody, and didn't live in a menagerie, and was never killed in a market, and was not a horse, or an ass, or a cow, or a bull, or a tiger, or a dog, or a pig, or a cat, or a bear. At every fresh question that was put to him, this nephew burst into a fresh roar of laughter; and was so inexpressibly tickled, that he was obliged to get up off the sofa, and stamp. At last the plump sister, falling into a similar state, cried out:

'I have found it out! I know what it is, Fred! I know what it is!'

'What is it?' cried Fred.

'It's your uncle Scro-o-o-o-oge!'

Which it certainly was. Admiration was the universal sentiment, though some objected that the reply to 'Is it a bear?' ought to have been 'Yes;' inasmuch as an answer in the negative was sufficient to have diverted their thoughts from Mr Scrooge, supposing they had ever had any tendency that way.

'He has given us plenty of merriment, I am sure,' said Fred, 'and it would be ungrateful not to drink his health. Here is a glass of mulled wine ready to our hand at the moment; and I say, 'Uncle Scrooge!'

'Well! Uncle Scrooge!' they cried.

'A merry Christmas and a happy New Year to the old man, whatever he is!' said Scrooge's nephew. 'He wouldn't take it from me, but may he have it, nevertheless. Uncle Scrooge!'

Uncle Scrooge had imperceptibly become so gay and light of heart, that he would have pledged the unconscious company in return, and thanked them in an inaudible speech, if the Ghost had given him time. But the whole scene passed off in the breath of the last word spoken by his nephew; and he and the Spirit were again upon their travels.

Much they saw, and far they went, and many homes they visited, but always with a happy end. The Spirit stood beside sick beds, and they were cheerful; on foreign lands, and they were close at home; by struggling men, and they were patient in their greater hope; by poverty, and it was rich. In almshouse, hospital, and gaol, in misery's every refuge, where vain man in his little brief authority had not made fast the door, and barred the Spirit out, he left his blessing, and taught Scrooge his precepts.

It was a long night, if it were only a night; but Scrooge had his doubts of this, because the Christmas holidays appeared to be condensed into the space of time they passed together. It was strange, too, that, while Scrooge remained unaltered in his outward form, the Ghost grew older, clearly older. Scrooge had observed this change, but never spoke of it until they left a children's Twelfth-Night party, when, looking at the Spirit as they stood together in an open place he noticed that its hair was grey.

'Are spirits' lives so short?' asked Scrooge.

'My life upon this globe is very brief,' replied the Ghost. 'It ends tonight.'

'Tonight!' cried Scrooge.

'Tonight at midnight. Hark! The time is drawing near.'

The chimes were ringing the three-quarters past eleven at that moment.

'Forgive me if I am not justified in what I ask,' said Scrooge, looking intently at the Spirit's robe, 'but I see something strange, and not belonging to yourself, protruding from your skirts. Is it a foot or a claw?'

'It might be a claw, for the flesh there is upon it,' was the Spirit's sorrowful reply. 'Look here.'

From the foldings of its robe it brought two children; wretched, abject, frightful, hideous, miserable. They knelt down at its feet, and clung upon the outside of its garment.

'Oh, Man! look here! Look, look, down here!' exclaimed the Ghost.

They were a boy and girl. Yellow, meagre, ragged, scowling, wolfish; but prostrate, too, in their humility. Where graceful youth should have filled their features out, and touched them with its freshest tints, a stale and shrivelled hand, like that of age, had pinched, and twisted them, and pulled them into shreds. Where angels might have sat enthroned, devils lurked and glared out menacing. No change, no degradation, no perversion of humanity, in any grade, through all the mysteries of wonderful creation, has monsters half so horrible and dread.

Scrooge started back appalled. Having them shown to him in this way, he tried to say they were fine children, but the words choked themselves, rather than be parties to a lie of such enormous magnitude.

'Spirit! are they yours?' Scrooge could say no more.

'They are Man's,' said the Spirit, looking down upon them. 'And they cling to me, appealing from their fathers. This boy is Ignorance. This girl is Want. Beware of them both, and all of their degree, but most of all beware this boy, for on his brow I see that written which is Doom, unless the writing be erased. Deny it!' cried the Spirit, stretching out its hand towards the city. 'Slander those who tell it ye! Admit it for your factious purposes, and make it worse! And bide the end!'

'Have they no refuge or resource?' cried Scrooge.

'Are there no prisons?' said the Spirit, turning on him for the last time with his own words. 'Are there no workhouses?'

The bell struck Twelve.

Scrooge looked about him for the Ghost, and saw it not. As the last stroke ceased to vibrate, he remembered the prediction of old Jacob Marley, and, lifting up his eyes, beheld a solemn Phantom, draped and hooded, coming like a mist along the ground towards him.

THE LAST OF THE SPIRITS

The Phantom slowly, gravely, silently approached. When it came near him, Scrooge bent down upon his knee; for in the very air through which this Spirit moved it seemed to scatter gloom and mystery.

It was shrouded in a deep black garment, which concealed its head, its face, its form, and left nothing of it visible, save one outstretched hand. But for this, it would have been difficult to detach its figure from the night, and separate it from the darkness by which it was surrounded.

He felt that it was tall and stately when it came beside him, and that its mysterious presence filled him with a solemn dread. He knew no more, for the Spirit neither spoke nor moved.

'I am in the presence of the Ghost of Christmas Yet to Come?' said Scrooge.

The Spirit answered not, but pointed onward with its hand.

'You are about to show me shadows of the things that have not happened, but will happen in the time before us,' Scrooge pursued. 'Is that so, Spirit?'

The upper portion of the garment was contracted for an instant in its folds, as if the Spirit had inclined its head. That was the only answer he received.

Although well used to ghostly company by this time, Scrooge feared the silent shape so much that his legs trembled beneath him, and he found that he could hardly stand when he prepared to follow it. The Spirit paused a moment, as observing his condition, and giving him time to recover.

But Scrooge was all the worse for this. It thrilled him with a vague uncertain horror to know that, behind the dusky shroud, there were ghostly eyes intently fixed upon him, while he, though he stretched his own to the utmost, could see nothing but a spectral hand and one great heap of black.

'Ghost of the Future!' he exclaimed, 'I fear you more than any spectre I have seen. But as I know your purpose is to do me good, and as I hope to live to be another man from what I was, I am prepared to bear you company, and do it with a thankful heart. Will you not speak to me?'

It gave him no reply. The hand was pointed straight before them.

'Lead on!' said Scrooge. 'Lead on! The night is waning fast, and it is precious time to me, I know. Lead on Spirit!'

The Phantom moved away as it had come towards him. Scrooge followed in the shadow of its dress, which bore him up, he thought, and carried him along.

They scarcely seemed to enter the City; for the City rather seemed to spring up about them, and encompass them of its own act. But there they were in the heart of it; on 'Change, amongst the merchants; who hurried up and down, and chinked the money in their pockets, and conversed in groups, and looked at their watches, and trifled thoughtfully with their great gold seals; and so forth, as Scrooge had seen them often.

The Spirit stopped beside one little knot of business men. Observing that the hand was pointed to them, Scrooge advanced to listen to their talk.

'No,' said a great fat man with a monstrous chin, 'I don't know much about it either way. I only know he's dead.'

'When did he die?' inquired another.

'Last night, I believe.'

'Why, what was the matter with him?' asked a third, taking a vast quantity of snuff out of a very large snuff-box. 'I thought he'd never die.'

'God knows,' said the first with a yawn.

'What has he done with his money?' asked a red-faced gentleman with a pendulous excrescence on the end of his nose, that shook like the gills of a turkey-cock.

'I haven't heard,' said the man with the large chin, yawning again. 'Left it to his company, perhaps. He hasn't left it to *me*. That's all I know.'

This pleasantry was received with a general laugh.

'It's likely to be a very cheap funeral,' said the same speaker; 'for, upon my life, I don't know of anybody to go to it. Suppose we make up a party, and volunteer?'

'I don't mind going if a lunch is provided,' observed the gentleman with the excrescence on his nose. 'But I must be fed if I make one.'

Another laugh.

'Well, I am the most disinterested among you, after all,' said the first speaker, 'for I never wear black gloves, and I never eat lunch. But I'll offer to go if anybody else will. When I come to think of it, I'm not at all sure that I wasn't his most particular friend; for we used to stop and speak whenever we met. Bye, bye!'

Speakers and listeners strolled away, and mixed with other groups. Scrooge knew the men, and looked towards the Spirit for an explanation.

The Phantom glided on into a street. It's finger pointed to two persons meeting. Scrooge listened again, thinking that the explanation might lie here.

He knew these men, also, perfectly. They were men of business: very wealthy, and of great importance. He had made a point always of standing well in their esteem: in a business point of view, that is; strictly in a business point of view.

'How are you?' said one.

'How are you?' returned the other.

'Well!' said the first. 'Old Scratch has got his own at last, hey?'

'So I am told,' returned the second. 'Cold, isn't it?'

'Seasonable for Christmas-time. You are not a skater, I suppose?'

'No. No. Something else to think of. Good morning!'

Not another word. That was their meeting, their conversation, and their parting.

Scrooge was at first inclined to be surprised that the Spirit should attach importance to conversations apparently so trivial; but, feeling assured that they must have some hidden purpose, he set himself to consider what it was likely to be. They could scarcely be supposed to have any bearing on the death of Jacob, his old partner, for that was Past, and this Ghost's province was the Future. Nor could he think of any one immediately connected with himself, to whom he could apply them. But nothing doubting that, to whomsoever they applied, they had some latent moral for his own improvement, he resolved to treasure up every word he heard, and everything he saw; and especially to observe the shadow of himself when it appeared. For he had an expectation that the conduct of his future self would give him the clue he missed, and would render the solution of these riddles easy.

He looked about in that very place for his own image; but another man stood in his accustomed corner, and, though the clock pointed to his usual time of day for being there, he saw no likeness of himself among the multitudes that poured in through the Porch. It gave him little surprise, however; for he had been revolving in his mind a change of life, and thought and hoped he saw his new-born resolutions carried out in this.

Quiet and dark, beside him stood the Phantom, with its outstretched hand. When he roused himself from his thoughtful quest, he fancied, from the turn of the hand, and its situation in reference to himself, that the Unseen Eyes were looking at him keenly. It made him shudder, and feel very cold.

They left the busy scene, and went into an obscure part of the town, where Scrooge had never penetrated before, although he recognised its situation and its bad repute. The ways were foul and narrow; the shops and houses wretched; the people half naked, drunken, slipshod, ugly. Alleys and archways, like so many cesspools, disgorged their offences of smell, and dirt, and life upon the straggling streets; and the whole quarter reeked with crime, with filth and misery.

Far in this den of infamous resort, there was a low-browed, beetling shop, below a pent-house roof, where iron, old rags, bottles, bones, and greasy offal were bought. Upon the floor within were piled up heaps of rusty keys, nails, chains, hinges, files, scales, weights, and refuse iron of all kinds. Secrets that few would like to scrutinise were bred and hidden in mountains of unseemly rags, masses of corrupted fat, and sepulchres of bones. Sitting in among the wares he dealt in, by a charcoal stove made of old bricks, was a grey-haired rascal, nearly seventy years of age; who had screened himself from the cold air without by a frouzy curtaining of miscellaneous tatters hung upon a line; and smoked his pipe in all the luxury of calm retirement.

Scrooge and the Phantom came into the presence of this man, just as a woman with a heavy bundle slunk into the shop. But she had scarcely entered, when another woman, similarly laden, came in too; and she was closely followed by a man in faded black, who was no less startled by the sight of them than they had been upon the recognition of each other. After a short period of blank astonishment, in which the old man with the pipe had joined them, they all three burst into a laugh.

'Let the charwoman alone to be the first!' cried she who had entered first. 'Let the laundress alone to be the second; and let the undertaker's man alone to be the third. Look here, old Joe, here's a chance! If we haven't all three met here without meaning it!'

'You couldn't have met in a better place,' said old Joe, removing his pipe from his mouth. 'Come into the parlour. You were made free of it long ago, you know; and the other two ain't strangers. Stop till I shut the door of the shop. Ah! How it skreeks! There an't such a rusty bit of metal in the place as its own hinges, I believe; and I'm sure there's no such old bones here as mine. Ha! ha! We're all suitable to our calling, we're well matched. Come into the parlour. Come into the parlour.'

The parlour was the space behind the screen of rags. The old man raked the fire together with an old stair-rod, and, having trimmed his smoky lamp (for it was night) with the stem of his pipe, put it into his mouth again.

While he did this, the woman who had already spoken threw her bundle on the floor, and sat down in a flaunting manner on a stool; crossing her elbows on her knees, and looking with a bold defiance at the other two.

'What odds, then? What odds, Mrs Dilber?' said the woman. 'Every person has a right to take care of themselves. *He* always did!'

'That's true, indeed!' said the laundress. 'No man more so.'

'Why, then, don't stand staring as if you was afraid, woman! Who's the wiser? We're not going to pick holes in each other's coats, I suppose?'

'No, indeed!' said Mrs Dilber and the man together. 'We should hope not.'

'Very well, then!' cried the woman, 'That's enough. Who's the worse for the loss of a few things like these? Not a dead man, I suppose?'

'No, indeed,' said Mrs Dilber, laughing.

'If he wanted to keep 'em after he was dead, a wicked old screw,' pursued the woman, 'why wasn't he natural in his lifetime? If he had been, he'd have had somebody to look after him when he was struck with Death, instead of lying gasping out his last there, alone by himself.'

'It's the truest word that ever was spoke,' said Mrs Dilber. 'It's a judgment on him.'

'I wish it was a little heavier judgment,' replied the woman; 'and it should have been, you may depend upon it, if I could have laid my hands on anything else. Open that bundle, old Joe, and let me know the value of it. Speak out plain. I'm not afraid to be the first, nor afraid for them to see it. We knew pretty well that we were helping ourselves before we met here, I believe. It's no sin. Open the bundle, Joe.'

But the gallantry of her friends would not allow of this; and the man in faded black, mounting the breach first, produced *his* plunder. It was not extensive. A seal or two, a pencil-case, a pair of sleeve-buttons, and a brooch of no great value, were all. They were severally examined and appraised by old Joe, who chalked the sums he was disposed to give for each upon the wall, and added them up into a total when he found that there was nothing more to come.

'That's your account,' said Joe, 'and I wouldn't give another sixpence, if I was to be boiled for not doing it. Who's next?'

Mrs Dilber was next. Sheets and towels, a little wearing apparel, two old-fashioned silver tea-spoons, a pair of sugar-tongs, and a few boots. Her account was stated on the wall in the same manner.

'I always give too much to ladies. It's a weakness of mine, and that's the way I ruin myself,' said old Joe. 'That's your account. If you asked me for another penny, and made it an open question, I'd repent of being so liberal, and knock off half-a-crown.'

'And now undo *my* bundle, Joe,' said the first woman.

Joe went down on his knees for the greater convenience of opening it, and, having unfastened a great many knots, dragged out a large heavy roll of some dark stuff.

'What do you call this?' said Joe. 'Bed-curtains?'

'Ah!' returned the woman, laughing and leaning forward on her crossed arms. 'Bed-curtains!'

'You don't mean to say you took 'em down, rings and all, with him lying there?' said Joe.

'Yes, I do,' replied the woman. 'Why not?'

'You were born to make your fortune,' said Joe, 'and you'll certainly do it.'

'I certainly shan't hold my hand, when I can get anything in it by reaching it out, for the sake of such a man as He was, I promise you, Joe,' returned the woman coolly. 'Don't drop that oil upon the blankets, now.'

'His blankets?' asked Joe.

'Whose else's do you think?' replied the woman. 'He isn't likely to take cold without 'em, I dare say.'

'I hope he didn't die of anything catching? Eh?' said old Joe, stopping in his work, and looking up.

'Don't you be afraid of that,' returned the woman. 'I an't so fond of his company that I'd loiter about him for such things, if he did. Ah! You may look through that shirt till your eyes ache; but you won't find a hole in it, nor a threadbare place. It's the best he had, and a fine one too. They'd have wasted it, if it hadn't been for me.'

'What do you call wasting of it?' asked old Joe.

'Putting it on him to be buried in, to be sure,' replied the woman with a laugh. 'Somebody was fool enough to do it, but I took it off again. If calico an't good enough for such a purpose, it isn't good enough for anything. It's quite as becoming to the body. He can't look uglier than he did in that one.'

Scrooge listened to this dialogue in horror. As they sat grouped about their spoil, in the scanty light afforded by the old man's lamp, he viewed them with a detestation and disgust which could hardly have been greater, though they had been obscene demons, marketing the corpse itself.

'Ha, ha!' laughed the same woman when old Joe, producing a flannel bag with money in it, told out their several gains upon the ground. 'This is the end of it, you see! He frightened every one away from him when he was alive, to profit us when he was dead! Ha, ha, ha!'

'Spirit!' said Scrooge, shuddering from head to foot. 'I see, I see. The case of this unhappy man might be my own. My life tends that way now. Merciful Heaven, what is this?'

He recoiled in terror, for the scene had changed, and now he almost touched a bed: a bare, uncurtained bed: on which, beneath a ragged sheet, there lay a something covered up, which, though it was dumb, announced itself in awful language.

The room was very dark, too dark to be observed with any accuracy, though Scrooge glanced round it in obedience to a secret impulse, anxious to know what kind of room it was. A pale light, rising in the outer air, fell straight upon the bed: and on it, plundered and bereft, unwatched, unwept, uncared for, was the body of this man.

Scrooge glanced towards the Phantom. Its steady hand was pointed to the head. The cover was so carelessly adjusted that the slightest raising of it, the motion of a finger upon Scrooge's part, would have disclosed the face. He thought of it, felt how easy it would be to do, and longed to do it; but had no more power to withdraw the veil than to dismiss the spectre at his side.

Oh, cold, cold, rigid, dreadful Death, set up thine altar here, and dress it with such terrors as thou has at thy command: for this is thy dominion! But of the loved, revered, and honoured head thou canst not turn one hair to thy dread purposes, or make one feature odious. It is not that the hand is heavy, and will fall down when released; it is not that the heart and pulse are still; but that the hand WAS open, generous, and true; the heart brave, warm, and tender; and the pulse a man's. Strike, Shadow, strike! And see his good deeds springing from the wound, to sow the world with life immortal!

No voice pronounced these words in Scrooge's ears, and yet he heard them when he looked upon the bed. He thought, if this man could be raised up now, what would be his foremost thoughts? Avarice, hard dealing, griping cares? They have brought him to a rich end, truly!

He lay, in the dark, empty house, with not a man, a woman, or a child to say he was kind to me in this or that, and for the memory of one kind word I will be kind to him. A cat was tearing at the door, and there was a sound of gnawing rats beneath the hearth-stone. What *they* wanted in the room of death, and why they were so restless and disturbed, Scrooge did not dare to think.

'Spirit!' he said, 'this is a fearful place. In leaving it, I shall not leave its lesson, trust me. Let us go!'

Still the Ghost pointed with an unmoved finger to the head.

'I understand you,' Scrooge returned, 'and I would do it if I could. But I have not the power, Spirit. I have not the power.'

Again it seemed to look upon him.

'If there is any person in the town who feels emotion caused by this man's death,' said Scrooge, quite agonised, 'show that person to me, Spirit, I beseech you!'

The Phantom spread its dark robe before him for a moment, like a wing; and, withdrawing it, revealed a room by daylight, where a mother and her children were.

She was expecting someone, and with anxious eagerness; for she walked up and down the room; started at every sound; looked out from the window; glanced at the clock; tried, but in vain, to work with her needle; and could hardly bear the voices of her children in their play.

At length the long-expected knock was heard. She hurried to the door, and met her husband; a man whose face was careworn and depressed, though he was young. There was a remarkable expression in it now; a kind of serious delight of which he felt ashamed, and which he struggled to repress.

He sat down to the dinner that had been hoarding for him by the fire, and, when she asked him faintly what news (which was not until after a long silence), he appeared embarrassed how to answer.

'Is it good,' she said, 'or bad?' to help him.

'Bad,' he answered.

'We are quite ruined?'

'No. There is hope yet, Caroline.'

'If *he* relents,' she said, amazed, 'there is! Nothing is past hope, if such a miracle has happened.'

'He is past relenting,' said her husband. 'He is dead.'

She was a mild and patient creature, if her face spoke truth; but she was thankful in her soul to hear it, and she said so with clasped hands. She prayed forgiveness the next moment, and was sorry; but the first was the emotion of her heart.

'What the half-drunken woman, whom I told you of last night, said to me when I tried to see him and obtain a week's delay; and what I thought was a mere excuse to avoid me; turns out to have been quite true. He was not only very ill, but dying, then.'

'To whom will our debt be transferred?'

'I don't know. But, before that time, we shall be ready with the money; and, even though we were not, it would be bad fortune indeed to find so merciless a creditor in his successor. We may sleep tonight with light hearts, Caroline!'

Yes. Soften it as they would, their hearts were lighter. The children's faces, hushed and clustered round to hear what they so little understood, were brighter; and it was a happier house for this man's death! The only emotion that the Ghost could show him, caused by the event, was one of pleasure.

'Let me see some tenderness connected with a death,' said Scrooge; 'or that dark chamber, Spirit, which we left just now, will be for ever present to me.'

The Ghost conducted him through several streets familiar to his feet; and, as they went along, Scrooge looked here and there to find himself, but nowhere was he to be seen. They entered poor Bob Cratchit's house; the dwelling he had visited before; and found the mother and the children seated round the fire.

Quiet. Very quiet. The noisy little Cratchits were as still as statues in one corner, and sat looking up at Peter, who had a book before him. The mother and her daughters were engaged in sewing. But surely they were very quiet!

'"And he took a child, and set him in the midst of them."'

Where had Scrooge heard those words? He had not dreamed them. The boy must have read them out, as he and the Spirit crossed the threshold. Why did he not go on?

The mother laid her work upon the table, and put her hand up to her face.

'The colour hurts my eyes,' she said.

The colour? Ah, poor Tiny Tim!

'They're better now again,' said Cratchit's wife. 'It makes them weak by candle-light; and I wouldn't show weak eyes to your father, when he comes home, for the world. It must be near his time.'

'Past it rather,' Peter answered, shutting up his book. 'But I think he has walked a little slower than he used, these few last evenings, mother.'

They were very quiet again. At last she said, and in a steady, cheerful voice, that only faltered once:

'I have known him walk with – I have known him walk with Tiny Tim upon his shoulder very fast indeed.'

'And so have I,' cried Peter. 'Often.'

'And so have I,' exclaimed another. So had all.

'But he was very light to carry,' she resumed, intent upon her work, 'and his father loved him so, that it was no trouble: no trouble. And there is your father at the door!'

She hurried out to meet him; and little Bob in his comforter – he had need of it, poor fellow – came in. His tea was ready for him on the hob, and they all tried who should help him to it most. Then the two young Cratchits got upon his knees, and laid, each child, a little cheek against his face, as if they said, 'Don't mind it, father. Don't be grieved!'

Bob was very cheerful with them, and spoke pleasantly to all the family. He looked at the work upon the table, and praised the industry and speed of Mrs Cratchit and the girls. They would be done long before Sunday, he said.

'Sunday! You went today, then, Robert?' said his wife.

'Yes, my dear,' returned Bob. 'I wish you could have gone. It would have done you good to see how green a place it is. But you'll see it often. I promised him that I would walk there on a Sunday. My little, little child!' cried Bob. 'My little child!'

He broke down all at once. He couldn't help it. If he could have helped it, he and his child would have been farther apart, perhaps, than they were.

He left the room, and went upstairs into the room above, which was lighted cheerfully, and hung with Christmas. There was a chair set close beside the child, and there were signs of someone having been there lately. Poor Bob sat down in it, and, when he had thought a little and composed himself, he kissed the little face. He was reconciled to what had happened, and went down again quite happy.

They drew about the fire and talked; the girls and mother working still. Bob told them of the extraordinary kindness of Mr Scrooge's nephew, whom he had scarcely seen but once, and who, meeting him in the street that day, and seeing that he looked a little – 'just a little down, you know,' said Bob, inquired what had happened to distress him. 'On which,' said Bob, 'for he is the pleasantest-spoken gentleman you ever heard, I told him. "I am heartily sorry for it, Mr Cratchit," he said, "and heartily sorry for your good wife." By-the-bye, how he ever knew *that* I don't know.'

'Knew what, my dear?'

'Why, that you were a good wife,' replied Bob.

'Everybody knows that,' said Peter.

'Very well observed, my boy!' cried Bob. 'I hope they do. "Heartily sorry," he said, "for your good wife. If I can be of service to you in any way," he said, giving me his card, "that's where I live. Pray come to me." Now, it wasn't,' cried Bob, 'for the sake of anything he might be able to do for us, so much as for his kind way, that this was quite delightful. It really seemed as if he had known our Tiny Tim, and felt with us.'

'I'm sure he's a good soul!' said Mrs Cratchit.

'You would be sure of it, my dear,' returned Bob, 'if you saw and spoke to him. I shouldn't be at all surprised – mark what I say! – if he got Peter a better situation.'

'Only hear that, Peter,' said Mrs Cratchit.

'And then,' cried one of the girls, 'Peter will be keeping company with someone and setting up for himself.'

'Get along with you!' retorted Peter, grinning.

'It's just as likely as not,' said Bob, 'one of these days; though there's plenty of time for that, my dear. But, however and whenever we part from one another, I am sure we shall none of us forget poor Tiny Tim – shall we – or this first parting that there was among us?'

'Never, father!' cried they all.

'And I know,' said Bob, 'I know, my dears, that when we recollect how patient and how mild he was; although he was a little, little child; we shall not quarrel easily among ourselves, and forget poor Tiny Tim in doing it.'

'No, never, father!' they all cried again.

'I am very happy,' said little Bob, 'I am very happy!'

Mrs Cratchit kissed him, his daughters kissed him, the two young Cratchits kissed him, and Peter and himself shook hands. Spirit of Tiny Tim, thy childish essence was from God!

'Spectre,' said Scrooge, 'something informs me that our parting moment is at hand. I know it, but I know not how. Tell me what man that was whom we saw lying dead?'

The Ghost of Christmas Yet To Come conveyed him, as before – though at a different time, he thought: indeed, there seemed no order in these latter visions, save that they were in the Future – into the resorts of business men, but showed him not himself. Indeed, the Spirit did not stay for anything, but went straight on, as to the end just now desired, until besought by Scrooge to tarry for a moment.

'This court,' said Scrooge, 'through which we hurry now, is where my place of occupation is, and has been for a length of time. I see the house. Let me behold what I shall be in days to come.'

The Spirit stopped; the hand was pointed elsewhere.

'The house is yonder,' Scrooge exclaimed, 'Why do you point away?'

The inexorable finger underwent no change.

Scrooge hastened to the window of his office, and looked in. It was an office still, but not his. The furniture was not the same, and the figure in the chair was not himself. The Phantom pointed as before.

He joined it once again, and, wondering why and whither he had gone, accompanied it until they reached an iron gate. He paused to look round before entering.

A churchyard. Here, then, the wretched man, whose name he had now to learn, lay underneath the ground. It was a worthy place. Walled in by houses; overrun by grass and weeds, the growth of vegetation's death, not life; choked up with too much burying; fat with repleted appetite. A worthy place!

The Spirit stood among the graves, and pointed down to One. He advanced towards it trembling. The Phantom was exactly as it had been, but he dreaded that he saw new meaning in its solemn shape.

'Before I draw nearer to that stone to which you point,' said Scrooge, 'answer me one question. Are these the shadows of the things that Will be, or are they shadows of the things that May be only?'

Still the Ghost pointed downward to the grave by which it stood.

'Men's courses will foreshadow certain ends, to which, if persevered in, they must lead,' said Scrooge. 'But, if the courses be departed from, the ends will change. Say it is thus with what you show me!'

The Spirit was immovable as ever.

Scrooge crept towards it, trembling as he went; and following the finger, read upon the stone of the neglected grave his own name, EBENEZER SCROOGE.

'Am *I* that man who lay upon the bed?' he cried upon his knees.

The finger still pointed from the grave to him, and back again.

'No, Spirit! Oh no, no!'

The finger still was there.

'Spirit!' he cried, tight clutching at his robe, 'hear me! I am not the man I was. I will not be the man I must have been but for this intercourse. Why show me this, if I am past all hope?'

For the first time the hand appeared to shake.

'Good Spirit,' he pursued, as down upon the ground he fell before it: 'your nature intercedes for me, and pities me. Assure me that I yet may change these shadows you have shown me by an altered life?'

The kind hand trembled.

'I will honour Christmas in my heart, and try to keep it all the year. I will live in the Past, the Present, and the Future. The Spirits of all Three shall strive within me. I will not shut out the lessons that they teach. Oh, tell me I may sponge away the writing on this stone!'

In his agony, he caught the spectral hand. It sought to free itself, but he was strong in his entreaty, and detained it. The Spirit, stronger yet, repulsed him.

Holding up his hands in a last prayer to have his fate reversed, he saw an alteration in the Phantom's hood and dress. It shrunk, collapsed, and dwindled down into a bedpost.

THE END OF IT

Yes! and the bedpost was his own. The bed was his own, the room was his own. Best and happiest of all, the Time before him was his own, to make amends in!

'I will live in the Past, the Present, and the Future!' Scrooge repeated as he scrambled out of bed. 'The Spirits of all Three shall strive within me. Oh, Jacob Marley! Heaven and the Christmas Time be praised for this! I say it on my knees, old Jacob; on my knees!'

He was so fluttered and so glowing with his good intentions, that his broken voice would scarcely answer to his call. He had been sobbing violently in his conflict with the Spirit, and his face was wet with tears.

'They are not torn down,' cried Scrooge, folding one of his bed-curtains in his arms, 'they are not torn down, rings and all. They are here – I am here – the shadows of the things that would have been may be dispelled. They will be. I know they will!'

His hands were busy with his garments all this time; turning them inside out, putting them on upside down, tearing them, mislaying them, making them parties to every kind of extravagance.

'I don't know what to do!' cried Scrooge, laughing and crying in the same breath; and making a perfect Laocoön of himself with his stockings. 'I am as light as a feather, I am as happy as an angel, I am as merry as a schoolboy. I am as giddy as a drunken man. A merry Christmas to everybody! A happy New Year to all the world! Hallo here! Whoop! Hallo!'

He had frisked into the sitting-room, and was now standing there: perfectly winded.

'There's the saucepan that the gruel was in!' cried Scrooge, starting off again, and going round the fire-place. 'There's the door by which the Ghost of Jacob Marley entered! There's the corner where the Ghost of Christmas Present sat! There's the window where I saw the wandering Spirits! It's all right, it's all true, it all happened. Ha, ha, ha!'

Really, for a man who had been out of practice for so many years, it was a splendid laugh, a most illustrious laugh. The father of a long, long line of brilliant laughs!

'I don't know what day of the month it is,' said Scrooge. 'I don't know how long I have been among the Spirits. I don't know anything. I'm quite a baby. Never mind. I don't care. I'd rather be a baby. Hallo! Whoop! Hallo here!'

He was checked in his transports by the churches ringing out the lustiest peals he had ever heard. Clash, clash, hammer; ding, dong, bell! Bell, dong, ding; hammer, clang, clash! Oh, glorious, glorious!

Running to the window, he opened it, and put out his head. No fog, no mist; clear, bright, jovial, stirring, cold; cold, piping for the blood to dance to; Golden sun-light; Heavenly sky; sweet fresh air; merry bells. Oh, glorious! Glorious!

'What's today?' cried Scrooge, calling downward to a boy in Sunday clothes, who perhaps had loitered in to look about him.

'EH?' returned the boy with all his might of wonder.

'What's today, my fine fellow?' said Scrooge.

'Today!' replied the boy. 'Why, CHRISTMAS DAY.'

'It's Christmas Day!' said Scrooge to himself. 'I haven't missed it. The Spirits have done it all in one night. They can do anything they like. Of course they can. Of course they can. Hallo, my fine fellow!'

'Hallo!' returned the boy.

'Do you know the Poulterer's in the next street but one, at the corner?' Scrooge inquired.

'I should hope I did,' replied the lad.

'An intelligent boy!' said Scrooge. 'A remarkable boy! Do you know whether they've sold the prize Turkey that was hanging up there? Not the little prize Turkey: the big one?'

'What! the one as big as me?' returned the boy.

'What a delightful boy!' said Scrooge. 'It's a pleasure to talk to him. Yes, my buck!'

'It's hanging there now,' replied the boy.

'Is it?' said Scrooge. 'Go and buy it.'

'Walk-ER!' exclaimed the boy.

'No, no,' said Scrooge, 'I am in earnest. Go and buy it, and tell 'em to bring it here, that I may give them the directions where to take it. Come back with the man, and I'll give you a shilling. Come back with him in less than five minutes, and I'll give you half-a-crown!'

The boy was off like a shot. He must have had a steady hand at a trigger who could have got a shot off half so fast.

'I'll send it to Bob Cratchit's,' whispered Scrooge, rubbing his hands, and splitting with a laugh. 'He shan't know who sends it. It's twice the size of Tiny Tim. Joe Miller never made such a joke as sending it to Bob's will be!'

The hand in which he wrote the address was not a steady one; but write it he did, somehow, and went downstairs to open the street-door ready for the coming of the poulterer's man. As he stood there, waiting his arrival, the knocker caught his eye.

'I shall love it as long as I live!' cried Scrooge, patting it with his hand. 'I scarcely ever looked at it before. What an honest expression it has in its face! It's a wonderful knocker! – Here's the Turkey. Hallo! Whoop! How are you? Merry Christmas!'

It *was* a Turkey! He never could have stood upon his legs, that bird. He would have snapped 'em short off in a minute, like sticks of sealing-wax.

'Why, it's impossible to carry that to Camden Town,' said Scrooge. 'You must have a cab.'

The chuckle with which he said this, and the chuckle with which he paid for the Turkey, and the chuckle with which he paid for the cab, and the chuckle with which he recompensed the boy, were only to be exceeded by the chuckle with which he sat down breathless in his chair again, and chuckled till he cried.

Shaving was not an easy task, for his hand continued to shake very much; and shaving requires attention, even when you don't dance while you are at it. But, if he had cut the end of his nose off, he would have put a piece of sticking-plaster over it, and been quite satisfied.

He dressed himself 'all in his best,' and at last got out into the streets. The people were by this time pouring forth, as he had seen them with the Ghost of Christmas Present; and walking with his hands behind him, Scrooge regarded every one with a delighted smile. He looked so irresistibly pleasant, in a word, that three or four good-humoured fellows said, 'Good morning, sir! A merry Christmas to you!' And Scrooge said often afterwards that, of all the blithe sounds he had ever heard, those were the blithest in his ears.

He had not gone far when, coming on towards him, he beheld the portly gentleman who had walked into his counting-house the day before, and said, 'Scrooge and Marley's, I believe?' It sent a pang across his heart to think how this old gentleman would look upon him when they met; but he knew what path lay straight before him, and he took it.

'My dear sir,' said Scrooge, quickening his pace, and taking the old gentleman by both his hands, 'how do you do? I hope you succeeded yesterday. It was very kind of you. A merry Christmas to you, sir!'

'Mr Scrooge?'

'Yes,' said Scrooge. 'That is my name, and I fear it may not be pleasant to you. Allow me to ask your pardon. And will you have the goodness ——' Here Scrooge whispered in his ear.

'Lord bless me!' cried the gentleman, as if his breath were taken away. 'My dear Mr Scrooge, are you serious?'

'If you please,' said Scrooge. 'Not a farthing less. A great many back-payments are included in it, I assure you. Will you do me that favour?'

'My dear sir,' said the other, shaking hands with him, 'I don't know what to say to such munifi——'

'Don't say anything, please,' retorted Scrooge. 'Come and see me. Will you come and see me?'

'I will!' cried the old gentleman. And it was clear he meant to do it.

'Thankee,' said Scrooge. 'I am much obliged to you. I thank you fifty times. Bless you!'

He went to church, and walked about the streets, and watched the people hurrying to and fro, and patted the children on the head, and questioned beggars, and looked down into the kitchens of houses, and up to the windows; and found that everything could yield him pleasure. He had never dreamed that any walk – that anything – could give him so much happiness. In the afternoon he turned his steps towards his nephew's house.

He passed the door a dozen times before he had the courage to go up and knock. But he made a dash, and did it.

'Is your master at home, my dear?' said Scrooge to the girl. Nice girl! Very.

'Yes, sir.'

'Where is he, my love?' said Scrooge.

'He's in the dining-room, sir, along with mistress. I'll show you upstairs, if you please.'

'Thankee. He knows me,' said Scrooge, with his hand already on the dining-room lock. 'I'll go in here, my dear.'

He turned it gently, and sidled his face in round the door.

They were looking at the table (which was spread out in great array); for these young housekeepers are always nervous on such points, and like to see that everything is right.

'Fred!' said Scrooge.

Dear heart alive, how his niece by marriage started! Scrooge had forgotten, for the moment, about her sitting in the corner with the footstool, or he wouldn't have done it on any account.

'Why, bless my soul!' cried Fred, 'who's that?'

'It's I. Your uncle Scrooge. I have come to dinner. Will you let me in, Fred?'

Let him in! It is a mercy he didn't shake his arm off. He was at home in five minutes. Nothing could be heartier. His niece looked just the same. So did Topper when *he* came. So did the plump sister when *she* came. So did every one when *they* came. Wonderful party, wonderful games, wonderful unanimity, won-der-ful happiness!

But he was early at the office next morning. Oh, he was early there! If he could only be there first, and catch Bob Cratchit coming late! That was the thing he had set his heart upon.

And he did it; yes, he did! The clock struck nine. No Bob. A quarter past. No Bob. He was full eighteen minutes and a half behind his time. Scrooge sat with his door wide open, that he might see him come into the tank.

His hat was off before he opened the door; his comforter too. He was on his stool in a jiffy; driving away with his pen, as if he were trying to overtake nine o'clock.

'Hallo!' growled Scrooge in his accustomed voice as near as he could feign it. 'What do you mean by coming here at this time of day?'

'I am very sorry, sir,' said Bob. 'I *am* behind my time.'

'You are!' repeated Scrooge. 'Yes. I think you are. Step this way, sir, if you please.'

'It's only once a year, sir,' pleaded Bob, appearing from the tank. 'It shall not be repeated. I was making rather merry yesterday, sir.'

'Now, I'll tell you what, my friend,' said Scrooge. 'I am

not going to stand this sort of thing any longer. And therefore,' he continued, leaping from his stool, and giving Bob such a dig in the waistcoat that he staggered back into the tank again: 'and therefore I am about to raise your salary!'

Bob trembled, and got a little nearer to the ruler. He had a momentary idea of knocking Scrooge down with it, holding him, and calling to the people in the court for help and a strait-waistcoat.

'A merry Christmas Bob!' said Scrooge with an earnestness that could not be mistaken, as he clapped him on the back. 'A merrier Christmas, Bob, my good fellow, than I have given you for many a year! I'll raise your salary, and endeavour to assist your struggling family, and we will discuss your affairs this very afternoon, over a Christmas bowl of smoking bishop, Bob! Make up the fires and buy another coal-scuttle before you dot another i, Bob Cratchit!'

Scrooge was better than his word. He did it all, and infinitely more; and to Tiny Tim, who did NOT die, he was a second father. He became as good a friend, as good a master, and as good a man as the good old City knew, or any other good old city, town , or borough in the good old world. Some people laughed to see the alteration in him, but he let them laugh, and little heeded them; for he was wise enough to know that nothing ever happened on this globe, for good, at which some people did not have their fill of laughter in the outset; and, knowing that such as these would be blind anyway, he thought it quite as well that they should wrinkle up their eyes in grins as have the malady in less attractive forms. His own heart laughed: and that was quite enough for him.

He had no further intercourse with Spirits, but lived upon the Total Abstinence Principle ever afterwards; and it was always said of him that he knew how to keep Christmas well, if any man alive possessed the knowledge. May that be truly said to us, and all of us! And so, as Tiny Tim observed, God Bless Us, Every One!

THE HAUNTED HOUSE

The Mortals in the House

Under none of the accredited ghostly circumstances, and environed by none of the conventional ghostly surroundings, did I first make acquaintance with the house which is the subject of this Christmas piece. I saw it in the daylight, with the sun upon it. There was no wind, no rain, no lightning, no thunder, no awful or unwonted circumstance, of any kind, to heighten its effect. More than that: I had come to it direct from a railway station: it was not more than a mile distant from the railway station; and, as I stood outside the house, looking back upon the way I had come, I could see the goods train running smoothly along the embankment in the valley. I will not say that everything was utterly common-place, because I doubt if anything can be that, except to utterly common-place people – and there my vanity steps in; but, I will take it on myself to say that anybody might see the house as I saw it, any fine autumn morning.

The manner of my lighting on it was this.

I was travelling towards London out of the North, intending to stop by the way, to look at the house. My health required a temporary residence in the country; and a friend of mine who knew that, and who had happened to drive past the house, had written to me to suggest it as a likely place. I had got into the train at midnight, and had fallen asleep, and had woke up and had sat looking out of window at the brilliant Northern Lights in the sky, and had fallen asleep again, and had woke up again to find the night gone, with the usual discontented conviction on me that I hadn't been to sleep at all; upon which question, in the first imbecility of that condition, I am ashamed to believe that I would have done wager by battle with the man who sat opposite me. That opposite man had had, through the night – as that opposite man always has – several legs too many, and all of them too long. In addition to this unreasonable conduct (which was only to be expected of him), he had had a pencil and a pocket-book, and had been perpetually listening and taking notes. It had appeared to me that these aggravating notes related to the jolts and bumps of the carriage, and I should have resigned myself to his taking them, under a general supposition that he was in the civil-engineering way of life, if he had not sat staring straight over my head whenever he listened. He was a goggle-eyed gentleman of a perplexed aspect, and his demeanour became unbearable.

It was a cold, dead morning (the sun not being up yet), and when I had out-watched the paling light of the fires of the iron country, and the curtain of heavy smoke that hung at once between me and the stars and between me and the day, I turned to my fellow-traveller and said, 'I *beg* your pardon, sir, but do you observe anything particular in me?' For, really, he appeared to be taking down, either my travelling-cap or my hair, with a minuteness that was a liberty.

The goggle-eyed gentleman withdrew his eyes from behind me, as if the back of the carriage were a hundred miles off, and said, with a lofty look of compassion for my insignificance, 'In you, sir? – B.'

'B, sir?' said I, growing warm.

'I have nothing to do with you, sir,' returned the gentleman; 'pray let me listen – O.'

He enunciated this vowel after a pause, and noted it down.

At first I was alarmed, for an Express lunatic and no communication with the guard, is a serious position. The thought came to my relief that the gentleman might be what is popularly called a Rapper: one of a sect for (some of) whom I have the highest respect, but whom I don't believe in. I was going to ask him the question, when he took the bread out of my mouth.

'You will excuse me,' said the gentleman contemptuously, 'if I am too much in advance of common humanity to trouble myself at all about it. I have passed the night – as indeed I pass the whole of my time now – in spiritual intercourse.'

'O!' said I, something snappishly.

'The conferences of the night began,' continued the gentleman, turning several leaves of his note-book, 'with this message: "Evil communications corrupt good manners."'

'Sound,' said I; 'but, absolutely new?'

'New from spirits,' returned the gentleman.

I could only repeat my rather snappish 'O!' and ask if I might be favoured with the last communication.

'"A bird in the hand,"' said the gentleman, reading his last entry with great solemnity, '"is worth two in the Bosh."'

'Truly I am of the same opinion,' said I; 'but shouldn't it be Bush?'

'It came to me, Bosh,' returned the gentleman.

The gentleman then informed me that the spirit of Socrates had delivered this special revelation in the course of the night. 'My friend, I hope you are pretty well. There are two in this railway carriage. How do you do? There are seventeen thousand four hundred and seventy-nine spirits here, but you cannot see them. Pythagoras is here. He is not at liberty to mention it, but hopes you like travelling.' Galileo likewise had dropped in, with this scientific intelligence. 'I am glad to see you, *amico. Come sta?* Water will freeze when it is cold enough. *Addio*!' In the course of the night, also, the following phenomena had occurred. Bishop Butler had insisted on spelling his name, 'Bubler,' for which offence against orthography and good manners he had been dismissed as out of temper. John Milton (suspected of wilful mystification) had repudiated the authorship of *Paradise Lost*, and had introduced, as joint authors of that poem, two unknown gentlemen, respectively named Grungers and Scadgingtone. And Prince Arthur, nephew of King John of England, had described himself as tolerably comfortable in the seventh circle, where he was learning to paint on velvet, under the direction of Mrs Trimmer and Mary Queen of Scots.

If this should meet the eye of the gentleman who favoured me with these disclosures, I trust he will excuse my confessing that the sight of the rising sun, and the contemplation of the magnificent Order of the vast Universe, made me impatient of them. In a word, I was so impatient of them, that I was mightily glad to get out at the next station, and to exchange these clouds and vapours for the free air of heaven.

By that time it was a beautiful morning. As I walked away among such leaves as had already fallen from the golden, brown, and russet trees; and as I looked around me on the wonders of creation, and thought of the steady, unchanging, and harmonious laws by which they are sustained; the gentleman's spiritual intercourse seemed to me as poor a piece of journey-work as ever this world saw. In which heathen state of mind, I came within view of the house, and stopped to examine it attentively.

It was a solitary house; standing in a sadly neglected garden: a pretty even square of some two acres. It was a house of about the time of George the Second; as stiff, as cold, as formal, and in as bad taste, as could possibly be desired by the most loyal admirer of the whole quartet of Georges. It was uninhabited, but had, within a year or two, been cheaply repaired to render it habitable; I say cheaply, because the work had been done in a surface manner, and was already decaying as to the paint and plaster, though the colours were fresh. A lop-sided board drooped over the garden wall, announcing that it was 'to let on very reasonable terms, well furnished'. It was much too closely and heavily shadowed by trees, and, in particular, there were six tall poplars before the front windows, which were excessively melancholy, and the site of which had been extremely ill chosen.

It was easy to see that it was an avoided house – a house that was shunned by the village, to which my eye was guided by a chuch spire some half a mile off – a house that nobody would take. And the natural inference was, that it had the reputation of being a haunted house.

No period within the four-and-twenty hours of day and night is so solemn to me, as the early morning. In the summer-time, I often rise very early, and repair to my room to do a day's work before breakfast, and I am always on those occasions deeply impressed by the stillness and solitude around me. Besides that there is something awful in the being surrounded by familiar faces asleep – in the knowledge that those who are dearest to us and to whom we are dearest, are profoundly unconscious of us, in an impassive state, anticipative of that mysterious condition to which we are all tending – the stopped life, the broken threads of yesterday, the deserted seat, the closed book, the unfinished and abandoned occupation, all are images of death. The tranquillity of the hour is the tranquillity of death. The colour and the chill have the same association. Even a certain air that familiar household objects take upon them when they first emerge from the shadows of the night into the morning, of being newer, and as they used to be long ago, has its counterpart in the subsidence of the worn face of maturity or age, in death, into the old youthful look. Moreover, I once saw the apparition of my father, at this hour. He was alive and well, and nothing ever came of it, but I saw him in the daylight, sitting with his back towards me, on a seat that stood beside my bed. His head was resting on his hand, and whether he was slumbering or grieving, I could not discern. Amazed to see him there, I sat up, moved my position, leaned out of bed, and watched him. As he did not move, I spoke to him more than once. As he did not move then, I became alarmed and laid my hand upon his shoulder, as I thought – and there was no such thing.

For all these reasons, and for others less easily and briefly statable, I find the early morning to be my most ghostly time. Any house would be more or less haunted, to me, in the early morning; and a haunted house could scarcely address me to greater advantage than then.

I walked on into the village, with the desertion of this

house upon my mind, and I found the landlord of the little inn, sanding his door-step. I bespoke breakfast, and broached the subject of the house.

'Is it haunted?' I asked.

The landlord looked at me, shook his head, and answered, 'I say nothing.'

'Then it *is* haunted?'

'Well!' cried the landlord, in an outburst of frankness that had the appearance of desperation – 'I wouldn't sleep in it.'

'Why not?'

'If I wanted to have all the bells in a house ring, with nobody to ring 'em; and all the doors in a house bang, with nobody to bang 'em; and all sorts of feet treading about, with no feet there; why, then,' said the landlord, 'I'd sleep in that house.'

'Is anything seen there?'

The landlord looked at me again, and then, with his former appearance of desperation, called down his stable-yard for 'Ikey!'

The call produced a high-shouldered young fellow, with a round red face, a short crop of sandy hair, a very broad humorous mouth, a turned-up nose, and a great sleeved waistcoat of purple bars, with mother-of-pearl buttons, that seemed to be growing upon him, and to be in a fair way – if it were not pruned – of covering his head and overrunning his boots.

'This gentleman wants to know,' said the landlord, 'if anything's seen at the Poplars.'

''Ooded woman with a howl,' said Ikey, in a state of great freshness.

'Do you mean a cry?'

'I mean a bird, sir.'

'A hooded woman with an owl. Dear me! Did you ever see her?'

'I seen the howl.'

'Never the woman?'

'Not so plain as the howl, but they always keeps together.'

'Has anybody ever seen the woman as plainly as the owl?'

'Lord bless you, sir! Lots.'

'Who?'

'Lord bless you, sir! Lots.'

'The general-dealer opposite, for instance, who is opening his shop?'

'Perkins? Bless you, Perkins wouldn't go a-nigh the place. No!' observed the young man, with considerable feeling; 'he an't over-wise, an't Perkins, but he an't such a fool as *that*.'

(Here, the landlord murmured his confidence in Perkins's knowing better.)

'Who is – or who was – the hooded woman with the owl? Do you know?'

'Well!' said Ikey, holding up his cap with one hand while he scratched his head with the other, 'they say, in general, that she was murdered, and the howl he 'ooted the while.'

This very concise summary of the facts was all I could learn, except that a young man, as hearty and likely a young man as ever I see, had been took with fits and held down in 'em, after seeing the hooded woman. Also, that a personage, dimly described as 'a hold chap, a sort of one-eyed tramp, answering to the name of Joby, unless you challenged him as Greenwood, and then he said, "Why not? and even if so, mind your own business,"' had encountered the hooded woman, a matter of five or six times. But, I was not materially assisted by these witnesses: inasmuch as the first was in California, and the last was, as Ikey said (and he was confirmed by the landlord), anywheres.

Now, although I regard with a hushed and solemn fear, the mysteries, between which and this state of existence is interposed the barrier of the great trial and change that fall on all the things that live; and although I have not the audacity to pretend that I know anything of them; I can no more reconcile the mere banging of doors, ringing of bells, creaking of boards, and such-like insignificances, with the majestic beauty and pervading analogy of all the Divine rules that I am permitted to understand, than I had been able, a little while before, to yoke the spiritual intercourse of my fellow-traveller to the chariot of the rising sun. Moreover, I had lived in two haunted houses – both abroad. In one of these, an old Italian palace, which bore the reputation of being very badly haunted indeed, and which had recently been twice abandoned on that account, I lived eight months, most tranquilly and pleasantly: notwithstanding that the house had a score of mysterious bedrooms, which were never used, and possessed, in one large room in which I sat reading, times out of number at all hours, and next to which I slept, a haunted chamber of the first pretensions. I gently hinted these considerations to the landlord. And as to this particular house having a bad name, I reasoned with him, Why, how many things had bad names undeservedly, and how easy it was to give bad names, and did he not think that if he and I were persistently to whisper in the village that any weird-looking old drunken tinker of the neighbourhood had sold himself to the devil, he would come in time to be suspected of that commercial venture! All this wise talk was perfectly ineffective with the landlord, I am bound to confess, and was as dead a failure as ever I made in my life.

To cut this part of the story short, I was piqued about the haunted house, and was already half resolved to take it. So, after breakfast, I got the keys from Perkins's brother-in-law (a whip- and harness-maker, who keeps the Post Office, and is under submission to a most rigorous wife of the Doubly Seceding Little Emmanuel persuasion), and went up to the house, attended by my landlord and by Ikey.

Within, I found it, as I had expected, transcendently dismal. The slowly changing shadows waved on it from the heavy trees, were doleful in the last degree; the house was ill-placed, ill-built, ill-planned, and ill-fitted. It was damp, it was not free from dry rot, there was a flavour of rats in it, and it was the gloomy victim of that indescribable decay which settles on all the work of man's hands whenever it is not turned to man's account. The kitchens and offices were too large, and too remote from each other. Above stairs and below, waste tracts of passage intervened between patches of fertility represented by rooms; and there was a moudly old well with a green growth upon it, hiding like a murderous trap, near the bottom of the back-stairs, under the double row of bells. One of these bells was labelled, on a black back-ground in faded white letters, MASTER B. This, they told me, was the bell that rang the most.

'Who was Master B.?' I asked. 'Is it known what he did while the owl hooted?'

'Rang the bell,' said Ikey.

I was rather struck by the prompt dexterity with which this young man pitched his fur cap at the bell, and rang it himself. It was a loud, unpleasant bell, and made a very disagreeable sound. The other bells were inscribed according to the names of the rooms to which their wires were conducted, as: 'Picture Room,' 'Double Room,' 'Clock Room,' and the like. Following Master B.'s bell to its source, I found that young gentleman to have had but indifferent third-class accommodation in a triangular cabin under the cock-loft, with a corner fireplace which Master B. must have been exceedingly small if he were ever able to warm himself at, and a corner chimney-piece like a pyramidal staircase to the ceiling for Tom Thumb. The papering of one side of the room had dropped down bodily, with fragments of plaster adhering to it, and almost blocked up the door. It appeared that Master B., in his spiritual condition, always made a point of pulling the paper down. Neither the landlord nor Ikey could suggest why he made such a fool of himself.

Except that the house had an immensely large rambling loft at top, I made no other discoveries. It was moderately well furnished, but sparely. Some of the furniture – say a third – was as old as the house; the rest was of various periods within the last half century. I was referred to a corn-chandler in the market-place of the county town to treat for the house. I went that day, and I took it for six months.

It was just the middle of October when I moved in with my maiden sister (I venture to call her eight-and-thirty, she is so very handsome, sensible and engaging). We took with us a deaf stable-man, my bloodhound Turk, two women servants, and a young person called an Odd Girl. I have reason to record of the attendant last enumerated, who was one of the Saint Lawrence's Union Female Orphans, that she was a fatal mistake and a disastrous engagement.

The year was dying early, the leaves were falling fast, it was a raw cold day when we took possession, and the gloom of the house was most depressing. The cook (an amiable woman, but of a weak turn of intellect) burst into tears on beholding the kitchen, and requested that her silver watch might be delivered over to her sister (2 Tuppintock's Gardens, Liggs's Walk, Clapham Rise), in the event of anything happening to her from the damp. Streaker, the housemaid, feigned cheerfulness, but was the greater martyr. The Odd Girl, who had never been in the country, alone was pleased, and made arrangements for sowing an acorn in the garden outside the scullery window, and rearing an oak.

We went, before dark, through all the natural – as opposed to supernatural – miseries incidental to our state. Dispiriting reports ascended (like the smoke) from the basement in volumes, and descended from the upper rooms. There was no rolling-pin, there was no salamander (which failed to surprise me, for I don't know what it is), there was nothing in the house, what there was, was broken, the last people must have lived like pigs, what could the meaning of the landlord be? Through these distresses, the Odd Girl was cheerful and exemplary. But within four hours after dark we had got into a supernatural groove, and the Odd Girl had seen 'Eyes' and was in hysterics.

My sister and I had agreed to keep the haunting strictly to ourselves, and my impression was, and still is, that I had not left Ikey, when he helped to unload the cart, alone with the women, or any one of them, for one minute. Nevertheless, as I say, the Odd Girl had 'seen Eyes' (no other explanation could ever be drawn from her), before nine, and by ten o'clock had had as much vinegar applied to her as would pickle a handsome salmon.

I leave a discerning public to judge of my feelings, when,

under these untoward circumstances, at about half-past ten o'clock Master B.'s bell began to ring in a most unfuriated manner, and Turk howled until the house resounded with his lamentations!

I hope I may never again be in a state of mind so unchristian as the mental frame in which I lived for some weeks, respecting the memory of Master B. Whether his bell was rung by rats, or mice, or bats, or wind, or what other accidental vibration, or sometimes by one cause, sometimes another, and sometimes by collusion, I don't know; but, certain it is, that it did ring two nights out of three, until I conceived the happy idea of twisting Master B.'s neck – in other words, breaking his bell short off – and silencing that young gentleman, as to my experience and belief, for ever.

But, by that time, the Odd Girl had developed such improving powers of catalepsy, that she had become a shining example of that very inconvenient disorder. She would stiffen, like a Guy Fawkes endowed with unreason, on the most irrelevant occasions. I would address the servants in a lucid manner, pointing out to them that I had painted Master B.'s room and balked the paper, and taken Master B.'s bell away and balked the ringing, and if they could suppose that that confounded boy had lived and died, to clothe himself with no better behaviour than would most unquestionably have brought him and the sharpest particles of a birch-broom into close acquaintance in the present imperfect state of existence, could they also suppose a mere poor human being, such as I was, capable by those contemptible means of counteracting and limiting the powers of the disembodied spirits of the dead, or of any spirits? I say I would become emphatic and cogent, not to say rather complacent, in such an address, when it would all go for nothing by reason of the Odd Girl's suddenly stiffening from the toes upward, and glaring among us like a parochial petrifaction.

Streaker the housemaid, too, had an attribute of a most discomfiting nature. I am unable to say whether she was of an unusually lymphatic temperament, or what else was the matter with her, but this young woman became a mere Distillery for the production of the largest and most transparent tears I ever met with. Combined with these characteristics, was a peculiar tenacity of hold in those specimens, so that they didn't fall, but hung upon her face and nose. In this condition, and mildly and deplorably shaking her head, her silence would throw me more heavily than the Admirable Crichton could have done in a verbal disputation for a purse of money. Cook, likewise, always covered me with confusion as with a garment, by neatly winding up the session with the protest that the Ouse was wearing her out, and by meekly repeating her last wishes regarding her silver watch.

As to our nightly life, the contagion of suspicion and fear was among us and there is no such contagion under the sky. Hooded woman? According to the accounts, we were in a perfect convent of hooded women. Noises? With that contagion downstairs, I myself have sat in the dismal parlour, listening, until I have heard so many and such strange noises, that they would have chilled my blood if I had not warmed it by dashing out to make discoveries. Try this in bed, in the dead of the night; try this at your own comfortable fireside, in the life of the night. You can fill any house with noises, if you will, until you have a noise for every nerve in your nervous system.

I repeat; the contagion of suspicion and fear was among us, and there is no such contagion under the sky. The women (their noses in a chronic state of excoriation from smelling-salts), were always primed and loaded for a swoon, and ready to go off with hair-triggers. The two elder detached the Odd Girl on all expeditions that were considered doubly hazardous, and she always established the reputation of such adventures by coming back cataleptic. If Cook or Streaker went overhead after dark, we knew we should presently hear a bump on the ceiling; and this took place so constantly, that it was as if a fighting man were engaged to go about the house, administering a touch of his art which I believe is called The Auctioneer, to every domestic he met with.

It was in vain to do anything. It was in vain to be frightened, for the moment in one's own person, by a real owl, and then to show the owl. It was in vain to discover, by striking an accidental discord on the piano, that Turk always howled at particular notes and combinations. It was in vain to be a Rhadamanthus with the bells, and if an unfortunate bell rang without leave, to have it down inexorably and silence it. It was in vain to fire up chimneys, let torches down the well, charge furiously into suspected rooms and recesses. We changed servants, and it was no better. The new set ran away, and a third set came, and it was no better. At last, our comfortable housekeeping got to be so disorganised and wretched, that I one night dejectedly said to my sister, 'Patty, I begin to despair of our getting people to go on with us here, and I think we must give this up.'

My sister, who is a woman of immense spirit, replied, 'No, John, don't give it up. Don't be beaten, John. There is another way.'

'And what is that?' said I.

'John,' returned my sister, 'if we are not to be driven out of this house, and that for no reason whatever, that is apparent to you or me, we must help ourselves and take the house wholly and solely into our own hands.'

'But the servants,' said I.

'Have no servants,' said my sister, boldly.

Like most people in my grade of life, I had never thought of the possibility of going on without those faithful obstructions. The notion was so new to me when suggested, that I looked very doubtful.

'We know they come here to be frightened and infect one another, and we know they are frightened and do infect one another,' said my sister.

'With the exception of Bottles,' I observed, in a meditative tone.

(The deaf stableman. I kept him in my service, and still keep him, as a phenomenon of moroseness not to be matched in England.)

'To be sure, John,' assented my sister; 'except Bottles.

And what does that go to prove? Bottles talks to nobody, and hears nobody unless he is absolutely roared at, and what alarm has Bottles ever given, or taken! None.'

This was perfectly true; the individual in question having retired, every night at ten o'clock, to his bed over the coach-house, with no other company than a pitchfork and a pail of water. That the pail of water would have been over me, and the pitchfork through me, if I had put myself without announcement in Bottle's way after that minute, I had deposited in my own mind as a fact worth remembering. Neither had Bottles ever taken the least notice of any of our many uproars. An imperturbable and speechless man, he had sat at his supper, with Streaker present in a swoon, and the Odd Girl marble, and had only put another potato in his cheek, or profited by the general misery to help himself to beefsteak pie.

'And so,' continued my sister, 'I exempt Bottles. And considering, John, that the house is too large, and perhaps too lonely, to be kept well in hand by Bottles, you, and me, I propose that we cast about among our friends for a certain selected number of the most reliable and willing – form a Society here for three months – wait upon ourselves and one another – live cheerfully and socially – and see what happens.'

I was so charmed with my sister, that I embraced her on the spot, and went into her plan with the greatest ardour.

We were then in the third week of November; but, we took our measures so vigorously, and were so well seconded by the friends in whom we confided, that there was still a week of the month unexpired, when our party all came down together merrily, and mustered in the haunted house.

I will mention, in this place, two small changes that I made while my sister and I were yet alone. It occurring to me as not improbable that Turk howled in the house at night, partly because he wanted to get out of it, I stationed him in his kennel outside, but unchained; and I seriously warned the village that any man who came in his way must not expect to leave him without a rip in his own throat. I then casually asked Ikey if he were a judge of a gun? On his saying, 'Yes, sir, I knows a good gun when I sees her,' I begged the favour of his stepping up to the house and looking at mine.

'*She's* a true one, sir,' said Ikey, after inspecting a double-barrelled rifle that I bought in New York a few years ago. 'No mistake about *her*, sir.'

'Ikey,' said I, 'don't mention it; I have seen something in this house.'

'No, sir?' he whispered, greedily opening his eyes. ' 'Ooded lady, sir?'

'Don't be frightened,' said I. 'It was a figure rather like you.'

'Lord, sir?'

'Ikey!' said I, shaking hands with him warmly: I may say affectionately; 'if there is any truth in these ghost-stories, the greatest service I can do you, is, to fire at that figure. And I promise you, by heaven and earth, I will do it with this gun if I see it again!'

The young man thanked me, and took his leave with some little precipitation, after declining a glass of liquor. I imparted my secret to him, because I had never quite forgotten his throwing his cap at the bell; because I had, on another occasion, noticed something very like a fur cap, lying not far from the bell, one night when it had burst out ringing; and because I had remarked that we were at our ghostliest whenever he came up in the evening to comfort the servants. Let me do Ikey no injustice. He was afraid of the house, and believed in its being haunted; and yet he would play false on the haunting side, so surely as he got an opportunity. The Odd Girl's case was exactly similar. She went about the house in a state of real terror, and yet lied monstrously and wilfully, and invented many of the alarms she spread, and made many of the sounds we heard. I had had my eye on the two, and I know it. It is not necessary for me, here, to account for this preposterous state of mind; I content myself with remarking that it is familiarly known to every intelligent man who has had fair medical, legal, or other watchful experience; that it is as well established and as common a state of mind as any with which observers are acquainted; and that it is one of the first elements, above all others, rationally to be suspected in, and strictly looked for, and separated from, any question of this kind.

To return to our party. The first thing we did when we were all assembled, was, to draw lots for bedrooms. That done, and every bedroom, and, indeed, the whole house, having been minutely examined by the whole body, we allotted the various household duties, as if we had been on a gipsy party, or a yachting party, or a hunting party, or were shipwrecked. I then recounted the floating rumours concerning the hooded lady, the owl, and Master B. with others, still more filmy, which had floated about during our occupation, relative to some ridiculous old ghost of the female gender who went up and down, carrying the ghost of a round table; and also to an impalpable jackass, whom nobody was ever able to catch. Some of these ideas I really believe our people below had communicated to one another in some diseased way, without conveying them in words. We then gravely called one another to witness, that we were not there to be deceived, or to deceive – which we considered pretty much the same thing – and that, with a serious sense of responsibility, we would be strictly true to one another, and would strictly follow out the truth. The understanding was established, that any one who heard unusual noises in the night, and who wished to trace them, should knock at my door; lastly, that on Twelfth Night, the last night of holy Christmas, all our individual experiences since that then present hour of our coming together in the haunted house, should be brought to light for the good of all; and that we would hold our peace on the subject till then, unless on some remarkable provocation to break silence.

We were, in number and in character, as follows:

First – to get my sister and myself out of the way – there were we two. In the drawing of lots, my sister drew her own room, and I drew Master B's. Next, there was our first cousin John Herschel, so called after the great astronomer: than whom I suppose a better man at a telescope does not breathe. With him, was his wife: a charming creature to whom he had been married in the previous spring. I thought it (under the circumstances) rather imprudent to bring her, because there is no knowing what even a false alarm may do at such a time: but I suppose he knew his own business best, and I must say that if she had been *my* wife, I never could have left her endearing and bright face behind. They drew the Clock Room. Alfred Starling, an uncommonly agreeable young fellow of eight-and-twenty for whom I have the greatest liking, was in the Double Room; mine, usually, and designated by that name from having a dressing-room within it, with two large and cumbersome windows, which no wedges *I* was ever able to make would keep from shaking in any weather, wind or no wind. Alfred is a young fellow who pretends to be 'fast' (another word for loose, as I understand the term), but who is much too good and sensible for that nonsense, and who would have distinguished himself before now, if his father had not unfortunately left him a small independence of two hundred a year, on the strength of which his only occupation in life has been to spend six. I am in hopes, however, that his banker may break, or that he may enter into some speculation guaranteed to pay twenty per cent.; for, I am convinced that if he could only be ruined, his fortune is made. Belinda Bates, bosom friend of my sister, and a most intellectual, amiable, and delightful girl, got the Picture Room. She has a fine genius for poetry, combined with real business earnestness, and 'goes in' – to use an expression of Alfred's – for Woman's mission, Woman's rights, Woman's wrongs, and everything that is a woman's with a capital W, or is not and ought to be, or is and ought not to be. 'Most praiseworthy, my dear, and heaven prosper you!' I whispered to her on the first night of my taking leave of her at the Picture-Room door, 'but don't overdo it. And in respect of the great necessity there is, my darling, for more employments being within the reach of Woman than our civilisation has a yet assigned to her, don't fly at the unfortunate men, even those men who are at first sight in your way, as if they were the natural oppressors of your sex;

for, trust me, Belinda, they do sometimes spend their wages among wives and daughters, sisters, mothers, aunts, and grandmothers; and the play is, really, not *all* Wolf and Red Riding-Hood, but has other parts in it.' However I digress.

Belinda, as I have mentioned, occupied the Picture Room. We had but three other chambers: the Corner Room, the Cupboard Room, and the Garden Room. My old friend, Jack Governor, 'slung his hammock,' as he called it, in the Corner Room. I have always regarded Jack as the finest-looking sailor that ever sailed. He is grey now, but as handsome as he was a quarter of a century ago – nay, handsomer. A portly, cheery, well-built figure of a broad-shouldered man, with a frank smile, a brilliant dark eye, and a rich dark eyebrow. I remember those under darker hair, and they look all the better for their silver setting. He has been wherever his Union namesake flies, has Jack, and I have met old shipmates of his, away in the Mediterranean and on the other side of the Atlantic, who have beamed and brightened at the casual mention of his name, and have cried, 'You know Jack Governor? Then you know a prince of men!' That he is! And so unmistakably a naval officer, that if you were to meet him coming out of an Eskimo snow-hut in seal's skin, you would be vaguely persuaded he was in full naval uniform.

Jack once had that bright clear eye of his on my sister; but, it fell out that he married another lady and took her to South America, where she died. This was a dozen years ago or more. He brought down with him to our haunted house a little cask of salt beef; for, he is always convinced that all salt beef not of his own pickling, is mere carrion, and invariably, when he goes to London, packs a piece in his portmanteau. He had also volunteered to bring with him one 'Nat Beaver,' an old comrade of his, captain of a merchantman. Mr Beaver, with a thick-set wooden face and figure, and apparently as hard as a block all over, proved to be an intelligent man, with a world of watery experiences in him, and great practical knowledge. At times, there was a curious nervousness about him, apparently the lingering result of some old illness; but, it seldom lasted many minutes. He got the Cupboard Room, and lay there next to Mr Undery, my friend and solicitor: who came down, in an amateur capacity, 'to go through with it,' as he said, and who plays whist better than the whole Law List, from the red cover at the beginning to the red cover at the end.

I never was happier in my life, and I believe it was the universal feeling among us. Jack Governor, always a man of wonderful resources, was Chief Cook, and made some of the best dishes I ever ate, including unapproachable curries. My sister was pastrycook and confectioner. Starling and I were Cook's Mate, turn and turn about, and on special occasions the chief cook 'pressed' Mr Beaver. We had a great deal of out-door sport and exercise, but nothing was neglected within, and there was no ill-humour or misunderstanding among us, and our evenings were so delightful that we had at least one good reason for being reluctant to go to bed.

We had a few night alarms in the beginning. On the first night I was knocked up by Jack with a most wonderful ship's lantern in his hand, like the gills of some monster of the deep, who informed me that he 'was going aloft to the main truck,' to have the weathercock down. It was a stormy night and I remonstrated; but Jack called my attention to its making a sound like a cry of despair, and said somebody would be 'hailing a ghost' presently, if it wasn't done. So, up to the top of the house, where I could hardly stand for the wind, we went, accompanied by Mr Beaver; and there Jack, lantern and all, with Mr Beaver after him, swarmed up to the top of a cupola, some two dozen feet above the chimneys, and stood upon nothing particular, coolly knocking the weathercock off, until they both got into such good spirits with the wind and the height, that I thought they would never come down. Another night, they turned out again, and had a chimney-cowl off. Another night, they cut a sobbing and gulping water-pipe away. Another night, they found out something else. On several occasions, they both, in the coolest manner, simultaneously dropped out of their respective bedroom windows, hand over hand by their counterpanes, to 'overhaul' something mysterious in the garden.

The engagement among us was faithfully kept, and nobody revealed anything. All we knew was, if any one's room was haunted, no one looked the worse for it.

THE GHOST IN MASTER B'S ROOM

When I established myself in the triangular garret which had gained so distinguished a reputation, my thoughts naturally turned to Master B. My speculations about him were uneasy and manifold. Whether his Christian name was Benjamin, Bissextile (from his having been born in Leap Year), Bartholomew, or Bill. Whether the initial letter belonged to his family name, and that was Baxter, Black, Brown, Barker, Buggins, Baker, or Bird. Whether he was a foundling, and had been baptized B. Whether he was a lion-hearted boy, and B was short for Briton, or for bull. Whether he could possibly have been kith and kin to an illustrious lady who brightened my own childhood, and had come of the blood of the brilliant Mother Bunch?

With these profitless meditations I tormented myself much. I also carried the mysterious letter into the appearance and pursuits of the deceased; wondering whether he dressed in blue, wore boots (he couldn't have been bald), was a boy of brains, liked books, was good at bowling, had any skill as a boxer, even in his buoyant boyhood bathed from a bathing-machine at Bognor, Bangor, Bouremouth, Brighton, or Broadstairs, like a bounding billiard ball?

So, from the first, I was haunted by the letter B.

It was not long before I remarked that I never by any hazard had a dream of Master B., or of anything belonging to him. But, the instant I awoke from sleep, at whatever hour of the night, my thoughts took him up, and roamed away, trying to attach his initial letter to something that would fit it and keep it quiet.

For six nights I had been worried thus in Master B's

room, when I began to perceive that things were going wrong.

The first appearance that presented itself was early in the morning when it was but just daylight and no more. I was standing shaving at my glass, when I suddenly discovered, to my consternation and amazement, that I was shaving – not myself – I am fifty – but a boy. Apparently Master B.!

I trembled and looked over my shoulder; nothing there. I looked again in the glass, and distinctly saw the features and expression of a boy, who was shaving, not to get rid of a beard, but to get one. Extremely troubled in my mind, I took a few turns in the room, and went back to the looking-glass, resolved to steady my hand and complete the operation in which I had been disturbed. Opening my eyes, which I had shut while recovering my firmness, I now met in the glass, looking straight at me, the eyes of a young man of four- or five-and-twenty. Terrified by this new ghost, I closed my eyes, and made a strong effort to recover myself. Opening them again, I saw, shaving his cheek in the glass, my father, who has long been dead. Nay, I even saw my grandfather too, whom I never did see in my life.

Although naturally much affected by these remarkable visitations, I determined to keep my secret, until the time agreed upon for the present general disclosure. Agitated by a multitude of curious thoughts, I retired to my room, that night, prepared to encounter some new experience of a spectral character. Nor was my preparation needless, for, waking from an uneasy sleep at exactly two o'clock in the morning, what were my feelings to find that I was sharing my bed with the skeleton of Master B.!

I sprang up, and the skeleton sprang up also. I then heard a plaintive voice saying, 'Where am I? What is become of me?' and, looking hard in that direction, perceived the ghost of Master B.

The young spectre was dressed in an obsolete fashion: or rather, was not so much dressed as put into a case of inferior pepper-and-salt cloth, made horrible by means of shining buttons. I observed that these buttons went, in a double row, over each shoulder of the young ghost, and appeared to descend his back. He wore a frill round his neck. His right hand (which I distinctly noticed to be inky) was laid upon his stomach; connecting this action with some feeble pimples on his countenance, and his general air of nausea, I concluded this ghost to be the ghost of a boy who had habitually taken a great deal too much medicine.

'Where am I?' said the little spectre, in a pathetic voice. 'And why was I born in the Calomel days, and why did I have all that Calomel given me?'

I replied, with sincere earnestness, that upon my soul I couldn't tell him.

'Where is my little sister?' said the ghost, 'and where my angelic little wife, and where is the boy I went to school with?'

I entreated the phantom to be comforted, and above all things to take heart respecting the loss of the boy he went to school with. I represented to him that probably that boy never did, within human experience, come out well, when discovered. I urged that I myself had, in later life, turned up several boys whom I went to school with, and none of them had at all answered. I expressed my humble belief that that boy never did answer. I represented that he was a mythic character, a delusion, and a snare. I recounted how, the last time I found him, I found him at a dinner party behind a wall of white cravat, with an inconclusive opinion on every possible subject, and a power of silent boredom absolutely titanic. I related how, on the strength of our having been together at 'Old Doylance's,' he had asked himself to breakfast with me (a social offence of the largest magnitude); how, fanning my weak embers of belief in Doylance's boys, I had let him in; and how, he had proved to be a fearful wanderer about the earth, pursuing the race of Adam with inexplicable notions concerning the currency, and with a proposition that the Bank of England should, on pain of being abolished, instantly strike off and circulate, God knows how many thousand millions of ten-and-sixpenny notes.

The ghost heard me in silence, and with a fixed stare. 'Barber!' it apostrophised me when I had finished.

'Barber?' I repeated – for I am not of that profession.

'Condemned,' said the ghost, 'to shave a constant change of customers – now, me – now, a young man – now, thyself as thou art – now, thy father – now, thy grandfather; condemned, too, to lie down with a skeleton every night, and to rise with it every morning——'

(I shuddered on hearing this dismal announcement).

'Barber! Pursue me!'

I had felt, even before the words were uttered, that I was under a spell to pursue the phantom. I immediately did so, and was in Master B's room no longer.

Most people know what long and fatiguing night journeys had been forced upon the witches who used to confess, and who, no doubt, told the exact truth – particularly as they were always assisted with leading questions, and the torture was always ready. I asserverate that, during my occupation of Master B's room, I was taken by the ghost that haunted it, on expeditions fully as long and wild as any of those. Assuredly, I was presented to no shabby old man with a goat's horns and tail (something between Pan and an old clothesman), holding conventional receptions, as stupid as those of real life and less decent; but, I came upon other things which appeared to me to have more meaning.

Confident that I speak the truth and shall be believed, I declare without hesitation that I followed the ghost, in the first instance on a broomstick, and afterwards on a rocking-horse. The very smell of the animal's paint – especially when I brought it out, by making him warm – I am ready to swear to. I followed the ghost, afterwards, in a hackney coach; an institution with the peculiar smell of which, the present generation is unacquainted, but to which I am again ready to swear as a combination of stable, dog with the mange, and very old bellows. (In this, I appeal to previous generations to confirm or refute me.) I pursued the phantom, on a headless donkey: at least, upon a donkey who was so interested in the state of his stomach that his head was always down there, investigating it; on ponies, expressly born to kick up behind; on roundabouts and swings, from fairs; in the first cab – another forgotten institution where the fare regularly got into bed, and was tucked up with the driver.

Not to trouble you with a detailed account of all my travels in pursuit of the ghost of Master B., which were longer and more wonderful than those of Sinbad the Sailor, I will confine myself to one experience from which you may judge of many.

I was marvellously changed. I was myself, yet not myself. I was conscious of something within me, which has been the same all through my life, and which I have always recognised under all its phases and varieties as never altering, and yet I was not the I who had gone to bed in Master B's room. I had the smoothest of faces and the shortest of legs, and I had taken another creature like myself, also with the smoothest of faces and the shortest of legs, behind a door, and was confiding to him a proposition of the most astounding nature.

This proposition was, that we should have a seraglio.

The other creature assented warmly. He had no notion of respectability, neither had I. It was the custom of the East, it was the way of the good Caliph Haroun Alraschid (let me have the corrupted name again for once, it is so scented with sweet memories!), the usage was highly laudable, and most worthy of imitation. 'O, yes! Let us,' said the other creature with a jump, 'have a seraglio.'

It was not because we entertained the faintest doubts of the meritorious character of the Oriental establishment we proposed to import, that we perceived it must be kept a secret from Miss Griffin. It was because we knew Miss Griffin to be bereft of human sympathies, and incapable of appreciating the greatness of the great Haroun. Mystery impenetrably shrouded from Miss Griffin then, let us entrust it to Miss Bule.

We were ten in Miss Griffin's establishment by Hampstead Ponds; eight ladies and two gentlemen. Miss Bule, whom I judge to have attained the ripe age of eight or nine, took the lead in society. I opened the subject to her in the course of the day, and proposed that she should become the Favourite.

Miss Bule, after struggling with diffidence so natural to, and charming in, her adorable sex, expressed herself as flattered by the idea, but wished to know how it was proposed to provide for Miss Pipson? Miss Bule – who was understood to have vowed towards that young lady, a friendship, halves, and no secrets, until death, on the Church Service and Lessons complete in two volumes with case and lock – Miss Bule said she could not, as the friend of Pipson, disguise from herself, or me, that Pipson was not one of the common.

Now, Miss Pipson, having curly light hair and blue eyes (which was my idea of anything mortal and feminine that was called fair), I promptly replied that I regarded Miss Pipson in the light of a Fair Circassian.'

'And what then?' Miss Bule pensively asked.

I replied that she must be inveigled by a merchant, brought to me veiled, and purchased as a slave.

(The other creature had already fallen into the second male place in the State, and was set apart for Grand Vizier. He afterwards resisted this disposal of events, but had his hair pulled until he yielded.)

'Shall I not be jealous?' Miss Bule inquired, casting down her eyes.

'Zobeide, no,' I replied; 'you will ever be the favourite Sultana; the first place in my heart, and on my throne, will be ever yours.'

Miss Bule, upon that assurance, consented to propound the idea to her seven beautiful companions. It occurring to me, in the course of the same day, that we knew we could trust a grinning and good-natured soul called Tabby, who was the serving drudge of the house, and had no more figure than one of the beds, and upon whose face there was always more or less black-lead, I slipped into Miss Bule's hand after supper, a little note to that effect: dwelling on the black-lead as being in a manner deposited by the finger of Providence, pointing Tabby out for Mesrour, the celebrated chief of the Blacks of the Hareem.

There were difficulties in the formation of the desired institution, as there are in all combinations. The other creature showed himself of a low character, and, when defeated in aspiring to the throne, pretended to have conscientious scruples about prostrating himself before the Caliph; wouldn't call him Commander of the Faithful; spoke of him slightingly and inconsistently as a mere 'chap;' said he, the other creature, 'wouldn't play' – Play! – and was otherwise coarse and offensive. This meanness of disposition was, however, put down by the general indignation of an united seraglio, and I became blessed in the smiles of eight of the fairest of the daughters of men.

The smiles could only be bestowed when Miss Griffin was looking another way, and only then in a very wary manner, for there was a legend among the followers of the Prophet that she saw with a little round ornament in the middle of the pattern on the back of her shawl. But every day after dinner, for an hour, we were all together, and then the Favourite and the rest of the Royal Hareem competed who should most beguile the leisure of the Serene Haroun reposing from the cares of State – which were generally, as in most affairs of State, of an arithmetical character, the Commander of the Faithful being a fearful boggler at a sum.

On these occasions, the devoted Mesrour, chief of the Blacks of the Hareem, was always in attendance (Miss Griffin usually ringing for that officer, at the same time, with great vehemence), but never acquitted himself in a manner worthy of his historical reputation. In the first place, his bringing a broom into the Divan of the Caliph, even when Haroun wore on his shoulders the red robe of anger (Miss Pipson's pelisse), though it might be got over for the moment, was never to be quite satisfactorily accounted for. In the second place, his breaking out into grinning exclamations of 'Lork you pretties!' was neither Eastern nor respectful. In the third place, when specially instructed to say 'Bismillah!' he always said 'Hallelujah!' This officer, unlike his class, was too good-humoured altogether, kept his mouth open far too wide, expressed approbation to an incongruous extent, and even once – it was on the occasion of the purchase of the Fair Circassian for five hundred thousand purses of gold, and cheap, too – embraced the Slave, the Favourite, and the Caliph, all round. (Parenthetically let me say God bless Mesrour, and may there have been sons and daughters on that tender bosom, softening many a hard day since!)

Miss Griffin was a model of propriety, and I am at a loss to imagine what the feelings of the virtuous woman would have been, if she had known, when she paraded us down the Hampstead Road two and two, that she was walking with a stately step at the head of polygamy and Mahomedanism. I believe that a mysterious and terrible joy with which the contemplation of Miss Griffin, in this unconscious state, inspired us, and a grim sense prevalent among us that there was a dreadful power in our knowledge of what Miss Griffin (who knew all things that could be learnt out of book) didn't know, were the mainspring of the preservation of our secret. It was wonderfully kept, but was once upon the verge of self-betrayal. The danger and escape occurred upon a Sunday. We were all ten ranged in a conspicuous part of the gallery at church, with Miss Griffin at our head – as we were every Sunday – advertising the establishment in an unsecular sort of way – when the description of Solomon in his domestic glory happened to be read. The moment that monarch was thus referred to, conscience whispered me, 'Thou, too, Haroun!' The officiating minister had a cast in his eye, and it assisted conscience by giving him the appearance of reading personally at me. A crimson blush, attended by a fearful perspiration, suffused my features. The Grand Vizier became more dead than alive, and the whole seraglio reddened as if the sunset of Bagdad shone direct upon their lovely faces. At this portentous time the awful Griffin rose, and balefully surveyed the children of Islam. My own impression was, that Church and State had entered into a conspiracy with Miss Griffin to expose us, and that we should all be put into white sheets, and exhibited in the centre aisle. But, so Westerly – if I may be allowed the expression as opposite to Eastern associations – was Miss Griffin's sense of rectitude, that she merely suspected apples, and we were saved.

I have called the seraglio united. Upon the question, solely, whether the Commander of the Faithful durst exercise a right of kissing in that sanctuary of the palace, were its peerless inmates divided. Zobeide asserted a counter-right in the Favourite to scratch, and the fair Circassian put her face, for refuge, into a green baize bag, originally designed for books. On the other hand, a young antelope of transcendent beauty from the fruitful plains of Camden Town (whence she had been brought, by traders, in the half-yearly caravan that crossed the intermediate desert after the holidays), held more liberal opinions, but stipulated for limiting the benefit of them to that dog, and son of a dog, the Grand Vizier – who had no rights, and was not in question. At length, the difficulty was compromised by the installation of a very youthful slave as deputy. She, raised upon a stool, officially received upon her cheeks the salutes intended by the gracious Haroun for other Sultanas, and was privately rewarded from the coffers of the Ladies of the Hareem.

And now it was, at the full height of enjoyment of my bliss, that I became heavily troubled. I began to think of my mother, and what she would say to my taking home at midsummer eight of the most beautiful of the daughters of men, but all unexpected. I thought of the number of beds we made up at our house, of my father's income, and of the baker, and my despondency redoubled. The seraglio and malicious Vizier, divining the cause of their lord's unhappiness, did their utmost to augment it. They professed unbounded fidelity, and declared that they would live and die with him. Reduced to the utmost wretchedness by these protestations of attachment, I lay awake, for hours at a time, ruminating on my frightful lot. In my despair, I think I might have taken an early opportunity of falling on my knees before Miss Griffin, avowing my resemblance to Solomon, and praying to be dealt with according to the outraged laws of my country, if an unthought-of means of escape had not opened before me.

One day, we were out walking, two and two – on which occasion the Vizier had his usual instructions to take note of the boy at the turnpike, and if he profanely gazed (which he always did) at the beauties of the Hareem, to have him bowstrung in the course of the night – and it happened that our hearts were veiled in gloom. An unaccountable action on the part of the antelope had plunged the State into disgrace. That charmer, on the representation that the previous day was her birthday, and that vast treasures had been sent in a hamper for its celebration (both baseless assertions), had secretly but most pressingly invited thirty-five neighbouring princes and princesses to a ball and supper: with a special stipulation that they were 'not to be fetched till twelve'. This wandering of the antelope's fancy, led to the surprising arrival at Miss Griffin's door, in divers equipages and under various escorts, of a great company in full dress, who were deposited on the top step in a flush of high expectancy, and who were dismissed in tears. At the beginning of the double knocks attendant on these ceremonies, the antelope had retired to a back attic, and bolted herself in; and at every new arrival, Miss Griffin had gone so much more and more distracted, that at last she had been seen to tear her front. Ultimate capitulation on the part of the offender, had been followed by solitude in the linen-closet, bread and water and a lecture to all, of vindictive length, in which Miss Griffin had used expressions: Firstly, 'I believe you all of you knew of it'; secondly, 'Every one of you is as wicked as another'; thirdly, 'A pack of little wretches'.

Under these circumstances, we were walking drearily along; and I especially, with my Moosulmaun responsibilities heavy on me, was in a very low state of mind; when a strange man accosted Miss Griffin, and, after walking on at her side for a little while and talking with her, looked at me. Supposing him to be a minion of the law, and that my hour was come, I instantly ran away, with the general purpose of making for Egypt.

The whole seraglio cried out, when they saw me making off as fast as my legs would carry me (I had an impression that the first turning on the left, and round by the public-house, would be the shortest way to the Pyramids), Miss

Griffin screamed after me, the faithless Vizier ran after me, and the boy at the turnpike dodged me into a corner, like a sheep, and cut me off. Nobody scolded me when I was taken and brought back; Miss Griffin only said, with a stunning gentleness, this was very curious! Why had I run away when the gentleman looked at me?

If I had had any breath to answer with, I dare say I should have made no answer: having no breath, I certainly made none. Miss Griffin and the strange man took me between them, and walked me back to the palace in a sort of state; but not at all (as I couldn't help feeling, with astonishment) in culprit state.

When we got there, we went into a room by ourselves, and Miss Griffin called in to her assistance, Mesrour, chief of the dusky guards of the Hareem. Mesrour, on being whispered to, began to shed tears.

'Bless you, my precious!' said that officer, turning to me: 'your Pa's took bitter bad!'

I asked, with a fluttered heart, 'Is he very ill?'

'Lord temper the wind to you, my lamb!' said the good Mesrour, kneeling down, that I might have a comforting shoulder for my head to rest on, 'your Pa's dead!'

Haroun Alraschid took to flight at the words; the seraglio vanished; from that moment I never again saw one of the eight of the fairest of the daughters of men.

I was taken home, and there was debt at home as well as death, and we had a sale there. My own little bed was so superciliously looked upon by a power unknown to me, hazily called 'The Trade,' that a brass coal-scuttle, a roasting-jack, and a birdcage, were obliged to be put into it to make a lot of it, and then it went for a song. So I heard mentioned, and I wondered what song, and thought what a dismal song it must have been to sing!

Then, I was sent to a great, cold, bare, school of big boys; where everything to eat and wear was thick and clumpy, without being enough; where everybody, large and small, was cruel; where the boys knew all about the sale, before I got there, and asked me what I had fetched, and who had bought me, and hooted at me, 'Going, going, gone!' I never whispered in that wretched place that I had been Haroun, or had had a seraglio: for, I knew that if I mentioned my reverses, I should be so worried, that I should have to drown myself in the muddy pond near the playground, which looked like the beer.

Ah me, ah me! No other ghost has haunted the boy's room, my friends, since I have occupied it, than the ghost of my own childhood, the ghost of my own innocence, the ghost of my own airy belief. Many a time have I pursued the phantom: never with this man's stride of mine to come up with it, never with these man's hands of mine to touch it, never more to this man's heart of mine to hold it in its purity. And here you see me working out, as cheerfully and thankfully as I may, my doom of shaving in the glass a constant change of customers, and of lying down and rising up with the skeleton allotted to me for my mortal companion.

Selected by HUGH LAMB

VICTORIAN NIGHTMARES

Phantom ships, bloodstained wedding-rings, bodies buried alive – Hugh Lamb has rescued from obscurity twenty-one unrivalled tales of unearthly happenings and terrible tragedy. From Scarborough to the South Seas, from wild moorland marshes to tranquil country gardens, the Victorian masters of nightmare return to chill us at the dead of night.

Edited by HUGH LAMB

THE TASTE OF FEAR: A HORROR ANTHOLOGY

The rats and the brother's revenge ...

The withered arm from beyond the grave ...

The monster spider in the health resort ...

The things beneath the Sargasso Sea ...

The possessed children and the mother's cure ...

The witching hour has struck, the pit has opened at your feet and you can now try for yourself THE TASTE OF FEAR in this baker's dozen of chillers old and new from masters of the macabre. But beware – that ghostly scream you hear just might not be your own!

CORONET BOOKS